THE ROGUE'S PLOT

The Untold Story of 1777

Ronald S. Gibbs

ISBN-13: 9798320398648
Imprint: Independently published

Cover design by: Judith Lippe and Howard Bomze

Cover figure of Washington on horseback adapted from "Washington Rallying the Americans at the Battle of Princeton" by William Ranney, 1848, Courtesy Princeton University Art Museum.

Cover map is detail from "Plan of the Operations of General Washington against the King's Troops in New Jersey..." by William Faden, 1777, courtesy Library of Congress

Printed in United States of America

Medicine and teaching are giving professions. I dedicate this book to my teachers of medicine and to my students, residents, and fellows.

Preface

At the height of the American Revolution, the British commander in chief made a bewildering strategic decision that fatally determined the outcome of the war and the future of United States. **The Rogue's Plot** provides a new background for what led to that strategy.

CONTENTS

ILLUSTRATIONS

Map 1. Battles of Trenton and Princeton

Map 2. Detail from map 1, showing Battle of Princeton

Map 3. Northern Part of New Jersey

Map 4. Detail from map 3 showing Princeton to Morristown

Map 5. Country from the Raritan River …to Elk Head

Map 6. Detail from map 5 showing surrounding area of Philadelphia

Map 7. Philadelphia and Parts Adjacent

Map 8. Detail from map 7, showing grid of Philadelphia

LINKS TO PORTRAITS AND PAINTINGS:

"Washington at Princeton" by Charles Wilson Peale
https://www.pafa.org/museum/collection/item/george-washington-princeton

"Lieutenant Colonel Banastre Tarleton" by Charles Wilson Peale, National Gallery, London
https://www.nps.gov/people/banastre-tarleton.htm

"General Charles Lee" by James Neagle, after an unknown artist,
https://www.americanrevolutioninstitute.org/asset/charles-

-engraving-ca-1813-by-james-neagle-after-barham-
,hbrooke/

/ashington Rallying the Americans at Battle of Princeton" by
lliam Ranney (1848)
tps://artmuseum.princeton.edu/collections/objects/22043

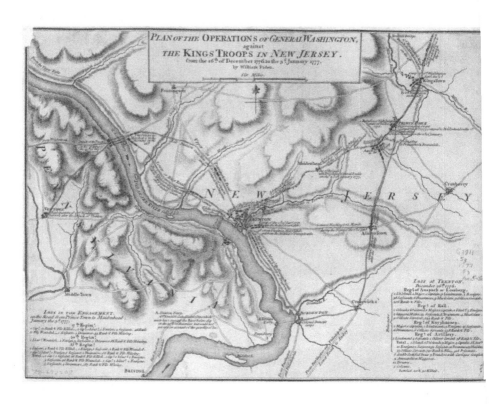

Map 1. Plan of the Operations of General Washington against The King's Troops in New Jersey, from 26th of December 1776 to the 3d January 1777," London, 15th April 1777 by Wm Faden. (Courtesy, Library of Congress)

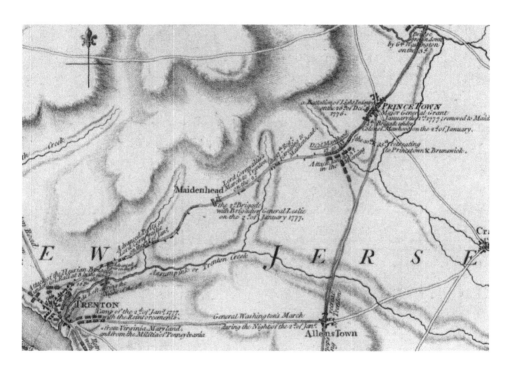

Map 2. Detail from Map 1 showing vicinity of Princeton. (Courtesy, Library of Congress)

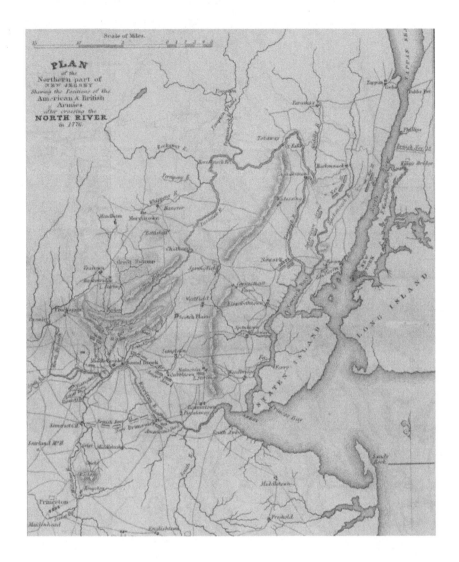

Map 3. "Plan of the Northern part of New Jersey...in 1776" from Atlas to Marshall's *Life of Washington*, J. Crissy, Philadelphia, 1832. Note "New York "(Manhattan Island) in center right, "Princeton" in lower left, "New Brunswick" to northeast of Princeton, and "Morristown" due west of upper Manhattan. Also note proximity of "South Amboy" and "New Brunswick" on the Raritan River. The town of New Brunswick was called Brunswick in most references of the time. (Map from author's family collection, image by Thomas Paper)

Map 4. Detail from Map 3, showing positions of "New York," "Morristown," and "New Brunswick." Note mountains east and south of Morristown. (Map from author's family collection, image by Thomas Paper)

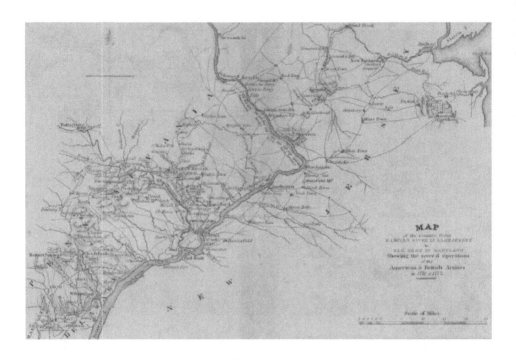

Map 5. "Map of the Country from the Raritan River in New Jersey to Elk Head in Maryland...in 1776 & 1777" from Atlas to *Marshall's Life of Washington,* J. Crissy, Philadelphia, 1832. Note "New Brunswick" in upper right, Philadelphia in center left, and Delaware River coursing generally north to south. (Map from author's family collection, image by Thomas Paper)

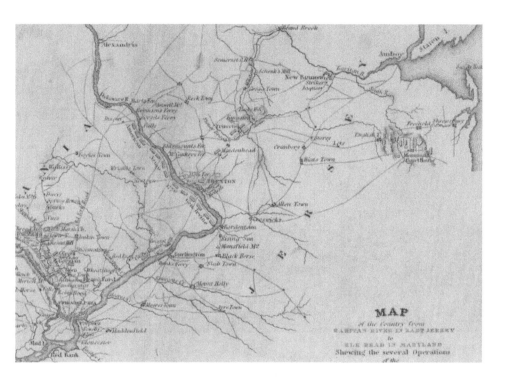

Map 6. Detail from Map 5, showing the area surrounding Philadelphia. (Map from author's family collection, image by Thomas Paper)

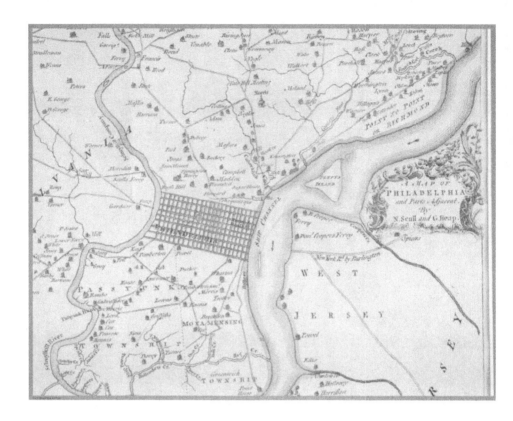

Map 7. "A Map of Philadelphia and Parts Adjacent by N. Scull and G. Heap," Second edition, Gentleman's Magazine, London, 1777. Philadelphia was the first capital of the new United States and with a population of 30,000 the largest city in North America. Capturing it was the object of British General Howe's Campaign of 1777. (Map from author's family collection, image by Thomas Paper)

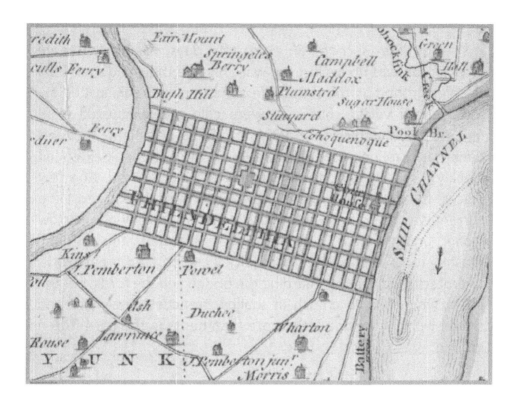

Map.8. Detail from map 7, showing city's location between the Delaware and Schuylkill Rivers and planned grid of streets. (Map from author's family collection, image by Thomas Paper)

Chapter 1- General Washington
Thursday Evening, January 2, 1777
Trenton, New Jersey

For the second time in ten days, General George Washington was up against the wall. His five thousand men held the high ground on the south side of Assunpink Creek, just below the Trenton village, but they were cold and exhausted from fighting and marching constantly since Christmas night. Their left flank was firmly on the Delaware River; the right flank extended weakly three miles up the Assunpink to Phillip's Ford. At a few places, the creek was fordable even in winter, but in most the current was so swift it was impossible to cross. Only one narrow stone bridge, near the Delaware, spanned the stream. Washington's artillerymen had quickly constructed breastworks to protect their cannon guarding the bridge and the fords, but the infantrymen had to crouch in shallow trenches. Their pick and shovel work had made little more than dents in the hard-frozen ground.

Late in the afternoon of January 2nd, British Major General Earl Cornwallis's advanced units entered Trenton on the north side of the Assunpink. The long column had been marching since morning to attack the Washington's army, but harassing musket and cannon fire from an American regiment delayed the British advance. When Cornwallis arrived at the creek, he was spoiling for a fight. A seasoned officer, Cornwallis usually showed tactical brilliance, but here he was overconfident and immediately threw his vanguard against the American positions. Cornwallis's attacks were piecemeal and in the gathering dusk were thrown back by determined American defenders.

Through his spyglass, in the waning light, Washington peered north across the creek, beyond the bloodied British and Hessians in the van, and saw the main enemy force moving into upper Trenton. He estimated they were over eight thousand in number, and they were marching jauntily to the music of their military bands. He thought to himself, "These are fresh, veteran soldiers, and they have gotten here much faster—and in much larger numbers—than I expected. Good Lord, our position here is dicey."

As dark descended, Washington turned to his aide-de-camp and said, "Call a council of war for eight o'clock sharp. We'll meet in the Douglass house."

Knowing of Washington's strict punctuality, the officers of the American council of war packed into the small, two-story, house early. As the grandfather clock struck eight, Washington entered the council room. Tall and powerful, Washington wore his commander in chief's uniform, complete with the blue sash signifying his ultimate rank. He took in the solemn mood of his senior officers. Washington addressed them confidently. "Gentlemen, on our front, we face General Cornwallis's larger force. Although we beat back their attacks late this afternoon, they will undoubtedly come with full force in the morning. They may come directly across Assunpink Creek, but we face a crafty foe in General Cornwallis, and I'd wager he'll try something else. Colonel Tilghman, please place the map in the center of the table." (1)

Lieutenant Colonel Tench Tilghman, a senior officer of the Life Guards and a favorite of Washington's, unrolled a pen-and-ink sketch of Trenton and its vicinity. Pointing to the American positions south of the Assunpink, Washington continued, "Here is our defensive line. Beyond our right flank is the impassable Great Bear Swamp. I believe the most likely point where General Cornwallis will attack is on our right, swinging around through Phillip's Ford."

Washington looked into the eyes of his trusted council

members. Before asking their opinions, he recounted what they had done together. "My fellow officers, ten days ago, we also were up against the wall. Our army was huddled on the Pennsylvania banks of the Delaware River. We had suffered defeat after defeat through the summer and autumn of 1776, and we had been forced to retreat all the way across New Jersey by early December. Our lads were losing heart, and most enlistments were expiring. And then, as the game seemed about up...as our cause looked darkest, we achieved a surprise victory over the German mercenary troops at Trenton on the day after Christmas. We took a thousand prisoners and marched safely back to Pennsylvania. Gentlemen, our brave American troops make me proud!"

Knowing his generals were eager for more, Washington continued assuredly, "Then, four days ago, after we received intelligence that West Jersey was open, we started our return march back to retake Trenton. But the enemy has arrived faster than we expected. I now ask your counsel."

Two of Washington's more faint-hearted generals advised retreating down the Jersey banks of the Delaware, but Washington pointed out that that would make the army still more vulnerable. Master of these councils, the commander in chief continued, "Let us now hear from my most reliable agent, John Honeyman. He has returned just this evening from a ride around the enemy."

Honeyman, who had provided critical intelligence for Washington in his surprise victory at Trenton ten days before, stepped to the map. He began, "Sirs, I know these roads like the back of my hand. Tonight, they'll be frozen solid, able to bear our wagons and artillery. There's a passable road running two miles to our rear, to Allen's Town, and from there, a good road heads straight north, right into Princeton."

Washington rarely smiled, but now he did slyly. "Gentlemen, we'll have one more surprise for our British cousins! Mr. Honeyman's line of march will get us out of this predicament and will give us Princeton and perhaps more. Our objective is to disengage from Cornwallis's army on his front, sweep around the British left, and strike at their rearguard in Princeton, twelve miles to the north. There, we will take British supplies and advance to Brunswick, where they have an even greater depot. But the plan has risk. If Cornwallis detects our movement across his front, he'll hit us in our left flank and put our entire force in jeopardy. Gentlemen, it's ten o'clock. We'll start moving in two hours, at precisely midnight. We are asking more of our troops than can be humanly expected, but tomorrow will be yet another day of victory!"

Washington's plan was ingenious in its maneuver and surprise, and it put all on the line. It was Washington at his best. It flew in the face of traditional tactics. Officers of all armies were trained that infantry had firepower to their front, not to their flank. Officers knew that exposing your flank to the enemy—even for a short time—risked withering enfilading fire which could not be returned. Yet, Washington was daring enough to risk this to gain an even better position for his army. For a few seconds, there was silence as the American generals absorbed the audacious plan. Then, as if in a chorus, they thumped the table and shouted, "Huzzah! Huzzah! Huzzah!" Washington folded his arms across his chest and nodded his head in affirmation and appreciation.

Sitting alone in the back of the room was a tall, thin, ill-appearing officer. Though he sat next to the fireplace, he shivered almost uncontrollably. His hair was matted from his heavy bouts of sweating, and his face was flushed. Lieutenant Colonel Tench Tilghman came over to him and said, "Dr. Grant, just in the two hours of the council meeting, you've begun to look like hell. You're the one who's the doctor, but you're worrying me. I'm getting you back to your own hospital right now."

As the council adjourned, Dr. Alexander Grant, Director of the General Hospital, stood up to leave the Douglass House but was so weak that he needed to grab the fireplace cornice. Tench steadied his dear friend. "Dr. Grant, I don't think you can make even the half mile ride to the hospital." Summoning a junior officer of General Washington's Life Guards, Tench called out, "Lieutenant, commandeer a wagon and teamster so that we can take Dr. Grant to The General Hospital—and, for God's sake, hurry!"

Within minutes, a burly teamster pulled up in front of the house, and he and Tench helped Alex into the open wagon. Though Tench was needed to prepare for the army's march to Princeton, he was desperate to assure Alex's safe arrival at the hospital. Tench hitched his horse to the rear of the wagon and climbed aboard to comfort Alex. The teamster made the journey over the rutted, frozen road in less than fifteen minutes, but in the bitterly cold night, Alex thought it was endless.

The American General Hospital was set up in the Blazing Star Ferry House, at the foot of Ferry Street where the Assunpink Creek flowed into the Delaware River. Two days before, when the American Army marched back into Trenton, Alex had selected the large, brick building because it suited his needs for a makeshift hospital almost perfectly. But now as the wagon approached the hospital, amidst Alex's febrile haze, he hardly recognized the building.

Dr. John Hobbs, Assistant Director of the Hospital, ran into the cold night to greet the wagon. Quickly assessing Alex's condition, Hobbs was aghast at how his colleague had deteriorated in just a few hours. "Dr. Grant, let's get you inside and warm you by the fireplace. We've got a strong tea on the fire to make you feel better, too!"

The ferry house contained one large front room with a small inner room and kitchen in the rear. In the front were the sick and wounded, carefully arranged on clean straw pallets. On the right side, a slender Black nurse ministered to the wounded soldiers, dressing them in clean bandages. On the other side of the ferry building, a stout surgeon's mate tended to the invalids, sick with fevers and coughs, skin rashes or diarrhea.

John Hobbs and Tench helped Alex to a freshly made straw pallet in the inner room, where the surgeon's mate and nurse awaited. Tench addressed the medical staff, "I'm turning Dr. Grant over to your good care. I must return to headquarters. The army is marching at midnight. We are going to slip away from the enemy on our front and surprise them in Princeton! Dr. Hobbs, with Dr. Grant so ill, please make dispositions for the sick and wounded. I'll arrange to get several wagons for those men you can move." To Alex, he added, "My good friend, you'll get well quickly. *Bon chance!*"

Now getting short of breath, Alex wheezed, "Colonel Tilghman, thank you for getting me here... Be safe!... Be victorious!" Tench left the ferry building and galloped back to Washington's headquarters.

Dr. John Hobbs, a native of Albany, New York, had taken his medical education in Scotland at the University of Edinburgh. (2) At dinner conversations at the hospital, he often reminisced about his service in the British Army in North America during the French and Indian War and his surgery practice in Albany afterwards. In 1776, he joined an Albany regiment in the American Continental Army as Regimental Surgeon. Just prior to the British invasion of Manhattan in September 1776, with his fine professional reputation, Hobbs was appointed as Assistant Director of the General Hospital, serving under Dr. Alexander Grant. Warm and nurturing by nature, Hobbs, as he was called by his friends, now quickly took charge.

Hobbs turned to his surgeon's mate and nurse. "It's going to get a bit hazardous here. The army will be marching shortly, and our hospital will follow in support. We've got... what?... twelve patients here. In just a minute, we'll assess each one: who is likely to recover and stay with us on the march and, er... who is just too ill to move. But right now, we must provide for Dr. Grant. Well, Dr. Grant, do you think you can move?"

Bravely, Alex volunteered to stay and care for the remaining invalids, but all knew Alex was too sick. The surgeon's mate, Willem Vander Voort, also from Upstate New York, begged to remain, but in the end the nurse's soft voice offered the best solution.

"May I make a suggestion, Dr. Hobbs?" she asked.

"Jesse, please proceed."

Jesse Jones, a formerly enslaved person in the household of a prominent New York family, had made her way to freedom during the chaos after the British invaded Manhattan. Soon after, she was assigned to the General Hospital and quickly added skills in dosing medication and wound care to her knowledge of the healing properties of native plants. "Dr. Hobbs," she began analytically, "You and Mate Vander Voort will be needed at Princeton. I think it makes perfect sense for me to stay here and take care of Dr. Grant and those too ill to move."

"Jesse, this is an extraordinarily brave proposition you make, but if you're certain, then it's the best idea. The British surgeons will be merciful in their care of Dr. Grant and, I hope, of you and our lads, too."

Jesse replied, "Dr. Hobbs, it's my firm desire. We'll be fine."

Outside the hospital, the main American army was forming its line along the road east to Allen's Town. Inside, Hobbs and Willem prepared ten of the invalids to go in ambulance wagons toward Princeton. The remaining two were officers, both already moribund. Hobbs stooped beside one, an infantry captain who was clutching his right thigh and moaning in pain. The short, empathic surgeon comforted him, "Captain, I'm Doctor Hobbs. You've been out of it for the last day since your leg wound got gangrene. To save your life, we had to amputate your leg."

Seeing the anguish on the officer's face, Hobbs added, "We'll keep you comfortable, and take good care of you." Yet, Hobbs had seen gangrene advancing up the captain's thigh and knew it was fatal. Hobbs lifted the captain's head and gave him a dose of laudanum from the hospital's dwindling supply. The captain managed a faint smile and shortly fell into a drug-induced sleep. Hobbs turned to the mate and said softly, "Ah, after amputation for gangrene, less than half our soldiers survive, and when gangrene advances, as in the case, no one makes it. The poor captain will stay here."

Hobbs saw the last patient: a partially obtunded lieutenant who had just been transferred from a New York regimental hospital. Hobbs still greeted him cheerfully, "I see by your regimental surgeon's note that you're from Albany. Well, good grief, I'm from Albany, too. So, we'll be sure you get better! Let's have a look at you."

The officer's head was burning hot to Hobbs' touch, and his pulse was rapid and weak. His hair was matted and greasy and his tongue dry, with a thick, yellow coating. The lieutenant's body was covered with nearly confluent red spots. When Hobbs and Willem looked closely, they saw small, black lice thickly in his hair and throughout his body. Hobbs walked over to Jesse and whispered, "The lieutenant has camp fever—and it's far advanced. (3) We'll leave him and the captain with leg gangrene here with you. I'm afraid they won't make it much longer. Keep them as comfortable as you can. I can spare only a few doses of laudanum."

With complete understanding, Jesse simply nodded. Hobbs and Willem moved the other ten sick and wounded to the ambulances and formed them at the rear of the American column, about to marching east.

While Jesse's other two patients fell into fretful sleep, she returned to Alex's side, placed a soothing poultice on his neck, and gave him sips of sassafras tea. Fortified a bit, Alex reflected, "Jesse, for the last three days, I cared for several officers who had fever and throat pain. One was a young lieutenant from Pennsylvania...he could hardly swallow and became short of breath...I applied throat poultices and bled him twice, but he died the next morning." Alex paused a moment to catch his breath and concluded, "Yesterday, I had an occasional chill myself and soreness in my throat. And this evening, as I was getting ready to go to the council of war to report on the sick and wounded, I started to feel worse. During the council, I thought I would collapse."

Even uttering these few words fatigued Alex, and with Jesse at his side he fell into an exhausted sleep. An hour later, Jesse heard cries of pain from the front room. With a lantern in hand, she went to the captain with the gangrenous leg. He was delirious and called out, "Mother, mother, help me." To comfort him, Jesse responded, "I am here, my son, right beside you. Now hold my hand." She reached for one of the last doses of laudanum and gave it to him with a few sips of water. While waiting for it take its merciful effect, she held his head against her chest. When he fell asleep, she turned the lantern to the lieutenant with camp fever. His mouth was agape, his breathing labored. He was unresponsive to Jesse's words. She covered him with a blanket for warmth and returned to Alex's side.

Just after dawn on January 3rd, Jesse was awakened by loud, husky voices outside the ferry building. She ran to the front just as an Irish sergeant and his squad of British Light Infantry barged through the door. The sergeant took in the two invalids and the small Black woman before him. The sergeant demanded, "Are you all that's left, and where have the rebels gone?"

Undaunted, Jesse replied, "I assist here at the General Hospital. As you can see, we have two dying officers. In the rear room is Dr. Alexander Grant, Director of the General Hospital, but he is frightfully ill himself. Can you please send for your regiment's surgeon?"

The Irish sergeant charged past Jesse and knelt beside Alex's pallet. Alex was waning but knew the red-coated sergeant's intent. "Doctor, I'll get our surgeon to see you and your invalids right off, but first you better tell me where your rebel army has gone."

With all his strength, Alex gathered his wits for one last ploy. "Sergeant, only for the sake of my patients do I tell you...Do I have your word that you'll send your surgeon?"

"Yeah, Yeah, immediately," grumped the sergeant impatiently.

"Then, the army has gone to Philadelphia," rasped Alex.

Jesse thought to herself, "How shrewd of Dr. Grant. Even through his agonizing illness, he still gives the enemy false intelligence."

While the sergeant rushed to General Cornwallis's headquarters with his news of Washington's retreat to the rebel capital, one infantryman guarded the new prisoners of war, and another tried to find where the British Regimental Surgeon might be. But even before the sergeant could get to Cornwallis, he heard distant thumping and recognized the sound of British field cannon, most likely six-pounders. With his keen ear, he estimated they were no more than eight to ten miles away. He smiled to himself and thought, "No need to rush to Cornwallis now. Our boys must already be attacking the retreating rebels!"

Jesse too heard the guns, starting before eight o'clock and continuing for more than an hour. The thumping awakened Alex, and to him, Jesse expressed her worry. "Goodness, those guns can't be too far away. I pray our army was not surprised by the redcoats!"

Alex nodded in agreement and lapsed into sleep again.

Later in the morning of January 3rd, a tired, disheveled lad, no more than twenty years old, rushed into the hospital. He wore a long red coat and a tricorn hat, but his uniform showed no rank. In his right hand, he carried a blood-stained, brown leather kit. The British infantryman guarding the hospital told him that the two American officers had already died and directed him to another officer and nurse in the back room. The red-coated lad saw Alex now barely responsive and told Jesse, "I'm the Surgeon's Mate to the 17th Regiment of Foot... I'm called Tom Smart. My surgeon is taking care of our wounded, so he sent me. Who are you, and who is this next to you?"

British Surgeon's Mate Smart quickly saw the seriousness of Alex Grant's condition and said worriedly to Jesse, "If I don't bleed your doctor, he's going to die!"

Seeing how young the mate was and knowing that surgeon's mates usually had little formal training, Jesse responded, "Mr. Smart, please do not take any offense, but have you done bleedings before?"

Tom Smart replied humbly, "I've been a mate for just about a year. Nearly all the bleedings are done by my surgeon, but he's directed me on several bleedings in case –like now—I needed to do them myself. Now, you can give me a hand?"

As Tom Smart opened his medical kit, Jesse noticed his fingernails were soiled with dried blood, most likely from soldiers he had cared for earlier that day. She shuddered for fear of his uncleanliness but could not say a word. Jesse placed Alex's left arm in a bowl of warm water for a few moments, and Smart placed a tourniquet around Alex's upper arm. After Alex's veins became engorged, Smart removed Alex's arm from the water and placed it above a pewter basin. Taking a silver lancet from his case, he sharply incised Alex's suffused arm vein. Alex barely noticed. Dark red blood flowed briskly into the graduated basin. When the mate had let fourteen ounces, he released the tourniquet and covered the vein with a cloth dressing.

"That should do it for now," Smart said. "Let's see how he responds. I'll be back in two hours. In the meantime, I've got to get back to my regiment. I'll also get the sentry outside to...er..dispose of the two deceased officers in your front room."

Alex seemed to rally initially as his breathing became easier, but only temporarily. With her alarm rising, Jesse applied a milk and bread poultice to Alex's neck. She gave him one of two doses of laudanum remaining in her supply and secreted the other inside her cloth sack. He opened his eyes and recognized Jesse. "I am feeling so poorly. I'm grateful you are here with me." She comforted him with a few tender strokes of her hand to his fevered brow. She thought, "Please, Lord, spare him. He has treated me—and everyone—so kindly, and we will need him.".

By late morning, Tom Smart returned in an ambulance wagon. He took in Alex's poor condition. "There's no more I can do here, but I'm taking this ambulance of wounded officers to the

British General Hospital in Brunswick. I made room for Dr. Grant. We'll be there by nightfall. Fortunately, one of the best doctors in the medical department will be in Brunswick on one of his regular visits from his main post. You see, he's the Director of His Majesty's Main General Hospital in New York City."

"Mr. Smart, I must go as well to take care of Dr. Grant. I can also help with your wounded."

The mate shrugged and responded, "Well, that makes sense. Besides, this is no place for you to be left alone. Let's get Dr. Grant warm and as comfortable as possible, and we'll be off for Brunswick."

Inside the ambulance, there were three wounded British officers. Jesse glanced at each of them, noted their cold, stony appearance, and grieved at their prospects. She covered Alex and herself with extra blankets, near the front of ambulance. Jesse hoped her own warmth would bring him some comfort. By early afternoon, Tom Smart's ambulance had made it well past the village of Maidenhead on the Trenton-Princeton Road. As they proceeded another three miles along the road, they approached Stony Brook Bridge. There, Smart took in a ghastly site and called out, "Jesse, for God's sake, come take a look at this!"

---

(1) Officers' ranks in both the British and American Armies were the same. In ascending order, they were: lieutenant, captain, major, lieutenant colonel (often shortened in conversation to "colonel"), colonel, brigadier general (often shortened to "brigadier"), major general, lieutenant general, and general.

(2) In 1777, there were approximately 3500 physicians in the United States, but the vast majority had never set foot in a medical school. Only ten percent had formal

medical education either in European schools or in the two new medical schools in America. The first American medical school was the Medical College of Philadelphia, founded in 1765, and later became the University of Pennsylvania School of Medicine. The other American medical school was King's College, later Columbia University School of Medicine. Fully ninety percent of American physicians got their training through apprenticeships, non-regulated, informal training from a senior practitioner.

(3) Camp fever, also called jail, ship, or hospital fever, was typhus, a disease recognized since ancient times. It is caused by microorganisms called rickettsia and is spread in crowded conditions by body lice. In the 18th Century, typhus had a high mortality. Today, it is cured with common antibiotics if diagnosed early.

Chapter 2 - The Brothers Howe
Evening, January 2, 1777
Mount Pleasant Mansion, British Headquarters, New York City

While Jesse and Alex shivered in the wagon carrying them to the redcoat General Hospital in Brunswick, British Commander in Chief, General Sir William Howe, overlooked New York City's East River from his headquarters office in Mount Pleasant mansion. (1) The large, two-story house was the Beekman family's elaborate estate, which had been abandoned in mid-September when the American army evacuated the city. Shortly afterwards, General Howe made it his headquarters as he found the elegant mansion much to his liking. Its exterior featured formal gardens and a large greenhouse containing many species exotic to New York, even orange trees and tropical plants. The luxurious interior had black marble mantels, highly ornamented fireplaces, and ornately carved banisters.

General Howe turned from the window to the man in the world he most trusted: his older brother, Admiral Lord Richard Howe, commander of the Royal Navy fleet in American waters. The admiral's right boot and sock were removed, his leg elevated on a hassock. "Good Lord, my toe feels like it's been bitten by a mangy dog." complained Lord Richard. "Look how red and swollen it is. Blast, these gout attacks have been coming all too commonly these days. (2) Sir William offered comfort. "Dick, here, let me get you another snifter of brandy. That should make you feel better." General William Howe, outgoing and affable by nature, appeared to be in typical high spirits. Just a few days before, a fast packet ship from London brought the gratifying news that he had been knighted for his victories over the American rebels the previous autumn. Now, his official title would be 5th Viscount Howe, Knight of the Bath, an honor dating from medieval times when recipients bathed as a sign of purification.

Admiral Richard Howe's persona was quite different. He was reserved, some thought him even remote, and always a man of few words. This night, despite the pain from his recurring gout, he managed to show his great family pride. "Savage," he said using an intimate family nickname for William, "I raise my glass and salute your great battlefield successes and the high honor you have brought to our family!"

"Dick," the general beamed, "I am thrilled to follow in your footsteps, as you were knighted previously. And on this night, I toast the beloved memory of our brother George, courageous in battle and idolized by the Regulars and by the militia. Good God, it's hard to believe he's been gone nearly twenty years." The brothers were now the pride of an already distinguished family. Both General William and Admiral Richard had earned reputations as popular, bold, and daring warriors during the French and Indian War. (3)

But underlying General William Howe's outward glow, he harbored misgivings. His mood began to change as he sought succor from his brother. "Dick, two weeks ago, we were cocksure we had this bloody rebellion quashed. Our forces defeated that American ragtag in battle after battle throughout 1776, and in December my agents reported that the rebels were down to less than three thousand half-frozen souls in Pennsylvania, on the bank of the Delaware River. With winter setting in, we secured our forces and expected the bitter weather to devastate the rebels. We thought we'd finish them off come spring. By God, I was looking forward to a comfortable winter in New York."

Even though the two brothers were close, there were often long pauses in their conversations. General Sir William reflected in silence on the two alarming dispatches he had received on the morning of December 27th. The first brought stunning news that the outpost at Trenton had been attacked by the American rebels the day before. Sixty-five miles from New

York and at the end of Howe's line, Trenton had been manned by fourteen hundred German mercenary allies and commanded by a veteran colonel. The second dispatch reported disaster. The German colonel had been killed, and a thousand Germans had been taken prisoner. Less than one in five managed to escape.

Lord Richard grunted in agreement. "Yes," he replied, "Setting up the posts was typical army doctrine." After another pause, he continued, "Bloody hell, you know the fortunes of war, and now you've sent your best regiments in pursuit of those damned rebels. We'll have a further report soon."

Indeed, William Howe had reacted promptly to the American attack at Trenton. Under his favorite and most courageous field general, Lord Earl Cornwallis, Howe sent a column of eight thousand men to pursue the American rabble. As if the admiral's words were prophetic, an express rider was ushered into headquarters late that evening. The brief report had been written that bitterly cold afternoon:

2nd January 1777
To Sir William Howe, KB, Commander in Chief:

I have the duty to report that the King's Forces under my command have found the rebel main body and have them pinned along the Assunpink Creek in Trenton. I will attack in the morning and expect to defeat them handily as we have them heavily outnumbered.

Your most obedient servant,
Charles Cornwallis, Major General, Commanding

Showing the dispatch to his brother, the general sneered, referring to Washington, "Now, we'll bag that Virginia planter!"

"Outstanding news, Savage," Lord Howe replied. "But with

my gouty right foot still so painful, the best place for me now is in bed. I bid you good night."

As Lord Richard hobbled to his room on the second floor, William rushed to his first-floor suite, far down the hall from the parlor. Awaiting him there was his paramour, Elizabeth Loring, the wife of one of his officers. "And what could possibly have kept you almost all evening?" she purred.

Earlier, Elizabeth had slipped into the general's suite through a private entrance. She spent several nights a week with the general, sometimes at the home of a loyalist or, as on this night, at Howe's headquarters.

Elizabeth Loring, age twenty-four, was twenty-three years younger than the general but was remarkably confident and assertive. General William Howe found her sensuous with long brown hair and full lips. He craved her from the moment they met at an officers' ball in late 1775 in Boston. The sole child of a wealthy Long Island family, she married Joshua Loring when she was seventeen. Joshua Loring had served in the British Army during the French and Indian War and subsequently had a series of modest British government posts. But by 1775 after six years of marriage, he had become lethargic, benefiting from Elizabeth's sizeable inheritance, and caroused regularly with his workmates. Elizabeth now found Joshua boring. When the powerful commander in chief Howe began to flirt with her, she could not resist. At first, their liaisons were discreet, but by summer of 1776 in New York, word of their affair was known throughout British circles. (4) When General Howe then appointed Joshua Loring to the lucrative post as Assistant Commissary for Prisoners, rumors spread that the appointment was Loring's "reward" for Howe's access to Elizabeth.

Howe often shared military matters with his younger lover, especially on evenings filled with sumptuous meals and his favorite wines. But this night, General Howe was not in the mood for tactical discussions. "Elizabeth, my dear, General Cornwallis has the American ragtag in his clutch and will finish them in the morning. For now, it's almost midnight, may we complete this night perfectly?" Elizabeth clutched William's hand and led him to bed.

Sir William arose at seven o'clock on January 3rd and arranged for his coachman to convey Elizabeth to her home. After his favorite breakfast of salmon and eggs, he busied himself attending to official reports and correspondence, all the while eagerly expecting word from General Cornwallis. Early in the afternoon, his orderly rapped on his office door with the much-awaited dispatch carried by Cornwallis's aide de camp. Howe ripped open the dispatch, and as he read the brief report, his face contorted.

---

(1) Location of Mount Pleasant today would be at 1st Ave and 51 St.

(2) Gout has been recognized since ancient times. Its manifestations include painful arthritis, typically of the great toe, and kidney stones. Because it has been long associated with rich foods and excessive alcohol, it has been referred to as "the disease of kings." General Howe provided his brother with brandy but was unaware that the alcohol might contribute to the condition. Today, gout is recognized as the result of abnormal metabolism of uric acid, and it is treated with drugs to decrease inflammation or decrease uric acid levels.

(3) In the French and Indian War, their older brother, Brigadier General George Howe, won an enduring place in the hearts of the Americans for his bravery against the French at Fort Ticonderoga in 1758. General George

Howe, aged thirty-six, was killed in that action.

(4) It was not uncommon for British officers to have extramarital affairs while on service in North America, but an affair with a subordinate officer's wife was unusual. General William Howe was married in 1765 to Frances "Fanny" Conolly, who was from an aristocratic Anglo-Irish family and thirteen years younger than he. They had no children.

Chapter 3 - The Battle at Princeton
Friday, January 3, 1777
Central New Jersey

Tom Smart squinted in the bright winter sunlight and saw bodies, all clad in scarlet uniforms, on both sides of the road. Jesse thrust her head through the ambulance's front canvas flap. "Heavens", she muttered to herself, "There must be forty of them lying out there!" Scattered among them were muskets and accoutrements, left by dead, dying or retreating British soldiers. Smart stopped the ambulance wagon near several men lying on the roadside, hoping to find some still alive. When he jumped down and rolled the first two over, he gasped. "Jesse, come here! This is desperate. They're all murdered, and every one of them from my own 17th Regiment of Foot. What in the devil's name happened here?"

****

Beginning just after midnight on January 3rd, Washington extricated his army from the British troops across the Assunpink Creek in Trenton. To deaden the sounds of their movement, the American Army even wrapped the gun carriage wheels in rags and marched in stealth east to Allen's Town. Stubbles of trees still hindered this part of the road, but the ground was frozen solid from the cold front that had just passed into West Jersey. The men, cannon, and heavy wagons were able to move quickly.

British General Cornwallis stayed put all night, fooled by the blazing American campfires, and expecting an easy victory in the morning. By first light, the Americans were already at Stony Brook, two miles south of Princeton. There, Washington divided his army. To his second in command, Washington barked out, "General Greene, your division will proceed to the left and take that stone bridge on the main road to Princeton." On the clear morning, Greene made out the bridge, a mile away across the valley. Washington continued, "You'll have General Hugh Mercer's 3rd Virginia brigade with you. General Cornwallis will no doubt awaken and be in a fury that we have eluded his grip. I'm sure he will come after us in force. Hold that bridge to delay his pursuit."

Major General Nathaneal Greene and Commander in Chief Washington understood each other perfectly. In 1775, at age thirty-three years, Greene had become the youngest brigadier general in the army, and through the 1776 campaign, he became the commander in chief's favorite—steady, loyal, and smart. General Hugh Mercer's 3rd Virginia Regiment was one of Washington's best, and Mercer himself, in good health at fifty-one years, was widely respected for his bravery and wisdom.

As Greene led his division toward the bridge, Washington said to his other division commander, "General Sullivan, I will ride with you. I want you to take the road to the right and attack Princeton from the east."

Hidden from Greene's division by the rolling terrain, three British regiments were approaching the stone bridge from the north. They had left Princeton at dawn, under orders to join Cornwallis in Trenton. As they crossed Stony Brook, their colonel caught the morning's sun flashing off the bayonets of Mercer's vanguard. He withdrew his scarlet-clad brigades back across the bridge and raced for good ground in a nearby orchard, but the Americans beat him to it. Now on the same side of the bridge, both the British and Americans quickly formed battle lines, no more than forty yards apart and began firing with muskets and small field cannon. General Mercer's horse fell after it was shot in leg, but Mercer continued to fight on foot. The British turned to their most fearsome tactic: a bayonet charge. As the redcoats closed with their seventeen-inch-long bayonets, Mercer's men panicked and ran in chaos. Mercer tried to rally his men but was knocked down by a British musket butt. Still fighting, he rose to defend himself with his sword but fell again. He was wounded seven times by British bayonets and was left for dead by the advancing red line.

From the road on the right, Washington heard the firing and galloped to Mercer's men. There, despite the hot fire and closeness of the British line, he waved his hat and called to his broken men. "Rally on me, my hearty Virginians! Rally on me!"

The British colonel yelled to his line, "Volley fire. Shoot those rebels and bring down that fool on the white horse!"

Washington was engulfed in smoke, but when the air cleared, he was still in the saddle, shouting encouragement to his troops. They cheered him and responded by rallying. Just then, Major General John Sullivan, a fiery New Hampshirite, led his division to reinforce the Virginians, and an American battery raked the redcoats with grape shot. (1) The redcoats reeled. Now well outnumbering the British, American units flanked them on both their right and left and had them nearly surrounded. But courage was high on both sides that day, and the gallant British commander was not about to surrender. He ordered another bayonet charge to break out of the developing encirclement and led a rapid retreat, leaving his dead and fatally wounded on the field.

Washington recovered his casualties and then marched his army into Princeton village. There the British rearguard, made up of men of the British 40th Regiment, had barricaded themselves in Nassau Hall, a strong stone edifice, the main building of the College of New Jersey. (2) The redcoats were quickly surrounded, and a New York Artillery Company brought up its two guns to point blank range. Captain Alexander Hamilton, commanding the battery, shouted, "Fire at the wooden doors and into the windows." The first cannon's six-pound solid ball smashed into the hall and ricocheted wildly through the rooms. It bounced off an interior, stone wall and tore off the leg of one private and then the shoulder girdle of another. Both redcoats fell to the floor, screaming in agony as bright red, arterial blood spurted through the room. A second later, a ball from the second cannon crashed into a first-floor window and instantly decapitated a sergeant who had just dared to peek out. His mangled, severed head rolled ghoulishly across the floor. More rounds were fired, killing and maiming the British defenders. They had had enough of the carnage, and a British captain waved a white flag from a second story window. Nearly two hundred redcoats surrendered.

Back at Stony Bridge, General Mercer, still alive, was taken to a nearby farmhouse. Despite his multiple stabbings, he was alert. A regimental surgeon hurried to his bedside and cut open the general's coat and breeches. "Sir," the surgeon said calmly, "I'm going to dress your leg wounds, but two of the wounds have entered your belly."

A veteran of many battles, Mercer did not need further explanation. He knew his wounds were fatal. The brigadier simply nodded in acceptance as the surgeon dressed his belly and administered medication for the pain. The next day, a senior physician arrived from Philadelphia, but by then Mercer was already moribund as his lacerated bowel leaked its contents into his abdomen. (3) Mercer struggled heroically and lingered a few more days before expiring.

In front of Nassau Hall, Washington called Greene and Sullivan to his side. "My intention was to strike at Brunswick, but the men have marched all night and fought like demons this morning. They are cold and worn. I can ask no more."

Sullivan nodded in agreement. Greene added, "Sir, an advance party of engineers is already at work in Morristown to set up camp. It's time to collect our trophies of war, shall we say, and prepare for winter there."

Washington savored the moment. As he led his army north to Morristown, he thought to himself, "Lord of Mercy, in ten days, we have had two victories over the best of the German and British regiments. We're now well stocked with captured supplies and arms, and from Morristown, we'll be able to counter any of Howe's moves. Yes, it's time to rest and refit the army. Indeed, we have given new life to the cause of independence. God willing, those in Philadelphia—and even those in London and perhaps Paris—will not miss the meaning of these victories."

****

That very afternoon General Howe received Cornwallis's dispatch. Indeed, what he read made him furious.

To Sir William Howe, Commander in Chief:
Sir,

I have the duty to report that at daybreak this morning, 3rd January, we commenced our attack on the rebel positions across the Assunpink Creek in Trenton and found that the Enemy had retreated from their positions during the night. Our rangers determined that their column was headed not to Philadelphia, but to Princeton. I immediately set out in pursuit. Meanwhile, the 17th, 40th and 55th Regiments which were marching south from Princeton to support me in Trenton encountered an Enemy column at the Stony Bridge, just south of Princeton village. These three regiments engaged the Enemy and caused them to retreat initially, but then a much larger Enemy force arrived making it necessary for our regiments to withdraw. Our losses were about three hundred men. The Enemy then advanced into the town and attacked soldiers of the 40th and 55th Regiments, who had barricaded themselves in Nassau Hall. The Enemy fired their cannon directly into the building and caused the surrender of the 194 defenders. With my main force from Trenton, I am now pursuing the Enemy, who we believe are heading toward Brunswick.

Your most obedient Servant,
Charles Earl Cornwallis, Major General, Commanding

With his world turned inside out, Sir William exclaimed out loud, "What? How could this happen to my finest regiments?"

Yet, in his inner mind, Howe knew that every setback in war provided an opportunity, and he was already planning his revenge. He called into the adjacent room to his military secretary, "Major Kemble, bring me the map case and request Admiral Howe's presence."

When Admiral Howe strode into his brother's office, Sir William looked up from the New Jersey map spread out before him and grunted a welcome. The grandfather clock struck three chimes.

After showing Lord Richard the new dispatch, Sir William continued, "Look here. At Trenton, Cornwallis was outsmarted by the rebel commander, but Cornwallis will take care of that rabble for now. Kemble already is dispatching my orders to the other posts at Bordentown and Brunswick to prepare for any possible enemy attack. But I presume Washington's army must be exhausted and will be heading for winter encampment. Dick, I've had enough of playing gently with these blasted rebels. I want to end this bloody rebellion at the outset of this coming spring campaign."

Sir William continued presciently, "Assuming the enemy encamps in the hills around Morristown, they'll find winter shelter there and will be in position to react to our moves. In early spring, I want to draw them out of those hills and into battle—on my terms! To do that, I say we move to capture their capital of Philadelphia. Their Congress will obligate Washington to defend the city, and then we'll finish them off once and for all. They'll have to meet my troops in the open, and then we'll show them what the King's Army can do!"

Then William placed his index finger on the map. "As to the route, eh, look. It's one hundred miles from here in New York to Philadelphia across the flat New Jersey plains. There are three main rivers to cross—the Hudson, the Raritan and then the Delaware, but these will provide no major obstacle because we can use existing ferries or bridges and even supplement them with pontoons my engineers will bring. Now, on closer inspection, we can make it an even easier expedition. Dick, if the Royal Navy would oblige me, we can transport my troops by your large flatboats from Manhattan inside New York Bay, through the Narrows, up Raritan Bay and, eh, disembark here on the south bank of the Raritan, across from Perth Amboy. From there, it is merely seventy miles of flatlands to Philadelphia, with only one river to cross—the Delaware. And Washington will have no choice but to engage us."

Admiral Richard Howe nodded knowingly, "Savage, The Royal Navy will be pleased to provide the flatboats for transporting your troops."

Sir William stood back from the map table and placed his thumbs in his vest pockets. In his own mind, he was now sure it would all turn out well. He called for his secretary, "Major Kemble, call for my Council of War to meet just as soon as General Cornwallis is back from the field. We've got work to do!"

(1) Grape shot is a type of cannon ammunition. It consisted of small caliber balls, wrapped in a canvas bag. When assembled, it looked like a cluster of grapes. It was used effectively for close in firing at infantry.

(2) Later Princeton University.

(3) Mercer's diagnosis was, in modern medical language, peritonitis, even today a life-threatening condition caused by bacteria entering the abdominal cavity from injured bowel. In present day, it is treated by antibiotics and surgical repair of the bowel.

Chapter 4 - The American Nurse and the British Surgeon
Friday Evening, January 3, 1777
Brunswick, New Jersey

As Tom Smart put together the British disaster at Princeton, the toll of deaths stunned him. To Jesse, he grieved, "So many poor, young lads, and I know most of them. Yet, we've got the wounded from Trenton already in the ambulance to look after. There's no more we can do here. We'll have to leave it to a burial detail to care for these dead." He mounted the ambulance and headed toward Brunswick. Inside, Jesse looked after three wounded British soldiers, shielding them from the bitter cold with extra blankets and administering laudanum when they cried out in pain. But her main charge was Alex, whose fever, throat pain and difficulty breathing all worsened along the route. When his chills shook the wagon, Jesse nestled with him under a layer of blankets to share her warmth. She desperately wished she could do more to comfort him. Alex passed in and out of sleep, and Jesse worried once when she could not awaken him.

Four miles from Brunswick, Tom Smart heard thundering hoofbeats approaching from the south. He stopped the ambulance as three scarlet-coated officers with a small wagon overtook his ambulance. Immediately, Smart spotted insignias of the 17th Regiment on their uniforms. The captain recognized him. "You're the 17th's surgeon's mate. What in hell's name are you doing out here?"

When Smart explained he was bringing wounded officers to the Brunswick General Hospital, the captain warned him, "Holy Mother, don't you know this area is crawling with enemy troops? Look here, what's left of the 17th are coming along this road and are not far behind. I've got a lieutenant inside my wagon, and he's in bad shape. He took a musket ball to the side of his head. I must get him to the General Hospital in Brunswick but fear he won't make it. Our surgeon's missing. Who knows what in God's name happened to him in all the chaos? I wrapped the lieutenant's head with an extra shirt I had. It was all I could do. Can you have a look? I'd be very obliged. You see, he's my younger brother."

Smart replied, "Captain, we've been on this road for hours, and I've not seen any signs of the enemy. So right now, I can have a look at him."

Jesse exited the ambulance and offered, "Captain, perhaps I might also help with your brother?"

"And exactly how would you be able to help?" The captain's disdain was palpable.

"I'm a nurse with the Continental Army General Hospital, and I'm caring for my surgeon who is dreadfully ill inside here. He was taken prisoner in Trenton. I've also been looking after the wounded British officers inside this ambulance."

But the captain was unimpressed and muttered, "Just what we need: a prisoner of war who needs our medical care." But desperate to get care for his brother, he added, "Very well, then, see what you can do." In the small wagon, Tom Smart and Jesse found the wounded British lieutenant unconscious. The white shirt wrapped around his head was soaked with blood. The right side of his head was already contused, with dark bluish-black blood grotesquely undermining the skin of his face.

When Smart removed the dressing, they saw the lieutenant's skull was fractured, with a one-ounce musket ball firmly lodged in the bone, four finger breadths above his left ear. "It's a miracle he's still alive. The ball must have been at the end of its course. If the ball had gone another inch into his head, he'd have been killed instantly."

Noting the lieutenant's irregular, shallow breathing and his alarmingly slow pulse, Jesse immediately understood his condition. "Mr. Smart, I've seen this before. Wounded men with bleeding almost always have a fast pulse, but Dr. Grant said that with head wounds the brain swells and causes the heart to slow. The breathing becomes shallow as well. This lieutenant will need trepanning once we get to the hospital, but for right now that ball should be removed. Otherwise, the ball will likely compress his brain even more as the wagon bumps and bounces along this road... I saw a small medical pouch in the ambulance. I hope there's what we need in it."

Jesse brought the leather pouch from the ambulance and shook her head as she saw only old instruments. "All we have here are two small probes, a bullet forceps, and some dressings." She thought to herself, "Too bad we don't have Dr. Grant's full set. With Dr. Grant so ill, Dr. Hobbs must have taken all the instruments from the hospital to Princeton." Jesse continued, "Mr. Smart, will you try to remove the ball? I believe it's the lieutenant's only chance."

Smart shook his head. "I haven't even seen the procedure."

Jesse replied, "I saw Dr. Grant do this several times. We can't take the lieutenant along these rutted roads. With God's help, I think I can do this." Using a bullet forceps, she grasped the ball, but she could not get an adequate purchase, and the forceps slipped off twice. Despite the cold, sweat formed on her brow and under her arms. Her mouth was cottony and dry. She looked at Smart woefully. "If we don't remove the ball, the pressure will add to his brain swelling. Please hand me the steel probe."

Jesse wedged the probe under the ball inferiorly and gently tried to pry the ball loose. Jesse's heart raced as she heard the sickening crunch of the shattered skull bone under her probe. Tom Smart's eyes widened as he watched helplessly. Jesse assessed, "I'll have to try at another location. Lord, help us." Jesse replaced the probe on the ball's lateral side. Finding less resistance, she slid the probe gently under the ball in an arc. "Thank goodness," she sighed, "the ball's freer." Jesse re-grasped the lead ball with the forceps and extracted it. She placed it in a pewter basin and said, "Thank you, Lord. That will relieve some of the pressure. The lieutenant's skull bone is still depressed, but there's no bleeding. That's all we can do now."

Smart beamed gratefully at Jesse as she dressed the wound with clean bandages. The captain, duly impressed with her knowledge and skills, was uncharacteristically humble. "Nurse, I am most thankful for the care you've given my brother. We must all get to the General Hospital."

Just after nightfall, the captain and Smart brought the ambulance to the Brunswick General Hospital, set up in the Presbyterian Church on the Raritan River. Stiff and cold from the long journey, Smart climbed down from his perch and walked behind the captain into the building. They instantly noted its cleanliness and order. A roaring fire threw its heat into the room. They were greeted warmly. "Hello, I'm the Hospital Mate—I'm called Samuel Blackfield. You look like you could use a hot rum."

"I could at that," replied the captain, "but first the lieutenant has a severe head wound. He's my younger brother."

Smart added, "And there's an American surgeon—a prisoner of war—with bad throat inflammation plus three other British officers wounded this morning at Princeton. Is the Director of the Hospital here this evening? His reputation precedes him."

Hospital Mate Samuel Blackfield responded, "Your invalids must be nearly frozen. Bring the officers and the American over there to the clean pallets near the fire. The director is expected to return here any moment. He's on regularly scheduled inspections of the regimental hospitals."

Just as soon as they were all inside the hospital, a tall officer with thick, graying hair strode in the door. Projecting calm and competence, he said, "Good evening, I'm Dr. Walker, Director of His Majesty's Main General Hospital in New York. I am here on inspections and to help for the moment. I see we have our work cut out for us. Please tell me who you are and then what you know of the wounded."

Quickly, Dr. Walker assessed the situation. To the captain, Walker spoke directly, but compassionately, "The lieutenant will need trepanning to relieve the swelling in his brain. We cannot wait." Assuming it was Tom Smart who removed the ball, Walker praised his action. "Mr. Smart, I congratulate you on your wise decision there in the field. The lieutenant's condition is poor, but you've given him every possible hope."

Smart stammered, "Dr. Walker, I...I...I am honored....to be in your presence...but...but you see, Sir, the ball was removed by the American nurse."

Walker turned about to see the petite, Black woman. Graciously, Dr. Walker replied, "My good lady, in all my years in the medical department, I've rarely seen a surgeon's mate remove a bullet lodged in the skull, and never have I even heard of a nurse doing it. You must have worked with an extraordinary surgeon. I offer my heartfelt compliments to you... and my sincerest apologies. Would you kindly tell me your name?"

Jesse was immediately taken by Dr. Walker's humility and courtesy. She had rarely been treated so respectfully by American men and was astonished to receive it from a British officer. She responded with a gentle smile and her own innate tact. "Thank you, Dr. Walker. My name is Jesse Jones. Since last summer, I have been honored to work with the best surgeon in the

Continental Army. And, Sir, he is the officer over there with severe throat inflammation. His name is Dr. Alexander Grant, of Philadelphia."

Walker's face lit up as he recognized the name. He put his arm on Samuel Blackfield's shoulder. "Blackfield," he said with affection, "Please see the other wounded while I see Dr. Grant with Nurse Jesse. As soon as I'm able, I'll prepare for the trepanning.

Turning to Jesse, the director inquired, "Tell me more about Dr. Grant's illness. How long has he been ill, and what has been done for him?"

On a thick pallet next to the fire, Alex rallied a bit after the long exposure in the ambulance. Kneeling next to Alex, Walker spoke softly, "Dr. Grant, I am honored to meet you. I've been in North America for over fifteen years, and I've read your book on wounds and injuries. It's changed my practice."

Through his fever and pain, Alex acknowledged Dr. Walker's compliments with a weak smile and a nod. Walker held Alex's right hand. "For now, Dr. Grant, I'm sorry for your severe throat inflammation. I've been seeing lots of these cases this winter. I think we'll spare you any further bleedings. I've just not observed very good responses. Instead, we'll continue with the neck poultices and laudanum. Fortunately, I have a good supply right now. I want to keep up your nourishment with broths and teas, and I have a soothing gargle made with sassafras tea. I'm glad Nurse Jesse will be able to help provide care for you. We've just been inundated with sick and wounded. And it's clear she *is* an exceptionally talented nurse. Right now, I'm going to perform trepanning on the young lieutenant. I'll come back to see you soon."

To Jesse, he said, "Dr. Grant seems stable just now. Mr.

Smart will look after the other wounded. Would you please assist Mr. Blackfield and me in the operation?"

Dr. Walker's operating theater was in a large side room which Mate Blackfield kept clean and orderly. During the day, it was thoroughly aired and well-lit by windows on three sides, and this evening Blackfield made it as bright as possible with several banks of large candles. Blackfield, a veteran of many campaigns, had assisted Walker on hundreds of operations and had already placed the lieutenant in a low chair with his head firmly fixed against padded, wooden side pieces.

Dr. Walker began, "Blackfield, Keep the lieutenant's head completely still. He's not responsive now, but my incision may draw movement. Nurse, please stand on my right to assist us." Walker skillfully cut into the skin and tendon above the depressed fracture and extended the incision to determine the place for the trepanning. The fracture line extended one inch on each side of the depression.

"Nurse, please hold these retractors to pull back the skin. We had better not go right at the depression. The brain right under it is likely injured already. I'm going to go two inches anteriorly along the fracture line. Hold him fast and firm, Sammy!"

Deftly, the surgeon reached onto the adjacent table and removed his trephine from its velvet lined case. It had a bone handle which was affixed to a three-inch long steel shaft. At the other end was a cylindrical saw, three-fourths of an inch in diameter. Walker placed the teeth of the trephine against the skull and bore down into the bone with twisting pressure. The lieutenant groaned as the bone crunched under the saw. After a half-dozen twists, Walker withdrew the instrument to clean bone spicules from the cutting edges. He took a deep breath, replaced the trephine in its track and carefully cut the rest of the way through the skull. With forceps, he removed the disc of bone.

Underneath, Walker saw the dura mater lining the brain. Below the bulging dura, there was dark reddish-black fluid.

"Ah," he concluded, "look at how tense the dura is. This poor fellow has suffered bleeding in his brain and marked swelling, as well. This will not have a good ending. Blackfield, get me dry lint to fill the trepanned hole, and then please dress his head. I'll go see his brother."

It was nearly midnight when Dr. Walker saw the captain. Both were weary. "Captain, come sit with me by the fire. Our cook has made some fresh tea."

The captain was already prepared for devastating news. "Dr. Walker, I've seen many men with head wounds like my brother's. What will happen?"

"Your brother sustained an extensive skull fracture. He has been unconscious all along. In the operation, I saw signs of swelling and bleeding in his brain. He will not survive, but I can't tell you how long he will go on. My best estimate is a few days. I am sorry to have to give you this news. Would you like to be at his side?"

While the captain went to his brother, Walker returned to Alex's pallet. Alex was sleeping fitfully. Jesse reported that his breathing was once again labored and that his cough brought up foul yellow sputum. To Walker's touch, Alex's brow was feverish, and his pulse rapid and weak.

Jesse asked, "Dr. Walker, are you going to bleed him? When Dr. Benjamin Rush, the consulting physician from Philadelphia, saw American soldiers with fevers in our hospital, he always advised bleeding, often repeatedly."

"Yes, Nurse, I know of the esteemed Dr. Rush and his

advocacy for bleeding, but I am of a different mind. I'd wager in less than fifty years bleedings will have disappeared from practice. I don't have proof yet, but I suspect bleedings do more harm than good. I've been keeping a log of cases of severe fevers. On even-numbered months, I do bleedings while on odd-numbered months, I do not. (1) So, January being an odd-numbered month, I'll treat Dr. Grant without bleeding. Yet, with Dr. Grant having thick yellow sputum, I want him to breathe warm, moist vapors. I've developed a special device to do just that."

Walker called out to his surgeon's mate, "Please bring over the breathing hood and the vapor apparatus."

From the hospital's storeroom, Blackfield set up a small tent over Alex's pallet. Adjacent to the pallet, the mate placed a large pewter basin. He filled the basin with steaming hot water to which he added camphor crystals. As the hood over Alex filled with the aromatic vapors, Alex breathed in deeply.

"Dr. Grant, Nurse Jesse, this apparatus of mine has helped others this winter. I think it will make the breathing easier. My quarters are just upstairs. Call me immediately with any concerns."

As Dr. Walker left, Jesse felt confidence in his care and admired his approach. His manner was similar to Alex's, in his methodical, innovative approach to care and especially his empathic care. From a personal view, she was impressed by the way he respected her. She thought, "In the last few months, two other doctors have talked about their growing reluctance to apply bleedings—Dr John Hobbs, Assistant Director at the Continental Army General Hospital and Dr. Alexander Grant himself."

(1) Dr. Timothy Walker was conducting, in today's scientific terminology, a "controlled clinical trial." His research began with a question: is bleeding beneficial or harmful? His method was simple by modern standards, but his purpose was to answer the question as objectively as possible. The 18th Century was a time of enlightenment and of great progress in science. Dr. Grant and Dr. Walker may have even read of one of the first clinical trials, conducted in 1753 by the Royal Navy Surgeon James Lind, who published results of a trial using citrus to prevent scurvy.

Chapter 5 - The Rogue
Monday, January 6, 1777
British Headquarters, New York City

At sunset on Monday afternoon, January 6th, General William Howe called to order his council of war. The commander in chief sat at the head of a heavy oak table, and Admiral Lord Howe was strategically seated at the opposite end, his gouty, bare right foot elevated on a hassock. The commander in chief turned to the officer on his right, "My dear General Cornwallis, as you returned from the field just this afternoon, would you please apprise us of the situation in the Jerseys?" (1)

"Yes, Sir, General Howe. Two days ago, our forces concentrated in Brunswick to secure that base in case of enemy attack. By yesterday, however, our agents reported that the Americans had no intentions of resuming any offensive and were headed to winter quarters in Morristown. Given the deteriorating weather, the enemy's head start, and the exhaustion of my troops, it was impossible to pursue the rebel army."

General Howe concluded, "Well, if you could not overtake Washington's army, no one could have. The last two weeks have shown us a turn of events. The fighting season is now over, and we must plan wisely for the spring. That is our purpose this evening."

The council was unusually small since several senior officers, notably General Henry Clinton, Howe's second in command, had already sailed home for the winter. The remaining officer at the table, seated to Howe's left, respectfully raised his right hand.

In a heavy German accent, he added, "My colleagues, may I make a few observations, please?" General Baron Wilhelm von

Knyphausen was now the senior German officer, a sixty-year-old Hessian and veteran of numerous European campaigns. Despite his age, Knyphausen was slender and fit, with sharp Teutonic features. Among his troops and his peers, he had a rare reputation of being at once gentle but very much respected. Howe acknowledged his request respectfully, "Herr General, the floor is yours. We will benefit from your views."

"Danke," began the baron slipping into his native German. "I have been in America for just three months. You kindly gave me the honor of leading the main attack on Fort Washington last November, on the 16th, to be exact. When our combined forces easily captured that fort, I was convinced the rebellion would be crushed quickly. But, in the last ten days, General Washington has shown his own aggressiveness, with his victory against excellent German regiments in Trenton and his actions at Princeton. We must not underestimate him in our planning. That is all I wish to say."

Lord Richard squirmed in his chair at Knyphausen's remarks, feeling that the old German was inappropriately chiding his brother, but William Howe responded graciously. "Baron, we have all been surprised. Rest assure; we do not take the enemy lightly. Indeed, I have just written a dispatch to Lord Germain, Secretary of State for American Colonies, requesting guidance in our planning and re-enforcements of another fifteen thousand troops from England. Yet, with Lord Germain far off in London, we cannot expect a reply for another four months, and by then, any direction will probably arrive too late for our spring maneuvers. Lord Germain cannot fully appreciate the conditions in North America—the vast areas of wilderness, the intricacies of the coastlines, and the extensive time required to travel even modest distances. I expect that Lord Germain will give me great discretion in carrying out my orders." Lord Richard Howe and Lord Cornwallis nodded in support.

Earnestly recording minutes of the council meeting was Howe's Deputy Adjutant General, Major Stephen Kemble, who served as Howe's military secretary. Seated in a desk chair to William Howe's right, Kemble, a New Jersey Loyalist, was also head of Howe's intelligence service.

And behind Kemble, almost imperceptible in the shadows, was a junior officer whom General Howe had invited as an observer. He had soft, handsome features with auburn hair and a stocky, athletic build. At twenty-two years and already Lieutenant Colonel of the 16th Light Dragoons, Banastre Tarleton had earned Howe's respect for his boldness and for his capture of the American general Charles Lee in mid-December. "Ban," as he liked to be called, was a witty extrovert, but he also had his dark side. Howe knew that Tarleton was the second son of a highly successful Liverpool merchant. On occasion, Howe had observed his aristocratic officers slighting Tarleton. And while his family had great wealth from its large export-import firms, it was also tainted because "Tarleton's and Backhouse" dealt in the slave trade. Howe knew that Tarleton's father's ships carried English manufactured goods to Africa, then slaves to America, and finally American sugar, cotton, and tobacco back to England. The trade was extraordinarily profitable, but British aristocrats were beginning to look askance at those profiting from the human misery of slavery. Tarleton sensed this by his exclusion from some officers' circles, and he resented it fiercely. He wanted to be accepted by the officers born to aristocratic privilege. What made matters worse for Banastre Tarleton was that he had a restless personality and sought thrills at gaming tables and brothels. While still in London, he had lost hundreds of English pounds playing faro. He even had to borrow from his mother to buy his commission in 1775. Now in New York, his addictions continued to haunt him. But above all, Banastre Tarleton was ambitious, and he knew that General Howe could sponsor his career advancement. During the council meeting, he took exacting mental notes about the senior officers and their ideas.

"Gentlemen," General Howe began, "I want to end this rebellion in the spring by bringing our superior forces to bear." He then proposed the exact route he and Lord Richard Howe had discussed four nights previously. "Thus," Howe concluded, "when we begin maneuvers in The Jerseys and march toward the rebel capital, the enemy will have to come out from their Morristown stronghold and meet us in the field.

Cornwallis added, "I know the countryside. Most of it is wide open plains, ideal to deploy our army. With our rangers and light infantry covering our flanks, there will be no surprises."

Lord Richard sat in silence, feeling no need to add any weight to the decision, and Knyphausen simply nodded and uttered two German words of support: "*Sehr gut.*"

"With your approval then," William Howe continued, "I will send another dispatch to Lord Germain in London telling him of our decision to move south in the spring to take Philadelphia. (2) I know that General Burgoyne is in London now meeting with Lord Germain about a separate action from Canada. In due course, I'm sure Germain will coordinate the plans. I have no doubt that the Americans can put only one large army on the field, and it will be under George Washington. General Cornwallis, General Knyphausen, may I ask that your staff begin to work on a detailed plan for our march to Philadelphia? Please be certain to coordinate your plans with Lord Richard, who will assure naval support for the crossing from Manhattan to West Jersey. That concludes our business for this evening. Would you now join me dinner? I believe our cook has prepared roasted duck."

* * * * * * * * *

While the senior officers walked to the Howe's dining room, Banastre Tarleton took the cue that it was time for him to leave, and he did that eagerly. He had enough of old men's thoughts for one night. In Tarleton's mind, Howe's war plans were always too cautious and depended too much on what the enemy *might do*. Tarleton knew that rebellions were not put down by capturing capital cities, but only by destroying the rebels' fighting ability. As he walked to his quarters, his mind was already at work on just how to achieve that end. But now, he was ready to enjoy the night. After changing from his uniform into his best black velvet suit, he rode to his favorite gaming establishment, The Black Cat Club, on Broadway across from St. Paul's Church. On route, he drank lustily from his flask of whiskey. When he arrived at close to eleven o'clock, the club was packed with gentlemen, including successful merchants, journalists, attorneys, and British officers, many still in uniform.

"Ah, look who's graced us with his presence," taunted one British colonel who knew Tarleton well. "What detained you until this hour, a little whoring, was it?"

Boldly, Tarleton placed a dismissive slap on the colonel's back and responded, "Well, Colonel, you would be surprised to know I was simply carrying out my duties for the senior officers. Now, would you please make room at your gaming table?"

Never knowing whether to take Tarleton at face value, the colonel snarled, "Keep it up, old boy, and maybe one day you'll get to my rank!"

Everyone in the gambling club focused silently on Tarleton and the colonel. The tension was palpable, but then the colonel returned the slap on Tarleton's back and burst into a hearty laugh. Relieved, everyone including Tarleton joined in. Tarleton ordered another round of whiskey and settled in for the game. The dealer, called the banker, was from the club, and there were four other players, called punters, at the hectic table. Feeling the effects of the alcohol, Tarleton missed that the banker was using a marked deck. By midnight, he had lost over fifty English pounds, a large sum considering his pay was less than a pound per day. Tarleton turned in his few remaining chips, walked one short block south on Broadway, and entered a brightly lit, two-story building.

A voluptuous blond woman greeted him, " 'ello, Ban, what's bin keepin' ya' away from m' establishmen'? I 'aven't seen ya' in weeks?"

"Well, Kate, it's just good to see you. You're looking so fine this evening, and this cold weather has brought color to your cheeks."

Kate, the proprietor of the brothel, knew Tarleton well as he frequented her house regularly. Because most of her visitors were now British officers or rank and file, Kate had to accommodate them, but personally she despised the British. She found the officers so haughty, and the foul rank and file often tried to cheat her. Yet, she had taken a liking to Tarleton. His handsomeness and wit aside, he always treated her courteously and never looked down upon her women. They all said he was an attentive lover. After more banter with Kate, Tarleton got to his real interest. "And would the lovely Miss Desirée be here this evening?"

Desirée greeted him with an affectionate smile, grabbed his hand, and led him up the stairs. At this hour, with few other clients in the house, Kate could hear their love making. When Tarleton emerged from Desirée's room an hour later, she looked at him fetchingly. "Come see me again soon, Ban."

Although it was now nearly two o'clock, Kate invited Tarleton for a night cap to ward off the chill during his ride back. From the night's drinking and revelry, his guard was down as he eagerly accepted her invitation. In her private room, she poured him a stout whiskey and a weak one for herself. She leaned forward exposing her ample cleavage and purred, "Well, Ban, this whiskey's on th' 'ouse. Ya' know, ya' never did tell m' what ya' been up t'."

Wanting to impress Kate, he replied, "Kate, my dear, I've been in General Howe's close company. You might say I've become part of his military family. Indeed, just tonight, I was an observer at his council meeting."

"I've heard a lot about 'im, but what's 'owe really like?" Kate asked feigning great interest.

"He's not like many of the other generals. He's brave and fights courageously alright, but he's not formal. He is liked by his men, and he enjoys good food and grand wines." Tarleton kept his criticism of Howe's strategy to himself.

Then, sounding innocent enough, Kate asked, "So, what does a general discuss at his council?" But this was not an innocent question at all for she often pried critical intelligence from loose-tongued British officers and then passed it on to the American command, for a handsome price.

Tarleton began evasively, "Oh, it was just formalities—reports of sick and wounded, correspondence from London and the like."

Tarleton finished his whiskey, gave Kate a peck on the cheek, and rode up the island to his quarters. Kate was certain that Tarleton had much more to tell and that she'd be able to gather it through her guiles on another night.

---

(1) Maps of the 18th Century show East and West Jersey as separate regions, hence, "The Jerseys."

(2) Time and distance worked against the British in coordinating their operational plans for America throughout the war. Even with favorable winds, it would take four to six weeks or more to send a dispatch across the Atlantic Ocean. Once a dispatch arrived in London, replies often took additional weeks to formulate owing to an extensive bureaucracy. Then getting the reply back to America required an additional month or more at sea. For the Campaign of 1777, the lack of central coordination proved critical.

Chapter 6 - The Plot Conceived
Tuesday, January 7, 1777
British Headquarters, New York City

Tarleton awoke in mid-morning with sensuous thoughts about his carousing. He thought lustily about Desirée and fantasized about seducing Kate during another visit. Since he had no duties that morning, Tarleton had slept late. He walked to the window, opened the curtains, and took in the three inches of newly fallen snow. Now in bright sunshine, New York had a wintry brilliance. He thought to himself, "Snow in London always seemed dreary and gray from the soot and smoke. Here in America, it's invigorating."

At two o'clock, Tarleton had an appointment with Major Stephen Kemble, General Howe's military secretary and chief of intelligence. Kemble had previously given him several discreet reconnaissance missions but had not yet told Tarleton the purpose of that afternoon's meeting. While Tarleton leisurely ate his lunch of oysters, ham, fried potatoes, and tea at The Queen's Head Tavern, he tried to imagine what Kemble wanted of him. Would it be another reconnaissance, or would it be something more exciting like capturing a high-ranking rebel officer? Thirty minutes before the appointment, Tarleton left the tavern and rode to British Headquarters at Mount Pleasant Mansion.

Tarleton saluted the two sentries at the entrance to headquarters and entered a small room in the rear of the first floor, Kemble's office. He knocked on the door. Kemble unlatched it from the inside and gave him a subdued welcome. The intelligence chief was in his mid-forties but looked younger. He had a scholarly appearance, well-attired with short brown hair and wire rim spectacles.

"Good morning, Colonel. I've arranged for another officer

to join our meeting."

As the door swung open, Tarleton saw a tall, painfully thin officer slouching in a chair. He had an unusually large nose, and two dogs sat quietly at his feet. Tarleton could not hide his astonishment that the officer wore scarlet.

Kemble smiled slyly as he said, "Lieutenant Colonel Tarleton, I believe you already know General Charles Lee. You are no doubt surprised to see him wearing a British uniform. Well, after his capture, his uniform of the rebel forces was so filthy that it had to be burned. In the last weeks, General Lee has been most helpful. Even though officially a prisoner of war, he has been given a British army uniform. We simply had nothing else suitable for him."

Indeed, Banastre Tarleton knew Charles Lee very well for the dragoon officer had led the capture of the American general just over three weeks previously while Lee was encamped in New Jersey, with only a small guard and far from his main force. The prisoner of war's career flashed through Tarleton's mind. "At outbreak of rebellion, Lee...the most experienced military officer in the American Army... had been a brave officer in the British Army in the French and Indian War... seriously wounded... the next year, served valiantly in Portugal under Burgoyne... later, in Polish Army, became general... but became embittered when passed over for promotion... came to America... quickly impressed the American Congress and appointed Washington's second in command in 1775...but soon began to resent his treatment by American Congress (1) ... rationalizing that the American cause was lost... arranged his capture in exchange for influence and gold."

Lee rose slowly from the chair and stood just inches from Tarleton, towering over the much shorter officer. The American general snorted, "Tarleton, Major Kemble here wants you to work for me on matters of high priority. I trust you'll agree."

Tarleton reeled from Lee's fetid breath and dominating presence. Tarleton was nearly always cocky, but this afternoon Lee clearly intimidated him. Even though Tarleton had "captured" him, Lee wanted Tarleton to know with certainty who would be in control.

Sizing up the mismatch, Kemble broke the tension. "Gentlemen, my steward will bring in tea in just a moment. General Lee has already provided us with detailed intelligence about the American Army. I must meet with General Howe, but I hope you two will get well acquainted and see how you might...eh...collaborate, to our advantage. You'll be able to use my office the rest of the afternoon. General Lee, when you're finished, please call my steward who'll arrange for your return to your quarters and dinner with two of our senior staff." (2)

As soon as Kemble left, Lee appeared to warm up to Tarleton. "Colonel, thank you for playing along with my ruse. I wanted Kemble, that bore, to think I disliked you, but in fact from our interactions last month, I quite admire your record. Now, you must wonder whether you can trust me, after all. You're quick-witted and must want to know why I arranged to be captured, eh? Am I right, Colonel?"

Still not sure how to interpret Lee's behavior, Tarleton answered cautiously, "Yes, General, we had no chance to talk when my dragoons captured...I mean, Sir, no chance to talk in New Jersey, but I do know of your career going back to the French and Indian War."

"Very well, then, you know I have far greater battlefield experience than the Virginia tobacco planter who is now the American commander in chief, and you must have no doubt that, if I'd been in command, I would have avoided his losses last year.

But the crones in the American Congress are infatuated with that bloody amateur. And that buggering combination— Washington and Congress—is a disaster. As a loyal subject to the Crown and as a true patriot, I see there is only one course: end the rebellion this year with minimal casualties to the Crown's forces. Don't you agree?"

Tarleton had heard that Lee was rewarded with a huge sum—on the order of five thousand British pounds—but he was not about to mention that. Instead, he stroked Lee's huge ego by acknowledging, "Yes, Sir, I fully concur and want to put down the rebellion."

"I know from your record, Tarleton, that you've been bold and loyal. That's exactly what I like to see in future generals. Tell me, in full confidence, how do you view General Howe's plan for the coming campaign?"

Tarleton, who still did not trust Lee sufficiently to speak frankly, began cautiously, "General Howe has an incredible record in North America going back to the French and…"

Lee cut him off abruptly and erupted, "Spare me the equivocation. We both know that if Howe had more fucking energy, the rebellion could have been ended easily at least four different times last year. Let's stop beating around the bush. Give me your straight opinion."

"Howe intends to capture Philadelphia, hoping to draw Washington into an open battle on our terms," Tarleton began rapidly. "But Washington may not take the bait at all, or he may not allow himself to fall into the trap. Capturing capital cities may end a war in Europe, but not with these American rebels. In my opinion, we must destroy their army's fighting ability."

"Well put, Tarleton, and there are two ways to do just that:

kill them or...weaken them before they even come to the battlefield."

Tarleton was usually quick to understand even vague inferences, but here his face reflected his uncertainty. Charles Lee reacted immediately, "Surely, you see what I am suggesting, don't you, Colonel." Lee rose from his chair and stalked around the small room, making Tarleton even more uncomfortable.

"Tarleton, breathe no word of this conversation to anyone else, or it will be your undoing. Agreed?" Tarleton could only nod affirmatively.

"Very well, then, the American army's officers and men mainly come from farms and small villages. Most hadn't travelled more than a day's ride from their homes prior to the war. Do you see what that means?"

Tarleton still looked perplexed.

"Well, Colonel," Lee spewed. "I'll have to spell it out for you. The American army is vulnerable to diseases—smallpox, in particular. Few have gotten the natural disease, and fewer took the inoculation. Take it from me, I know how they view it; they fear the inoculation. Almost the whole damned army is ripe for smallpox. The American army will be shattered by that scourge if it is spread in their camp!"

Tarleton was taken aback and responded deliberately. "I see, Sir, but will General Howe approve the plan?"

"For the love of Christ, Tarleton," Lee exploded, "He won't know, at least not officially. Look here, during the past war, British officers introduced smallpox among Indian tribes siding with the French, and when the British were surrounded in Boston last winter, they intentionally sent townspeople with smallpox into the American camp. There's precedent for spreading scourges among the Indian tribes and even among fellow Englishmen—those in open rebellion against the Crown. Oh, right, the commander in chief, touting his English sense of fair play, might be able to say he knew nothing about this plot, but he'd merely be turning a blind eye. Right now, Howe will do anything to put down this rebellion. We'll keep him in the dark for now, and when the plot succeeds, I'll assure that you get all due credit. You see, I want this rebellion to be ended just as much as you. I have my own score to settle, and you have to gain all the recognition you deserve. I know the inside of the American organization, and you know the British establishment. Do you think you can complete this scheme?"

Knowing what Lee expected, he replied, "Yes, Sir, I can, and I will."

"Excellent, excellent!" Lee exhorted, "Let's have you flesh out the details, and we'll meet privately as soon as possible."

As Banastre Tarleton exited British Headquarters, he gazed skyward and noted the thick, stony-gray clouds which had formed over Manhattan. The sun would be setting in less than an hour, and the air was cold and biting, matching his own inner spirits. He had dealt with many high-ranking and powerful men, his own father, for example, and a score of British generals, but he had never met anyone quite like General Charles Lee. In the two hours Lee and he were together, Lee was abusive, bullying and cunning one moment but supportive, open and even mentoring the next. Tarleton's mind flashed back to all the times the aristocratic officers taunted him about his merchant background and especially about his family's profiting from the slave trade, as though they were not themselves the beneficiaries of their families' previous generations of such trade and plantation ownership. The resentment roiled him every day, but now Tarleton saw his chance to end the rebellion—and get full credit.

Tarleton's mind quickly prioritized his needs: a source of smallpox secretions, a fool-proof method to get the pox into the American camp, and a means to conceal his own involvement. He'd also need perfect intelligence and unknowing accomplices to achieve his aim.

Yet, he worried about who the real General Charles Lee was. How could he trust a man who had just turned his back on his own army? Tarleton also fretted about his own predicament. He was now in league with the traitorous American general, and he had better carry out the scheme— or he feared the intimidating Lee would surely tear him to pieces.

---

(1) In the summer of 1776, Lee was in South Carolina, involved in the successful defense of Charleston, but he felt that theater of war was a sideshow to the great battles in New York. Even though Congress lauded his actions in the South, in his own mind, Lee still felt slighted. He despised Washington, whom he considered a rank amateur in military matters.

(2) By the 18th Century code of military honor, captured high ranking officers were considered brothers in arms and usually treated with great courtesy by their captors.

Chapter 7 - The Surgeon as a Patient
Wednesday, January 8, 1777
Brunswick, New Jersey

Early on the morning of January 8th, Timothy Walker fretted as he looked at his American patient. Alex Grant was asleep, but his face was flushed and his respirations rapid. Walker heard Alex's harsh, high-pitched breathing sounds. Jesse, who had been at his bedside, reported, "Dr. Walker, he's had hectic fevers and shaking chills through most of the night, and his coughing spells...they've been frightful. At one point, he had so much thick mucus that he could barely catch his breath."

Shortly, Alex awoke, prostrate, confused, and anguished. Walker asked comfortingly, "Dr. Grant, how are you feeling now?"

Alex was uncertain where he was but managed to respond hoarsely, "The pain on swallowing is ...marked. At times, I cannot... get... enough air."

Walker had been applying gentle treatments for several days, and there had been no improvement. This morning, when Walker examined Alex's throat, he saw both tonsils were dusky red and coated with a grayish-yellow exudate. The left tonsil was so swollen that it covered over half his pharynx. Upon lightly palpating Alex's tonsils with his examining index finger, Walker found them tense and tender. Even this gentle pressure was agonizingly painful to Alex.

To Alex and Jesse, Walker assessed the picture. "Dr. Grant, there is no doubt that you have a severe case of quinsy. As you know, it usually runs its course over about four to seven days, but I'm concerned about the degree of swelling and suppuration in his throat."

Walker had to say no more. In clear-headed moments, Alex had thought of quinsy as his diagnosis while Jesse worried about Alex's airway closing over and suffocating him.

Walker explained, "I expect the suppuration will localize. Often, an abscess forms and drains spontaneously, but if not, I may have to incise it. We'll watch him closely."

"Nurse, you must be exhausted now. Please get some rest. Mates Blackfield and Smart will help me this morning."

"Thank you, Sir, but I'm feeling fine and would prefer to stay with Dr. Grant."

Across the room, Mate Blackfield knelt by the young lieutenant who had the trepanning operation. As Walker and Smart approached, Blackfield shook his head and reported, "He's remained unconscious and had a seizure just before dawn." His brow was hot to Dr. Walker's touch, and his head dressing oozed yellow-brown pus.

Walker frowned. "This is just what I feared. The lad will not last much longer. Please send a messenger to his brother, the captain, so that he can see him before it's too late."

The next morning, Thursday, January 9th, Alex awoke with even worse pain on the left side of his throat. His breathing became labored, rattling and even more rapid. Alex gazed at Jesse with a wide-eyed, anguished look, and she immediately called for Dr. Walker and Mate Blackfield. As soon as the British surgeon examined Alex's throat, he knew exactly what needed to be done. He explained to Jesse and Blackfield, "There is an abscess in his left tonsil. It is obstructing his airway. If I delay, he will suffocate. By God's grace, the abscess is already coming to a head. I should be able to incise it quickly. Once I do, a large amount of pus will discharge. I'll immediately place his head down so that the pus

70

will drain into this pewter basin. We must not let the pus get into his airway for he will surely drown in it. Are you both ready? Hold him, Blackfield, fast and firm!"

In the bright morning sunlight, Blackfield held Alex upright in a high-backed chair while Jesse held a mirror to direct the light. Walker opened Alex's mouth as widely as he could and wedged a roll of gauze dressing between his teeth. Walker placed his left index finger behind the abscessed left tonsil and, with a pencil-sized scalpel, deftly incised the abscess where it had already come to a head. Immediately, copious amounts of foul, creamy-yellow pus exuded. Alex gagged at first, but Blackfield and Jesse forced his head down. Reflexively, Alex spat out the foul exudate which was now streaked with bright red blood. Almost instantly, for the first time in days, his breathing became noticeably easier.

Later that morning, Walker beamed as he looked at his patient. "Dr. Grant, you look like you are feeling better already." Indeed, Alex's toxicity and confusion had cleared promptly. In a raspy voice, he acknowledged, "I owe you a great debt. My throat feels much less painful, but Good Lord, what a horrid taste I have in my mouth."

"And that we can take care of easily," replied Walker pleasantly. "Nurse Jesse, would you please bring Dr. Grant the cooled mint tea. I want him to gargle and spit with that until it returns clear. Then, continue the neck poultices throughout the day. While the tonsil still drains, we'll keep Dr. Grant on a liquid diet, but let's give him plenty of fluids."

Alex, following Dr. Walker's counsel to sleep on his stomach, with his head down. had his most restful night in over a week and awoke feeling alert and hungry. Jesse greeted him with a broad smile, saying, "Good morning, Dr. Grant, are you feeling better today?"

"Much better, indeed, Jesse. Please tell me where I am. My memory is so vague since we left Trenton."

To Jesse's hand, Alex's brow felt cool. She reassured him. "Heavens, Doctor, you've been through an ordeal. You were delirious, off and on. No wonder your memory's hazy." After filling Alex in, she added, "Dr. Walker incised an abscess in your tonsil. He should be here shortly. Let's get you freshened up and give him a nice surprise!"

When Walker saw Alex, he beamed. "Dr. Grant, you had us all sick with worry! I can tell already your fever is gone, and your breathing is slower. Let's have a look at your throat."

After the examination, Dr. Walker nodded. "Hmm, the right tonsil is almost back to its normal size, and the left one no longer has any pus and is one-fourth the size it was yesterday. "

Alex grinned, "Now that I can breathe and swallow easily, I'm getting very hungry."

"I'm delighted with your good appetite. Our cook will have breakfast up shortly, but I must keep you on liquids until the incision site heals. I don't want any food particles getting lodged in there. Nurse, I think we can stop the laudanum, but let's continue the poultices three times today. Dr. Grant, so gratified you're on the mend. In the hospital, there are more invalids than we can keep up with, and over in the prisoners' wing, I'm looking after several American wounded. I would very much appreciate your help, just as soon as you're ready. There's a spare room adjacent to my quarters. After all, it's the practice for captured surgeons to care for their own, and I think we can learn from each other."

By Friday, January 17th, Alex had fully regained his strength. The timing was fortuitous as he had begun the morning by assuming care for the wounded American prisoners in the British General Hospital. Just as he finished his rounds, Mate Blackfield came rushing into the prisoners' wing.

"Dr. Grant," he exclaimed, "Dr. Walker would like your assistance in the operating theatre immediately!"

****

Earlier on the morning of January 17th, Major John Redmond of the Royal Engineers stood less than half a mile from the hospital, on the Raritan River's east bank, facing the wide bridge. Redmond was tall and burly with flaming red hair and beard. As he inspected the span with his junior officer, he fumed, "Horrible. This bridge is rotting in so many spots. It looks like termites have been having at it. Don't these bloody colonials know how to keep their bridges in order? This blasted structure won't bear the weight of cavalry much less the bloody artillery!"

The junior engineer officer, a lieutenant, had served under Redmond for over six months since arriving in America. The lieutenant revered Redmond, who was widely regarded as among the best in the Royal Engineers. From a working-class family, Redmond had made his way through the ranks by sheer skill and grit. As a tribute to his brilliant red hair, his feisty temper and spirited language, everyone referred to him as "Red Jack," and he didn't mind that a bit. He had a brotherly bond with his men. Despite his crusty exterior, he looked after them, and, contrary to 18th Century protocol, he often called his rank-and-file lads by their first names. In turn, they would do anything for him.

Red Jack continued, "Lieutenant, for the time being, we'll have to shore up the bridge's pilings and its twin arches and replace all the decayed planks. It's a bloody miracle that we've got a clear day and the wagon loads of supplies are even here. For once, the idiotic commissary officers have managed to get us what we need. You take one platoon to the west side of the bridge, and I'll start with the other boys over here."

To his senior sergeant, Red Jack then bellowed, "Now, Paddy, get the lads to work. Off load those planks from the first wagon and get the pilings and beams for the arches off the second. Get their cods moving. We haven't got all bloody day!"

Although the temperature did not rise above the mid 40s, the day was still and sunny. Red Jack began to sweat and took off his heavy wool tunic as he walked among his platoon giving words of encouragement and inspecting their work. To a young private who was carrying an arm load of planks, Red Jack called out, "William, that's putting your back into it! Strong work, my boy."

Later in the morning, Red Jack Redmond watched carefully as his senior sergeant prepared to fit a new wooden beam between the bridge's arches. The sergeant tied ropes at each end of the six-inch wide joist and drew the ropes through pulleys attached to the arches. From the pulleys, the ropes were hitched to a team of four draft horses. Atop the bridge, three engineer's mates stood ready to fit the new beam into place.

When the horses lurched forward, the ropes became taught, and the huge beam inched its way toward the top of the arch. Unseen by the sergeant or the men atop the bridge, one of the ropes slipped off its track inside the pulley. As the sergeant whipped the horses forward, the rope got hot from the friction and started to fray. With the other pulley working smoothly, the heavy beam upended placing increased friction on the fraying rope. The rope unraveled and then snapped, sending the beam angling downwards in a wide arc— right at Red Jack. Despite his height and bulk, he was agile and jumped down the steep embankment just as the beam careened inches above his head and thudded into the muddy ground. Red Jack's first thought was relief that he had escaped sudden death, but on the sharply inclined embankment he tripped over a root and fell heavily. With gathering momentum, he rolled towards the river. He placed his arms alongside his head and vainly tried to slow his descent. And then, Redmond felt a searing pain in his right arm, a thump to his head.

From the other side of the bridge, the lieutenant watched in horror as he saw the beam arc wildly downward toward his mentor. He sprinted across the span. The senior sergeant had his back to the river but heard the whoosh of the beam and its thud. When he turned, he saw Red Jack's body rolling down the embankment. He and the lieutenant arrived at Red Jack's side simultaneously. They found him unconscious, lying face up on gently sloping ground. He had come to rest just below a jagged stump which had torn through his shirt and punctured his right arm. The wound was oozing dark red blood.

The lieutenant barked, "Sergeant, he's still breathing. Get that wagon over here. Bloody hell, we've got to get the major to hospital. Send one man ahead to tell Dr. Walker what's happened. I'll wrap his wound with the remnants of his white shirt. And private, you there, get his tunic so that we can keep him warm!"

By the time Redmond's injured body arrived at the hospital, Drs. Walker and Grant had already prepared the operating table. Mate Blackfield stood by ready to assist. When the stout major was placed on the table, Walker and Alex quickly examined him. Alex reported, "His breathing's regular, and his pulse is rapid but strong." Walker saw an egg-sized soft lump on the back of his head and a few scratches on his face. To Alex, he said, "I feared this would be much worse. Let's have look at his arm." As they probed the wound, Red Jack groaned.

"Well, that's a good sign," remarked Walker. "He's regaining consciousness. Look here, Dr. Grant, the skin is lacerated and contused. A puncture extends deep with flecks of mud, slivers of rotted wood, and material from his shirt drawn in. It's not bleeding very much. The main artery has been spared, but from the extent of the wound and all the debris, I think this will not heal unless we amputate."

Alex inspected the wound carefully and drew Walker to the corner of the room. "The muscle looks mostly viable, and the bone is intact. Do you mind if I offer an alternative to amputation? In my laboratory in Philadelphia, we have created experimental wounds in goats so that we can improve treatment. When we've made puncture wounds like this one, even those contaminated with foreign materials, we have cures without amputation by laying open the wound, washing it out thoroughly, and excising the debris and any devitalized tissues. Then, rather than closing such contaminated wounds, we leave them open to heal from the bottom up. Sometimes it takes months, but we've been able to save the limb."

"Interesting," replied Walker somewhat dubiously, "but have you used this approach in humans?"

"I wish we had," Alex reported, "but I think this is the right case to try it."

"Well, let's see if the major is game for your approach. If so, I'll assist you," agreed Walker somewhat hesitantly.

On the table, the big major regained consciousness. "Where the hell am I, and what in name of God has happened to my bloody arm?"

Walker spoke comfortingly. "Major Redmond, you're lucky to be alive. You're in the General Hospital in Brunswick. I'm Dr. Walker, and this is Dr. Grant. At the bridge, a wooden beam broke loose and just missed you, but you fell down the embankment and sustained a nasty wound to your right arm. You also hit your head, but no serious injury there so far as we can tell."

"No need to sugar coat this, Surgeon," said Red Jack with resignation. "I've seen plenty of injuries in my days. If you need to amputate my bloody arm, I'm ready. For Christ's sake, get on with it."

"Hold on a minute, Major," Walker continued. "There's another option. This is Dr. Grant. He's an American, now a prisoner of war, but one of the best surgeons in North America. We believe there's a good chance of saving your arm by removing the dirt and debris and having the wound heal from inside out. We'll have to watch you carefully because amputation might still be necessary. Whatever we do, we must proceed promptly. Do you understand?"

Red Jack needed little time. He replied a bit skeptically, "Well, if there's a chance of keeping my arm, you bet I'm for it."

As the surgeon's mate gave the major a dose of laudanum, Alex added, "Dr. Walker, might I ask: do you happen to have any carbolic acid?"

Walker was intrigued as he nodded his head. "We have plenty of acetic acid, as vinegar solution, and just last week I saw a few bottles of carbolic acid in the medicine chests. I've never used it though."

"Then," responded Alex, "if you agree, I suggest we wash our hands with soap and water and then rinse thoroughly with diluted carbolic acid. Before beginning the surgery, we'll also wash Major Redmond's arm and rinse with it as well. And cleanse the instruments the same way. I've found these hygienic practices lead to faster healing." (1)

Smiling indulgently and a bit doubtfully at his innovative

American colleague, Walker remarked, "I'm eager to observe the results. After we're done, I'll inquire from the commissary about getting more carbolic acid."

Jesse and Mate Blackfield strapped the major onto the table with his right arm extended. Jesse washed the wound and gave Red Jack a second dose of laudanum.

Alex spoke softly to the major who was now feeling heavily sedated. "Major Redmond, you'll feel my nurse and surgeon's mate restraining you a bit, and I'm going to place this wooden rod between your teeth." Alex felt no need for a tourniquet and then moved swiftly and surely. With his forceps, he removed the debris in the wound and then extended the wound with his scalpel so that he could see the injury to the muscle.

"The damage to his biceps is more extensive than I thought, and there are many slivers of rotted wood and still a fair amount of dirt," observed Alex. "I'll debride the necrotic areas of the skin and muscle to excise all the foreign material. Jesse, Blackfield, hold him fast!" While Walker retracted the incision, Alex trimmed away the unhealthy skin and excised the heavily contaminated muscle. He then placed sutures on oozing vessels and irrigated the wound copiously.

To his surgical team, Alex continued, "There's no further bleeding, and the wound now looks clean. I'm going to pack it with clean dressing and then wrap the arm. The major should be coming to shortly. We'll inspect the wound in two days. I expect he'll do well."

Yet, as this surgical treatment was still unproved, Walker thought to himself, "For his sake and mine—and yours, Dr. Grant, I pray so." Red Jack rested comfortably over the next two days with no fever and only modest arm discomfort. When Alex removed the dressing, he beamed, "Dr. Walker, come look. The wound is clean and is already beginning to granulate nicely. I'm going to irrigate it with this warm water and redress it."

In the next week, Red Jack's arm required modest debridement on three days. On the seventh morning at Jack's bedside, Dr. Walker added jovially, "Major, your arm is showing good healing. The timing is quite good. You see, I'm returning to the His Majesty's Main General Hospital in New York to handle a heavy case load there. Dr Grant, still my prisoner, is coming with me so he can help care for both the British and some American wounded. And because your arm still needs some attention, we're taking you with us. That way, you'll be in good company. Get your things together. We'll leave at eleven o'clock by ambulance wagon."

---

(3) By using these cleansing techniques, Dr. Alexander Grant was introducing techniques that are today called "antisepsis," but he was nearly a century ahead of recorded medical science. Modern microbiology had its founding with the pioneering work of Louis Pasteur in France and Robert Koch in Germany in the late 19th Century, and clinical use of antiseptics is credited to Joseph Lister in Scotland in 1867.

Chapter 8 -The First Smallpox Outbreak
Mid-January 1777
The American Winter Encampment, Morristown, New Jersey

General Washington's ragged army of fewer than five thousand men had dragged into their Morristown encampment by the end of the first week of January. The village's fifty houses, single church, and sole tavern could not quarter many troops, but Washington's advanced party of engineers picked Morristown because of its superb natural defenses. The engineers saw that it rested on a plateau, protected on its sides by steep ascents and in its rear by Thimble Mountain. The army would be safe from British attack because the only approach from New York was through a series of easily defendable hills. From Morristown, they reasoned Washington could counter a move by the British either south to Philadelphia or north up the Hudson River. Washington immediately made Freeman's Tavern his headquarters, and senior officers quartered in the town's homes. Initially, the rank and file had no other shelter than their summer tents, but they quickly set to work building huts. The engineers provided specifications: each was made of logs, with mud daubed in between, measuring fourteen by sixteen feet, and with a fireplace at one end. Crude, stacked beds were built in along the walls, for twelve men per hut. Built by the hundreds, these huts were crowded, smoky and drafty, but provided some protection from the mid-Atlantic winter. By mid-January the encampment was respectable and secure.

Across the village green from headquarters, Dr. John Hobbs, acting as Continental Army General Hospital Director in Alex Grant's captivity, had set up beds in the church. One evening, John Hobbs was putting his well-known culinary skills to work in the church kitchen. For the first few weeks in camp, fresh food was in short supply, but the commissary officer had just brought in a herd of cattle. When the army's butchers slaughtered the stock, the first cuts went to the hospital and staff. Assigned to the hospital was a cook, but he had no experience and regularly ruined the vegetables and toughened the meat. This evening, Hobbs announced he was making dinner for all: freshly baked bread and a savory stew with tender chunks of beef, a few potatoes, carrots, turnips, and selections from his carefully husbanded spices. On the table, Hobbs placed a bottle of red wine from the hospital supply. Mate Vander Voort asked, "Dr. Hobbs, what's the special occasion?"

"Tonight, indeed, is very special, Vander Voort. Not only is this the first time in weeks that we've had fresh meat, but we're having a guest, Lieutenant Colonel Tilghman. You'll remember him from his visits to our hospital during last year's campaign. We haven't seen him in a while and have lots to catch up about. He'll be here at six o'clock."

Adopting Washington's habit of punctuality, Tench arrived exactly on time and greeted Hobbs and Vander Voort robustly. "By Jove, it's good finally to see you both. Our duties have kept us apart for far too long. And whatever you're preparing for dinner smells wonderful."

Hobbs smiled devilishly and teased Tench, "Oh, it's just an old family recipe: opossum and garden snake stew!" While the cook served portions of the stew to the invalids, Tench, Hobbs, and Vander Voort ate leisurely at a small table by the kitchen's fire. Tench complimented the host, "Dr. Hobbs, seriously, your stew is hearty and delicious. Indeed, it's even better than what they make for the headquarters staff, but don't tell anyone I said that."

"Well, very kind of you, Colonel Tilghman, but tell me, what have you been doing?"

"Just as soon as I get a second helping of your stew." When

Tench returned to the table, he poured another glass of wine and began, "It's been a difficult time since we got here. Of course, it's been bitter cold. The old men in Congress are useless. They grumble constantly among themselves. They have little authority to raise funds for food and supplies, and the commissary rarely can get us enough blankets, warm clothing, or fresh meat. The rotting potatoes and turnips they supply us with are not fit for consuming. Tonight's meal is the prized exception. Indeed, the situation with Congress became so contentious recently that General Washington sent The Commandant of Life Guards, Lieutenant Colonel Gibbs, to Philadelphia as his liaison. He's written me two letters describing how difficult President Hancock is—vain, haughty, and ...erm...not very quick. He expects to return from Philadelphia in February. As for the men, they're all billeted in new huts. Enough from me. What's the situation here in the hospital?"

"Not a pretty picture here either, colonel. We've got a full load of seriously wounded and a dozen or so with frostbite, camp fever, or pneumonia. We're all right at the moment, but with Dr. Grant and Jesse gone, Mate Vander Voort and I will be overwhelmed if there's any disease outbreak. By the way, has headquarters received any word about Dr. Grant? He was dreadfully ill when we pulled out of Trenton."

Tench winced as he replied, "Dr. Hobbs, we just have no way of knowing. I suppose we should trust in Providence."

"Now about the soldiers' huts," remarked Hobbs, "the conditions there are prime for disease to spread. They're crowded and will quickly become foul. There's no telling when something dread will start to run through camp. Colonel Tilghman, when you are with General Washington, might you be able to put in a word about sending us a few lads we can train as hospital mates? That would really help."

"I'll see what I can do, Dr. Hobbs. General Washington prizes all your work at the hospital."

"Very well', replied Hobbs. "Let's change the topic to something a bit more positive. After dinner, let's play a round of faro."

Grand idea!" said Tench. "How about penny a point, just to make it interesting?"

Less than a week afterwards, a worried-looking young officer rushed into the General Hospital. "Dr. Hobbs," he began hesitantly, "I'm the regimental surgeon for the 4th New York. We formed up near Albany. I understand that's where you're from. May I have a word?"

Putting the young surgeon at ease, Hobbs replied, "Come in. Come in. I'm always delighted to meet new friends from Albany. I'm just brewing some tea. I'll get you a cup. How may I help?"

"Dr. Hobbs, my regiment is encamped on the west side of the Morristown plateau. From one hut, I have two privates with nearly identical stories, but I can't figure it out. They're both in my regimental hospital in a private home nearby. Two days ago, each reported having repeated chills, accompanied by severe headache, back pain, and vomiting. Both have fever, and one is delirious."

Hobbs inquired, "Does either have a rash?"

When the reply was "No," Hobbs then asked, "Have any men from that hut left camp?"

Rubbing his chin in thought, the regimental surgeon said softly, "Well, ten days ago, they were detached to a foraging party. They returned late, admitting they visited with some camp followers."

Hobbs jumped on these points. "Good Lord, I must go to see them myself. I fear I know the diagnosis."

When John Hobbs examined the two men, he found them restless and anxious. The delirious one had to be restrained in bed. To Hobbs's careful examination, their skin was dry, and their faces flushed, but neither had a rash.

Turning to the young surgeon, Hobbs explained, "It is early in the course, but I'll wager we are dealing with my worst fear: smallpox."

"But...but," the surgeon replied, "they have no rash or pustules!"

"Mark my words, the rash will appear tomorrow. Now, we must act quickly. Isolate these two men in an upstairs room by themselves. I'm writing a dispatch to your regiment's colonel to isolate all the men in that hut, to have their food brought to them, and to have a separate necessary dug for them. (1) Do you know if any in the regiment have been inoculated?"

"I got inoculated when I was a lad, but, sir, these men all come from farms outside Albany. Inoculation is not very popular among them. They fear the illness that follows, and they always believe they'll never get a natural case of it. I doubt any have had it."

Hobbs continued, "I feared that also, but you'll be protected. Check with your surgeon's mate about his inoculation. I'm going to headquarters. If my diagnosis is correct, we've got trouble ahead. For now, keep these two invalids on a light diet with tea and barley-water. If they continue to have severe back or head pains, give them laudanum if you have any. I'm afraid I have none to spare from the General Hospital stock. (2) I'll come back to see them with you at nine o'clock tomorrow."

John Hobbs returned to the General Hospital, put on a fresh uniform, and crossed the green to headquarters. To his relief, he immediately found Tench in the front room.

"Colonel Tilghman," he announced formally, "May I speak with you?"

Tench and Hobbs slipped into a hall where Hobbs explained his suspicions. Then, Hobbs concluded, "Most of our lads are from the country with few likely to have been inoculated. If there are two men with findings of early smallpox now, there are bound to be dozens of other cases brewing. Smallpox can spread though this camp like fire through dried grass. So, we must be ready. I'm just the Assistant Hospital Director and have never met General Washington. Can you get me in to see him?"

Twenty minutes later, Tench ushered Hobbs into Washington's office, a large room with south-facing windows. The general rose from his desk. Nervously, Hobbs saluted, as he took in Washington's imposing figure. The commander in chief looked every bit the part. Hobbs estimated he was over six feet tall and was powerfully built. His brownish hair was beginning to turn gray at the temples. As the general approached to offer his hand, Hobbs noted scars on the general's face from earlier smallpox.

Washington extended a warm welcome. "Dr. Hobbs, I thank you for the splendid job you've been doing at the General Hospital since Dr. Grant has been a prisoner. Colonel Tilghman tells me that you think we have smallpox in a New York regiment. This would be a huge threat to the entire encampment, but exactly how sure are you?"

"Your Excellency, smallpox has a very characteristic early presentation. While there are similarities to the findings of camp or hospital fever, I'd stake six months' pay on my diagnosis."

Hobbs' offer brought a rare chuckle from the commander. "That's a hearty wager, Dr. Hobbs. What do you recommend?"

"Sir, I have already made recommendations to the regiment's colonel and surgeon to isolate the two sick men in the regimental hospital and to quarantine the soldiers from their same hut. If smallpox is the diagnosis, we'll see the diagnostic rash in twenty-four hours. In the meantime, I'd find out who among the senior officers has had smallpox or the inoculation. And I'll find out what instruments we have for performing the inoculation. I think it would also be good to keep the camp closed starting now—no one in and no one out."

Outside, heavy snow had been falling, and the temperature fell well below freezing. Washington continued, "Very precise, Dr. Hobbs. Colonel Tilghman, please see to these recommendations. So as not to spread alarm just yet, say the camp is buttoning up because of the winter storm. Is there anything else?"

"Sir, well, yes, if you don't mind my asking. Have you heard anything about Dr. Grant?"

"Dr. Hobbs, I've been anxious about him also, but we've had no word. That's not necessarily bad. You see, I'd expect to have news from the British commander in chief only about general grade officers as prisoners of war. We'll have to keep faith. Please return tomorrow when you have examined the New York lads. Dr. Hobbs, I am most thankful for your skills in these cases."

At precisely nine o'clock the next morning, Hobbs returned to the New Yorkers' regimental hospital. In the isolation room on the second floor, the two invalids looked distressed. Exactly as Hobbs had predicted, one now had small red spots on his forehead and wrists; the other had papules on his face, arms, and trunk.

The regimental surgeon added, "Dr. Hobbs, an hour ago, another soldier...er, from the neighboring New Jersey Regiment...was brought to our hospital. His regimental surgeon left camp two days ago to attend his sick wife, and I'm covering his regiment. You must see this new patient...in the next room."

Lying on a straw pallet was a young private, whose face was covered with grayish-yellow pustules. Between the lesions, his skin was red, and his eyelids were swollen shut. He moaned in pain even though he had received laudanum.

"There can be no doubt now," concluded Hobbs. "Quarantine the New Jersey Regiment as well. Have you done smallpox inoculations?"

"Sir, I have not, but I've read about it, and I know there are lancets in my medical kit."

"Read up again," retorted Hobbs. "I'll be back as soon as possible with orders. We'll need to transfer these sick men to the General Hospital, where I'll set up a smallpox ward. Right now, I must report to headquarters."

When Hobbs reported the smallpox cases to General Washington, the commander in chief summoned his two most trusted senior officers. Promptly, a barrel-chested major general and a beefy brigadier general arrived. Also present was Tench Tilghman serving as secretary to the meeting.

Washington began in earnest, "Gentlemen, you have met Dr. Hobbs, now Acting Director of the General Hospital. This morning, Dr. Hobbs confirmed the diagnosis of smallpox in three privates, two from a New York Regiment and another from a New Jersey Regiment. I'll now ask Dr. Hobbs for his assessment."

"Sirs, Good afternoon. With three cases already evident, we'll clearly see others. Our encampment is ripe for a devastating outbreak. The men are crowded into small, dirty huts, and few men have either had the natural disease or have taken the inoculation. With death expected in about a quarter of those afflicted, the army faces a grave threat."

Washington added, "Dr. Hobbs has made recommendations which he'll now describe."

"Thank you, Your Excellency. To control the outbreak, I advise three measures: First, isolate those with diagnosed smallpox in a separate room in the Continental Army General Hospital. Second, quarter the New York and Jersey troops in small units, preferably in houses if any are available in the village. Third, begin immediate inoculation of all soldiers and villagers, unless they are already protected by previous disease or inoculation."

Seated to Washington's right, Major General Greene asked, "Dr. Hobbs, I salute your rapid diagnosis and thoughtful recommendations. I had smallpox when I was young during the 1752 outbreak which claimed the lives of hundreds. Please tell us about the inoculations. The men fear it. Last winter in Boston, there was a huge smallpox outbreak among the townspeople. The disease spread to our ranks, but not so extensively. To protect our troops, our surgeons in Boston quarantined the afflicted, but they did not use inoculation. I'd like your frank opinion."

Hobbs had met Greene briefly with Alex Grant on several occasions and knew that Greene was quick minded and honest.

"General, Sir, inoculation has unfairly gotten a bad name among the rank and file and among everyday citizens. It frightens many because it means cutting the skin and inoculating a small amount of material from smallpox pustules. Inevitably, an illness which can last up to a couple of weeks follows. During this illness, the inoculated individual can spread smallpox. And there is about a one to two percent death rate. The death rate from natural smallpox is fifteen to twenty-five percent, even as high as forty percent or more at times. Among citizens, it's generally the poor and rural families who are less likely to be inoculated. And that's where many of our soldiers come from. Outside the army, the cost to inoculate is often large, up to two to five English pounds...But inoculation prevents illness and saves lives."

"Well, then, Dr. Hobbs, how do you convince the men?" posed Greene.

"Sir, it's a push and pull. A general order from the commander in chief plus explanations from the Medical Department officers about the clear benefit to the lads—and to the camp followers."

In the opposite corner of the room, the newly appointed brigadier was recognized next by General Washington. Still in his mid-twenties, Henry Knox asked, "Please explain your inoculation technique. I understand there have been modifications in the last few years."

Hobbs knew of Knox's heroic achievements as artillery chief. Indeed, in an epic feat in winter 1775-1776, Knox and his attachment transported sixty cannon and mortars from captured Fort Ticonderoga in upstate New York to the Siege of Boston. Some of the large mortars weighed over a ton each. Knox's party built forty sledges and acquired eighty oxen for the three hundred mile, six-week long journey through the frozen New York-New England wilderness. When Knox brought the artillery train to the siege, Washington used these guns to force the British to evacuate Boston in March 1776. Knox's reputation was forever established. Facing an uphill battle, as Hobbs anticipated the smallpox inoculation effort would be, he thought, "Henry Knox is a man I want on my side."

"General Knox, you're quite right. About ten years ago, a London doctor—I recall his name was Sutton—simplified inoculation. He did away with the days of dietary preparation and emetics and used a shallow incision on the arm. I adhere to these changes."

But Washington was still unconvinced. "As recently as May of last year in New York, I favored quarantining but not inoculation. Indeed, I issued a general order against inoculation. I thought inoculation was not necessary then, and I did not want to have many men ill or even some dying from inoculation. Now, Dr Hobbs, I must have additional information. What can you tell me about the status of smallpox in the British Army? And in our army, is there any difference in our New England troops compared with those from the Middle Colonies?"

"General Howe's army is in much better shape than ours. Many of their troops had natural smallpox by growing up in big English cities, and from my time serving in the King's Army during the French and Indian War, I know that the British army started to order inoculations about twenty years ago. But some redcoats still avoided getting it out of fear. Among Americans, those from New England are more susceptible to smallpox than those from the Middle Colonies. The inoculation is just more feared in New England, but I have never known why. This is a special problem since so many of our regiments are made up of lads from Massachusetts, Connecticut, and Rhode Island. Fortunately, Sir, those of us with prior inoculation or natural smallpox do not spread the disease."

Still undecided, Washington noted, "I want you to know that I had smallpox when I sailed to Barbados with my brother when I was nineteen years old. You see the pox marks on my face. I recall being ill for over three weeks, not even able to make diary entries. General Greene has also had the natural smallpox. General Knox, what is your status?"

The artillery chief replied, "During the large smallpox outbreaks in Boston when I was a lad, I got the inoculation."

Turning to Tench, Washington nodded, "And your history?"

"Growing up on a farm in Maryland, I had no exposure to smallpox, and, Sir, I've not had the inoculation either."

Registering thinly veiled alarm about one of his favorite aides, the commander in chief directed, "Well, then, let's be sure to keep you away from the afflicted. Gentlemen, what is your opinion on accepting Dr. Hobbs' three recommendations? Colonel Tilghman, please record the vote."

General Greene offered a temporizing proposal, "Your Excellency, I'd favor proceeding with quarantining and quartering the troops in small units, but I'd not begin general inoculations just yet. I'd want to see what happens with these two measures." Knox nodded in agreement.

Hobbs felt the outbreak might spread, but he had lost the argument and could say no more.

"Gentlemen," Washington concluded, "Thank you for your wise counsel. Colonel Tilghman, please prepare the orders accordingly. We're adjourned."

As Hobbs dejectedly walked across the green toward the hospital, Tench caught up with him. "Dr. Hobbs, I was persuaded to start inoculations, but, of course, didn't have a vote. But I'll tell you this: just as soon as His Excellency comes around to ordering inoculations, I want to be the first one who gets it."

---

(1) A "necessary" was an 18th Century military term for a latrine.

(2) Medical supplies were in chronically short supply in the Continental Army. At the outbreak, there were simply not enough medications to support a war effort. To make matters worse, most apothecaries were loyalists, and even the patriotic apothecaries were loath to accept the nearly worthless Continental currency from Congress. Commissary officers had to scrounge civilian supplies, obtain French medications, or rely upon privateers to raid enemy ships to get medicines.

Chapter 9-The Plot Ripened
Tuesday, January 14, 1777
New York City and Brunswick

On an unseasonably warm afternoon in mid-January, a British major dismounted his horse and strode into His Majesty's Main General Hospital in lower Manhattan. He was short and graying, and his quartermaster's uniform fit tightly over his protruding belly. Seeing no one as he entered the foyer, he bellowed, "Who's in charge here?"

A surgeon's mate ran from the quarantine room and saluted the major, "Sir, Director Walker 'n' others on th' staff 'r' in Jers'y inspectin' other 'ospitals. I'm th' only mate 'ere. 'ow may I 'elp ya'?"

"Now see here," the major began impatiently. "The Quartermaster General is requisitioning regimental medical chests from London for the upcoming campaign. I must know how many chests you already have in stock?"

When the mate replied that he did not know, the quartermaster officer gruffly ordered him to find out, ending with, "And be quite accurate about it. I must get my exact report in by this evening. The dispatch goes by ship tomorrow. I'll wait here while you do the inventory."

"But, Sir," replied the mate, "I'm tendin' t' m' wounded 'n' sick."

"Well, if you were a decent mate," the major continued imperiously, "you'd already know about the inventory of chests. So, get the inventory done, and then you may return to your invalids. Do I make myself clear?"

"Yes...yes, Sir, th' chests, they're in th' basemen' storeroom."

As the mate rushed down to the storeroom, the major slipped toward the quarantine room. Three men whose faces, torsos, and extremities were covered with pustules lay on clean straw bedding. They lay motionless and unresponsive. The major knelt next to the nearest soldier and removed a small steel scalpel from his dispatch case. He folded back the soldier's shirt and gagged at the malodorous, nearly confluent pustules. "Good Lord," he thought to himself, "these poor bastards won't last much longer." With the scalpel, he took scrapings from numerous chest pustules and placed the material into glass tubes. The smallpox victim groaned only slightly. After covering up the first soldier's chest, he moved to the second soldier and repeated the collections, this time from the right leg. Finally, he knelt by the third soldier who had even more advanced pustules. The major felt nauseated but managed to collect four tubes of secretions from the moribund lad's abdomen and then covered his belly. As the major left the quarantine room, he stoppered the dozen tubes, wrapped them in soft cloth, and gently placed them in his dispatch case.

Twenty minutes later, the mate came up the stairs and reported, "Sir, th' count is forty-four regiment'l chests. All 'r' full and 'ave their contents listed inside each chest. I double checked." (1)

"Very good, mate. You may now return to your other...er...duties," the major said condescendingly. He jotted a note in his book and walked from the hospital. The surgeon's mate was miffed, but with his low station in the army structure he had come to accept such supercilious treatment from officers. Yet, of this haughty quartermaster officer, he already had become suspicious.

Indeed, the suspicion was well placed for the quartermaster officer's uniform, complete with gray wig and padding for his middle, was a disguise crafted by Banastre Tarleton.

Tarleton rode north up Broadway, crossed over to Bowery Lane, and turned left to a hillock. Behind the prominence, while concealed by a thick clump of tall shrubs, he retrieved a satchel that he had hidden there that morning. He removed the elements of his disguise and from the satchel, then removed a green jacketed uniform of the 16th Dragoons and dressed himself quickly. Tarleton thought to himself, "This worked perfectly. I knew the director would be on inspection in Jersey with his other mates, leaving that one dupe by himself! Now I've got my specimens from the sickest of patients—and safely so thanks to my inoculation back in London. These specimens will remain potent, and I already know how I'm going to deliver them to the American camp. It will be my Trojan Horse!" Almost gleefully, Tarleton rode to his quarters to stash the satchel and hide the tubes of pustular secretions deep in a desk drawer.

But despite Tarleton's clandestine ways, he had already left a perceptible trail. At the Main General Hospital, completely unnoticed by Tarleton, when the surgeon's mate was about to return to the ward from the basement storeroom, he glimpsed "the major" exiting the quarantine room and placing something in his dispatch case. Perplexed, the mate withdrew to the basement storeroom for several minutes while his mind raced with what "the major" was doing. Once the mate got control of his feelings, he came back to the ward and reported the inventory to "the major."

****

Two afternoons later, Tarleton rode to General Charles Lee's quarters, a small, two-story brick house. It was a suitable accommodation for so high ranking a prisoner, and it was a quarter mile from British Headquarters. Arriving punctually at two o'clock, Tarleton returned the salute from the sole guard and entered the house. In the small parlor, Lee was handing his two dogs scraps of meat left over from lunch. The larger dog, a black Pomeranian, snarled at Tarleton.

"Oh, don't mind *Spado*, Colonel," Lee said calmly. "You just interrupted his meal. Now, let's hear what has happened since we last met?"

When Tarleton reported on his collection of the smallpox specimens, Lee rubbed his hands together. "Excellent, Tarleton, excellent!" he said with false affection. "Now, how do you plan to get the pox into the rebel camp?"

Tarleton moved closer to Lee so as not to be overheard. *Spado* growled and lunged at Tarleton. "*Spado*, here!" commanded Lee, and the Pomeranian retreated to Lee's heels. Tarleton moved back also and then described his detailed plan. Lee jumped from his chair and clapped his hands together.

"By Jesus, Tarleton, that's brilliant!"

****

After his meeting with Tarleton, Charles Lee schemed to cover his own tracks. In his entire career, he never lost sight of one goal: his own advancement, no matter what the cost to others. And he was expert at it. Now his calculating mind turned to the possibility that the smallpox plot would be revealed and tied to Tarleton and to him. "Yes," he analyzed, "I am collaborating with the British high command, but I also needed to keep my avenues open with the American command. I cannot afford to be implicated in this plot against my own army. Lee stewed over the matter. Then, one evening, he impulsively turned to the British soldier guarding him at his quarters, "Private, I have an urgent matter for General Howe. I demand you accompany me to headquarters."

Lee was expert at bullying those of lower rank, even as a prisoner of war. Already intimidated, the soldier replied hesitantly, "General Lee, I...I...I've no orders t' take you t' 'eadquarters. M' sergeant will...eh...be back in an 'our, and I...I could ask 'im then."

"Damn your soul, private. My matter cannot wait an hour. I am a major general, and I demand your obedience. If I do not get to General Howe right now, you're going to be responsible for a calamity. Look here, I'm already wearing the scarlet uniform. You either come with me or get out of the way while I go by myself."

It was after eight o'clock in the evening when Charles Lee with the British private entered Howe's headquarters. The captain of the guard recognized General Lee instantly and as a matter of courtesy for the high-ranking prisoner saluted him. Lee returned the salute and whispered, "Captain, I have an urgent matter for General Howe." As the captain relayed the message, Lee stepped into the foyer and smiled to himself relishing his influence in both armies.

When the captain of the guard returned to the foyer, he snapped, "General Lee, His Excellency General Howe is...indisposed right now."

Lee immediately understood the reply for he had glimpsed General Howe's carriage just outside headquarters entrance. Now, he realized that his own impulsiveness had resulted in terribly poor timing. He thought to himself, "Christ, Howe's in bed with his mistress!"

"Very well, captain. My matter is urgent, but it can wait until General Howe is available later this evening. I'll make myself comfortable here in the foyer."

Inside his office suite, General Howe fumed, his plans for the evening with Elizabeth Loring already disrupted. He muttered to her, "Damned fool, that Lee! Who in the heaven's name does he think he is, invading my privacy this evening? He's a major general with the rebels, but in our army, he was merely a major. I don't know what he's up to, but I'm going to put him in his place right now!"

Opening the door to his office, Howe bellowed, "Show him into my office now!"

Charles Lee was often poor at reading others, but as soon as he walked into General Howe's office, he knew he had erred badly. Rather than acting boldly, he knew to begin obsequiously. Howe tore into him, "You are my prisoner, and you are a traitor to England. I have afforded you selected courtesies in exchange for certain intelligence you provided, but you have violated every common courtesy. The idea, indeed, of barging...barging into the commander in chief's office! Why, I should have you hung, for the treason you have committed! I'm done with you!"

"Your Excellency," Lee began submissively, "I apologize for interrupting you at this hour, but I do have new, urgent intelligence. May I redeem myself by disclosing it to you?"

"This had better be good, or surely you'll find yourself on a short rope!"

"Today, Sir, a dragoon officer sought my knowledge of the American Army for he had formulated a plot which he was about to spring." Noting that Howe's interest was piqued, the scheming American general continued revealing half-truths. "Sir, I had no idea of his planning, but the officer seemed motivated to bring you victory. Nevertheless, because of the...shall I say, *unusual nature* of the plot, I had to inform you as soon as possible, Sir."

Howe was immediately suspect of Charles Lee's intentions. He thought, "Can I trust anything Lee tells me? And there are some developments that I as commander in chief and a gentleman must never be officially aware of. Yet, Lee does have access to unique information." Accordingly, Howe cautiously allowed his high-ranking prisoner to proceed. "General Lee, go on, but I will tell you when to stop. Then, you must not utter one more word. Do you understand?"

Lee was aware of the games that commanders had to play so that they could deny involvement, when necessary, but Lee was eager to get Howe the whole story. "Well, yes, Sir. The dragoon officer came up with the scheme to decimate the enemy even before the spring campaign begins. By doing so, he believes he will save British lives, bring you still more honors, and gain recognition from you for his own advancement."

"Stop that thought right there!" General Howe's mind was now quickly running through several possible scenarios, none of which he wanted to deal with. Yet, he was eager for some further information. He continued, "You say that this officer came to you because of your knowledge of the enemy, but how did he know you in the first place?"

"Sir," replied Lee softly, "The dragoon officer has known me for months. He's the bold lad from the Liverpool merchant family: Banastre Tarleton."

"Now, that all fits. For the love of God, this can come to no good. I'm going to have Major Kemble put an end to this plan right away!"

"Your Excellency, please wait one minute," begged Lee. Knowing that Howe hungered for revenge, Lee grabbed his attention by saying, "Sir, this plot may well ravage the enemy allowing you to end the rebellion at minimal cost to the British Army. In the end, Sir, if anything were to go awry, you could easily make him the scapegoat."

Howe was intrigued by Lee's arguments, his anger assuaged. "Very well, General Lee, I'll take your intelligence under advisement. Under penalty of death, you will speak of this plot to no one, and I shall act accordingly. You may now return to your quarters with your guard."

Yet, unknown to General Howe, their excited voices carried through the commander's suite, and another pair of ears had been listening intently.

Howe took some time before returning to Elizabeth. He thought to himself, "Yes, I do want to end this rebellion in the coming campaign. And yes, I still do not trust Lee's true motives. So, if it were to my advantage, I could easily also sacrifice that crude American traitor." As Howe walked back to Elizabeth's side, he thought, "I have only to let this plot evolve, whatever it is about. There was no way the scheme could be traced to me."

---

(1) In contrast to the chronic shortages of medical supplies in the Continental Army, The British Army was mainly well-supplied, but every vial, every box of lint, and every instrument had to come from England. Accordingly, even in the British hospitals, there were delays in getting supplies and mismatches between what was available compared to what was needed.

Chapter 10 - In the Name of Mercy
Sunday, January 26, 1777
New York and Morristown

In the very early hours of January 26th , Elizabeth Loring awoke with excruciating pain in her belly. She reached beside her and shook William. "Darling, please wake up. I...I need your help."

The commander in chief's head was groggy. The prior evening, a Saturday, William and Elizabeth had a sumptuous dinner including two of his favorite bottles of claret. They retired to his bedroom and after lovemaking fell asleep at nearly two o'clock. When Elizabeth woke William, he lit the lamp and saw on the grandfather clock that it was six o'clock. "Elizabeth, what's wrong?"

"I don't know, my dear. During our lovemaking last night, I felt uncomfortable, but I did not want to say anything. I woke up a while ago, with pain coming and going in my belly. Oh, it's gotten worse now." She grimaced and paused at the height of the pain. "Now, I feel sick to my stomach. I've never felt like this before. Childbirth was easy compared to these pains."

Alarmed, Sir William summoned his steward. "Get Dr. Walker over here from the hospital right away, but don't tell anyone why. It's a good thing he recently returned from Brunswick."

Howe's steward rushed the director to headquarters as the new day dawned. General Howe met him outside the bedroom. Dr. Walker saw the anguish on the general's face and got his account of the night.

"Indeed, General Howe, let us visit Mrs. Loring." As Walker entered the room, he observed her in between bouts of pain.

"Good morning," he said warmly, "I'm Army surgeon Dr. Walker. General Howe has asked me to see you."

As he had done thousands of times before, Walker elicited the medical history exactingly and empathically. He immediately gained her confidence and then asked, "May I now examine you to help find out what's wrong?"

Elizabeth nodded. General Howe, who stood by the bedside, looked increasingly distraught. Walker discreetly covered her with a sheet as he palpated her abdomen. When Walker completed the examination, he asked General Howe to step outside with him. He then summarized to the commander in chief, "Sir, I have the diagnosis, but I know of no one who can save her...except, by the grace of God, the American prisoner of war, Dr. Alexander Grant."

Howe stammered, "But...but Dr. Walker, I thought you were the best in the army here in North America."

Walker explained, "Elizabeth almost certainly has developed a large tumor of her ovary, and it is bleeding. I've seen these cases before, and the outcome has been an excruciatingly painful death. I haven't done surgery in the abdomen, and neither have any other of our army surgeons here, but Dr. Grant has (1). He's written about it, and we've talked about it. He's fully recovered from his own illness—a devastating case of quinsy, and I've seen him perform surgery on wounded men. General Howe, Dr. Grant has excellent judgement and far advanced skills. I recommend we have him see Mrs. Loring immediately."

Howe looked perplexed and added, "But...but he's a prisoner of war."

"With respect, Sir, being a prisoner in this case is irrelevant," Walker replied without hesitation. "He's a doctor first and foremost. He's treated everyone I've asked him to—American prisoners and British soldiers alike! He came here with me from Brunswick. We have no time to waste."

"Very well, Dr. Walker, see to it. I'd like to meet Dr. Grant immediately."

Walker rode back to the His Majesty's Main General Hospital and found Alex at Major Redmond's bedside. Alex smiled to Walker and proudly showed him how well the engineer's arm was healing. Red Jack bellowed, "I'm feeling fit and can move my arm and all the fingers." Dr. Walker glanced cursorily but quickly took Alex aside. "I'm delighted with Major Redmond's recovery, but now I've got a bigger case for you. Grab your surgical kit and come with me to headquarters!" As an afterthought, Walker called back to Red Jack, "Apologies, we'll be back later."

On route, Walker explained Elizabeth's condition to Alex. The general was almost always the picture of composure, but now Alex saw a man shaken because of worry. Howe's coat was off, and he wrung his hands constantly. The general began slowly, "Dr. Grant, I understand that...um... the fortunes of war...bring you to see...um...Mrs. Loring this morning. Our esteemed Dr. Walker has recommended you highly. No doubt, he has filled you in and... given his diagnosis. I am grateful if you'd provide your care."

"Sir, I am honored to meet you. I am eager to see the patient."

Entering the room, Alex saw that Elizabeth was now in constant pain. Although she smiled bravely to him, she looked ashen. When Alex examined her abdomen, it was now more tender than at Walker's examination just an hour before. He nodded to Walker and turned to General Howe and Elizabeth. "I concur with Dr. Walker's diagnosis. Because of her worsening condition, it is urgent that we remove the tumor and stop the hemorrhage."

"When will you begin?" General Howe asked hesitantly.

"Since it is only a quarter mile from here, we'll move the patient to the General Hospital by ambulance and begin as soon as possible. There, the operating theater is already clean and prepared. Under less pressing circumstances, I'd prefer to have my regular assistant surgeon and my own surgical instruments for the case. But with Dr. Hobbs and my full set of instruments in Morristown, under these conditions, we cannot wait. Fortunately, we'll have Nurse Jesse, who is familiar with the care. The surgery may have its complications, but there is no other choice. Dr. Walker and I and his excellent mates will see the case through, but in the meantime...."

General Howe knew exactly what Alex was about to propose and made it easy. "Dr. Grant, in this extraordinary situation, I'll send my aide-de-camp, under a flag of truce, to General Washington, with a letter from you –covered by mine— to get your assistant surgeon here as soon as possible. As General Washington is a gentleman, I am certain he will agree." (2)

Alex administered a dose of laudanum to Elizabeth. As two surgeon's mates carried Elizabeth to the awaiting ambulance, General Howe took Alex aside and whispered, "You will have my eternal gratitude. If you save her life, I will grant you a prompt parole."

****

General Howe's senior aide-de-camp, Major Richard Leffingwell, left British Headquarters and boarded the army ferry as it was leaving Manhattan for Paulus Hook, New Jersey. From there, his mission was to ride toward the American camp in

Morristown and under a white flag deliver two letters addressed to George Washington. Howe picked Major Leffingwell because of his superb diplomatic skills which would be essential for the mission's success. Aboard the ferry, the major thought to himself, "Well, this is the most peculiar mission Howe has ever given me. I am to let myself get taken by enemy cavalry, show them the first letter from General Howe, and hope they will escort me to their commander, Washington. I hope I get to see old England again."

Before Major Leffingwell left New York, Howe had shown him the letters. Howe had written the first which read:

To His Excellency, General G. Washington,

Sir,

My senior aide-de-camp, Major Richard Leffingwell, carries a letter from your Director of the General Hospital, Dr. Alexander Grant, who is now a prisoner of war. At the time of this writing, Dr. Grant is conducting emergency surgery on a desperately ill member of my military household. In an accompanying letter, Dr. Grant personally requests that you dispatch his Assistant Surgeon, Dr. John Hobbs, to New York to assist with the recovery and any subsequent events. Dr. Hobbs is requested to bring Dr. Grant's full set of surgical instruments.

You shall be pleased to know that, under the care of British Army physicians, Dr. Grant has recovered fully from his severe throat disease and is now in good health. If you are agreeable, Major Leffingwell shall accompany Dr. Hobbs to New York and assure his safety on route and on his return.

In the name of mercy, I beg your assistance.

William Howe, K.B., General
Commander in Chief, His Majesty's Forces in North America

Leffingwell was instructed to show this letter to any American officers who would intercept him in New Jersey, but the second letter he was instructed to show only to Washington.

****

At His Majesty's Main General Hospital, set up in a large mansion south of headquarters, the two mates carried Elizabeth into the operating theater on the ground floor. It was a large room, previously the parlor for the Tory family who had lived there. The room was bright, catching the morning sun through its windows facing east and south. Despite the winter chill, the windows were partially opened to let in fresh air. In place of the furniture, Dr. Walker's sturdy, wooden operating table now stood in the center of the room. Adjacent to the operating table, on two smaller tables, the mates had already laid out a set of English surgical instruments and dressings. The mates carefully placed Elizabeth on the table and covered her with clean sheets. Jesse affixed large leather straps around her thighs and chest. Following Alex's practice before surgery, Dr. Walker, his chief mate, Jesse, and Alex thoroughly washed their hands with soap and water and applied a final rinse with carbolic acid solution. Alex instructed another mate on washing Elizabeth's abdomen similarly. Elizabeth's heart was racing, but she faced the operation courageously. When Alex and Walker moved next to her, she preempted them, saying gracefully, "I am thankful to be taken under the care of both of you. I have faith the operation will be successful."

Alex bent over to speak comfortingly into her ear. "Mrs. Loring, in just a minute, we shall begin. Here is another dose of laudanum. You will feel a sharp pain in your belly as we begin and then only some pulling and tugging. The operation will not take long. Here is a birch rod to place between your teeth. It's fine to bite down on it when you must. You are a brave woman. We will take good care of you and, afterwards, you will feel much better." Elizabeth gave a half smile and drifted into opium-induced semi-consciousness. Outside the operating theater, General William Howe, the most powerful British officer in the Americas, paced helplessly as the fate of his lover rested in the hands of an enemy surgeon.

Following Alex's unusual hygienic preliminaries, the medical team was ready. Standing to Elizabeth's right side, Alex palpated her abdomen once more before beginning. Through her lower belly, he felt the firm tumor protruding almost up to her umbilicus. Alex nodded to Walker, who was assisting him from Elizabeth's left, and to Mate Blackfield, who was next to Walker. As she stood next to Alex at the operating table, Jesse noted beads of sweat on his brow. She discreetly dabbed his forehead with a clean cloth. Surgeon's Mate Smart sat next to Elizabeth's head to assure she was breathing regularly. He nodded to Alex that she was.

Alex had performed three abdominal operations previously, two on men with farming injuries and one on a woman with a tumor like Elizabeth's. But none of the previous cases had his freedom riding on them. Fleetingly, Alex thought, "For her sake and for mine, this had better go well!" His mouth felt parched, but he addressed his colleagues in an authoritative tone, "Now then, Jesse, hand me the medium scalpel."

With that, Alex made a midline skin incision over the tumor's prominence. He carried it down through her thin subcutaneous tissue and clamped small bleeding vessels. Walker placed ligatures around the bleeders and quickly tied them. Elizabeth gasped once and then moaned softly but continued her normal breathing. While Walker retracted the skin, Alex incised the shiny, white tendon in the midline and retracted the underlying red muscles of her belly. Walker and he now peered at the peritoneum, the smooth, transparent lining of the abdominal cavity. Below this layer, they saw reddish fluid pressing upwards.

"Your diagnosis is correct, Dr. Walker. Inside the abdomen, there's a mixture of blood and fluid. I suspect that they are both coming from the ovarian tumor which is beginning to leak. We got here just in time. I'm going to open the peritoneum. Jesse, scissors please."

As Alex opened the abdominal cavity, copious amounts of bloody, serous fluid rushed out. Alex ladled much of the fluid into a basin and absorbed the remainder in towels. When Alex extended the incision, they were able to see a melon-sized, shiny, purplish-red tumor arising from an ovary.

Alex queried Walker, "This tumor is too large to excise through our incision, and with our limited pain control, I am reluctant to extend our incision any further. I'm in favor of draining the tumor so we can remove it more easily. What's your thought?" (3)

Walker presented his rationale, "Well, it appears the tumor has already been leaking into the abdomen. I'd agree that we should incise the tumor to collapse it and then excise it through our present incision."

Alex then swept his index finger around the tumor and found it free of adhesions. When he incised the tumor, much more fluid egressed. Alex noted, "Good Lord, this fluid is much bloodier, and there must be over one hundred ounces of it. Yet, now the tumor is collapsed." He used his steel ladle to remove the fluid from Elizabeth's belly.

With his extensive knowledge of anatomy, Alex found the tumor's blood supply, clamped the vessels, and cut and ligated them. He then removed the collapsed tumor sac from the abdomen. Alex observed, "The exterior of the tumor is completely shiny and smooth, and the inside has a few smaller cysts, but no growths. I don't see any other tumor in the abdomen, and the other ovary is a normal white, walnut-sized structure." (4)

Walker was awed, "Dr. Grant, this is the first time I've seen abdominal surgery, and you performed it swiftly and smartly."

Jesse looked at Alex admiringly as he took a deep breath and responded humbly, "We were lucky. It could have been dicey. Jesse, please hand me the suture to close her abdomen. If we get Mrs. Loring through the immediate recovery, she'll do very well."

As soon as the surgery was completed, Alex and Walker met a very anguished General Howe outside the operating theater. Alex began, "General Howe, I am pleased to report that all went well. While we did find a tumor on her ovary, it looks like a simple structure without any sign of spreading. She lost a fair amount of blood inside the abdomen before we started, but there's no further bleeding. She'll be sleepy for a few hours, but you may go in and see her now."

Relieved, General William Howe cautiously approached Elizabeth still on the operating table. At first, he did not notice the petite Black woman now standing a few feet away. Although Howe had witnessed great carnage on fields of battle, he suddenly felt light-headed when he saw Elizabeth's blood on the drapes and floor of the room. His own color paled, and he broke out in a profuse sweat. Jesse clutched the general's arm to steady him. Howe was visibly taken aback upon seeing Dr. Grant's nurse was a Black woman. Comfortingly, Jesse said, "It's all right, General, your dizziness will pass in a few minutes."

Howe nodded appreciatively. Dr. Walker flashed his commander a comforting smile and added, "Sir, I remember when I first saw surgery. I felt the same way."

Recovering, the general replied to Walker with a half grin, "Tell anyone about this, and you'll find yourself cashiered!"

"Indeed, Sir, I noticed nothing," Walker assured him.

****

Twenty miles to the west, Major Richard Leffingwell peered through his telescope at a troop of American cavalry riding toward him. "Now it's time to see if I'll get safely to the rebel camp and then ever home again." He attached a white flag to the muzzle of his carbine and slowed his horse to a walk. The cavalry troop captain, a veteran from New York, suspiciously approached the lone British rider.

"Halt, there, and state your business," the captain shouted.

"I am General Howe's aide-de-camp. I carry a letter from my commander in chief for General Washington. It is a matter of life and death."

"We see life and death every day, Major," said the New Yorker indifferently. "My sergeant will approach. Hand him your letter." Although the letter was addressed to "His Excellency, General G. Washington," the cavalry captain had the authority to open intercepted letters. He laughed ebulliently as he read the letter. "Major, I am delighted to read that Dr. Grant is well. We knew of his illness, and we feared his death. Now, as for seeing General Washington, we'll take you to camp all right, but you'll need to wear this blindfold as we approach Morristown. And one more requirement: I'll have to see the letter supposedly written by Dr. Grant—before we take you."

Leffingwell reneged. "Captain, my orders are to deliver

this letter o n l y to General Washington."

"And my orders, Major, are to interrogate anyone heading to Morristown. That means, I see the letter, or you become my prisoner. Clear?"

The British aide knew he was out maneuvered and handed Alex's letter to the American officer. The letter read:

To His Excellency, General George Washington, Commander in Chief,

Sir,

I humbly apologize for troubling you with this matter. I am about to perform surgery, at General William Howe's request, on a member of his military household. No British surgeon is adequately qualified. By the time you receive this letter, the surgery will have been completed with the assistance of the Director of the Main British General Hospital in New York, Dr. Walker. However, as complications may arise due to the extensive nature of the surgery, I humbly ask that Dr. John Hobbs be granted your permission to join me at British Headquarters in New York City until the patient is stable. I request that Dr. Hobbs also bring my personal full surgical chest as the British chests do not include fine as well as large clamps, scissors, retractors, and other special instruments that I am likely to need. I believe that Dr. Hobbs' role at our hospital can be assumed, during his anticipated short absence, by one of the excellent senior regimental surgeons in Morristown. I have been assured of Dr. Hobbs' safe passage by General Howe. I am feeling well now and look forward to my return.

Your most obedient servant,

A. Grant, Surgeon

The captain looked up. "Major, this sounds like something Dr. Grant would say. I am certain the letter is legitimate. I'll get you to Morristown before nightfall."

The New York cavalry troopers and Major Leffingwell rode the ten miles to the American encampment, arriving at sunset. With the aide blindfolded, they escorted him to Washington headquarters in Freeman's Tavern. Outside, the sentries halted the New York cavalry captain to ascertain the reason for bringing a British officer—even a blindfolded one— to see General Washington. One sentry went inside and returned a few minutes later with Lieutenant Colonel Tilghman.

Tench announced, "Captain, you may bring the British officer inside but keep him blindfolded."

Inside the American headquarters, Leffingwell's blindfold was removed by Tench, who extended the customary courtesy to a fellow officer. "Major Leffingwell, you've had a long ride on a cold day. His Excellency shall receive you shortly." But Major Leffingwell had to wait over an hour before being brought into Washington's office.

In full regalia, the American Commander in Chief rose from his desk and greeted Leffingwell formally. "Major, I trust you will give my regards to General Howe upon your return to New York. My aides have already explained the reason General Howe sent you here."

Leffingwell had heard much about Washington in British military circles, nearly all of it demeaning and denigrating. Yet, across the desk, rose a tall, powerful officer who exuded confidence and composure. Washington continued, "General Howe shall be glad to know that I have already authorized Dr.

Hobbs to go to New York with you. Colonel Tilghman, please show him in."

John Hobbs greeted Leffingwell openly. "Major, I am delighted to meet you and eager to learn details of our mission in New York. If Dr. Grant wants me there, I'm certain there is excellent reason."

As soon as all were seated around Washington's conference table, he queried Leffingwell, "Now, major, please fill us in on the details."

"Thank you, Sir. I humbly extend the gratitude of Sir General Howe for your prompt action to fulfill his and Dr. Grant's requests. You see, the surgery was removal of a tumor of a women's abdomen." Leffingwell knew that the request he carried was an extraordinary one. He surmised that the American commander had already guessed the woman must be very close to Howe, likely Elizabeth Loring. Knowing how the Americans despised Joshua Loring for his cruel treatment of prisoners, Leffingwell intentionally omitted the officer's name. He hoped he would not have to disclose the patient's identity.

Gracious and discreet, Washington simply added, "You must get a good night's rest for you will be off in the early morning. Colonel Tilghman, please see to it that Life Guards provide an escort to British lines. Major Leffingwell, you'll have quarters tonight in Dr. Hobbs's billet. I bid you all success in the care of General Howe's...um...*high priority* patient."

Leffingwell winced as he was now convinced that Washington had deduced Elizabeth Loring's identity. On the way to Hobbs' quarters, the American surgeon pressed Leffingwell for details of the surgery. "Do you know what organ the tumor arose from? And how was the patient doing when you left New York."

Leffingwell replied, "Not being a surgeon, I don't know the answer to your first question, and as to the second, the patient survived the surgery. I wish I had more I could tell you."

Then mischievously, Hobbs asked the burning question, "Major, do you at least know whose life Dr. Grant saved this morning?"

Leffingwell presumed that Hobbs had already figured out the answer and replied indirectly, "Dr. Hobbs, I regret that I am unable to officially reply officially, but of course you will find out as soon as you get to New York. "

Hobbs smiled to himself and nodded, "Of course."

---

(1) Dr. Grant's surgery to remove the ovarian tumor from Elizabeth Loring would not have been the first surgery of its kind. Credit for performing the first laparotomy (surgical opening of the abdomen) in America has usually been given to Dr. Ephraim McDowell, who removed a large ovarian tumor on his kitchen table in Danville, Kentucky in 1809. The woman survived. However, earlier, Dr. John Bard performed a laparotomy in 1759, and in 1785 Dr. John Warren (brother of the physician-general Joseph Warren, who died at Bunker Hill) carried out a similar operation in Boston. In the 1790s, Virginia surgeon William Baynham performed two laparotomies for tubal (ectopic) pregnancies. One recent source about early surgery is P-O Hasselgren's *Revolutionary Surgeons, Patriots and Loyalists on the Cutting Edge*, Knox Press, New York, 2021.

(2) To the 21st Century reader, it may seem astonishing that enemy commanders would have corresponded and

asked for a special consideration, even for a favor under extraordinary circumstances, as depicted in this chapter. Yet, in the 18th Century, high-ranking officers often had great respect for each other and considered themselves brothers-in-arms. These feelings were especially likely between British and Americans who shared a common language and heritage. Further, the bond between medical staffs of opposing armies was still stronger as they often envisioned themselves as doctors first and military personnel second. For example, after The Battle of Brandywine in Pennsylvania in September 1777, American surgeons were called by the British to help treat American wounded remaining on the battlefield even though the American army had retreated many miles to the east.

(3) In modern surgery, the practice is to remove ovarian tumors intact to prevent spread in case of cancer. However, given the limitations that Dr. Grant faced, decompression of the ovarian cyst was his best option.

(4) From Alex's description of the tumor, it likely would have been benign. In terms of pathology, the tumor would probably have been a serous cystadenoma, today recognized as one of the most common, benign ovarian neoplasms.

Chapter 11-The Plot in Full
Monday, January 27, 1777
New York and Brunswick

Tarleton's delayed his next move to minimize suspicion but chafed to get on with his scheme. Finally, in late January, disguised once again as the stocky quarter master major, he took the early morning ferry from Manhattan to Perth Amboy, New Jersey and then rode the remaining fourteen miles to Brunswick. On route, he thought through his plan to himself, "Blankets will be my perfect media to transmit the pox, especially during cold nights in the American mountain encampment. I've already prepared a forged requisition to get a shipment of wool blankets from the huge British army storehouse in Brunswick, and there I'll avoid the snooping eyes of bloody informers who are all over New York. Besides, from Brunswick, it's an easy passage to Morristown. To haul the shipment, I'll hire civilian contractors, and I've prepared a forged contract for them too. The army quartermaster is so overwhelmed that they'll never pick up the forgeries. My only incomplete piece is how to assure the British Army blankets get to Morristown, and I've got a good idea as to how to do just that."

At the huge British storehouse in Brunswick, he dismounted awkwardly because of the padding in his disguise and waddled to the counter. A thin, short lieutenant greeted him cheerfully, "Good afternoon, major, a bit chilly out there today. How may I help you?"

"Lieutenant," the major began haughtily, "I have a high priority requisition, signed by the Quartermaster General himself. We have intelligence that rebel forces are increasing activity to the northwest. General Howe is mobilizing part of the 42nd Highlanders to establish a strong point about twenty miles from here, but there's a need of supplies and ammunition. I'm told you are well stocked here. Look at the requisition, and you'll see it's for cartridges, salt pork, cheese, winter great coats, and above all blankets."

The young officer scanned the requisition order and frowned. "Major, no problem with the cartridges, coats, cheese, and salt pork—I've got lots of those, but this is a huge order for blankets. With the cold we've been having, I just don't have that many in store."

The major grew angry. "Look here, lieutenant, we'll have half a Regiment of Foot desperate for these supplies out there, freezing in this wintery weather and protecting our flank, while you stay warm in your storehouse all day and push papers. Don't tell me you don't have blankets for these warriors. The 42nd will have to prepare for winter at the new outpost. It will take them about three weeks. Prepare the full order any way you can but have it complete and ready to be hauled on February 20th, or I'll have you charged with insubordination!"

Smugly, the major turned and left the unnerved young lieutenant to solve the problem. Tarleton smiled to himself, "Damned good act, old boy, I must say. If that doesn't motivate that prissy lieutenant, I'll bet a year's pay."

As the sun was setting, Tarleton, still in disguise, rode to The White Horse Inn just outside Brunswick. He ate a simple meal of roast beef with potatoes and a half bottle of claret alone in his room. "This way," he thought, "I'll spend the night where no one will know that Lieutenant Colonel Tarleton was in Brunswick, and I'll quietly celebrate my successes."

Early the next morning, Tarleton washed, dressed in the quartermaster's uniform, settled his bill, and rode south of the town. One mile from the army storehouse, he found a small house with a stable to its side. Hanging on the fence was a sign, with crudely carved letters: "Williamson Bros, Teamsters."

As Tarleton entered the humble dwelling, a stout, unshaven man greeted him. "Mornin', Major, I'm Charles Williamson. What can I do for the major?"

"Mr. Williamson, I know you've done work for the army. I have an order here to haul a shipment to an outpost just twenty miles to the northwest. It would take two wagons and must be delivered by February 20th. The contract is to deliver cartridges, salt pork, great coats and blankets."

"Well, Major, my brother and me—well, we run a reliable company. We were set up New York City last fall and did many contracts with the King's forces. We moved our business to Brunswick last month so we could be near our sickly mum. I hear the army's commissary wagons are bein' used for large convoys. So, we'll be glad to make the shipment...but it'll cost dearly."

They quickly agreed, and the major replied, "Very well, then ten pounds the fee will be. You and your brother with two wagons will meet me at the army storehouse in Brunswick at nine o'clock in the morning on, Thursday, February 20th. I'll give you half the fee that morning and the rest upon your return. Agreed?"

"Not wantin' to be ungrateful, Sir," Williamson replied craftily, "but to cover our expenses, I'd like the King's treasury to put down at least two pounds today, three pounds next week, and the rest upon our return."

The major grew perturbed but needed Williamson's services. He took the contract from his dispatch case, made the revisions in the payment schedule, and asked Williamson to sign the bogus document. Williamson scrawled "CW," and the major scribbled an illegible signature on the line marked "By Order of The Quartermaster General." From his own purse, Tarleton handed Williamson two one-pound silver coins, neatly folded the contract into his dispatch case, and rode back toward Brunswick.

Tarleton thought to himself, "Now just one more piece of information to gather before I head back to New York." He rode to Brunswick's western outskirts and came to a British cavalry squadron's headquarters in a modest farmhouse. To the mounted sergeant outside, Tarleton inquired, "Is your commanding officer here now? I must see him presently."

The sergeant snapped a smart salute to the quarter master major. "Sir, my captain is in the parlor preparing a report. May I tell him your reason to see him?"

"Sergeant, kindly tell your captain that I have an urgent matter of intelligence to discuss. "

Showing deference to his senior officer, the cavalry captain hastened outside to greet the major. "Please, Sir, come inside on this chilly morning. Won't you have some tea?"

Sipping the hot tea, the putative quartermaster major convincingly told the captain his concocted story. "I am authorizing a secret shipment to an outpost, guarding our flank to the west. I have a need for security and secrecy. I'm certain you understand. I am not at liberty to reveal any more about the timing or escort, and you must not breath a word of my visit to anyone. Clear? But I have need for intelligence from you about enemy patrols to the west."

Tarleton had not raised any suspicion from the cavalry officer who gave him the exact answer he wanted. "Sir, rebel cavalry patrol out there all the time—from dawn to dusk! My troopers go only in force.

****

On the morning after Elizabeth Loring's surgery, Alex and Walker crossed the street from their quarters and strode into His Majesty's Main General Hospital in New York. Walker greeted his young Surgeon's Mate jauntily, "Good morning, MacLeish. I've been so busy that I haven't even had a chance to see you. Mate Archibald MacLeish, please meet Dr. Alexander Grant."

The mate, a tow-headed lad from Edinburgh, appeared nervous in the presence of the renowned American surgeon. "Pleas'd t' meet ya', Dr. Grant. Dr. Walker, may I 'ave a word?"

Walker replied, "Don't think of Dr. Grant as a prisoner. He's my outstanding colleague. Whatever you have to say, you may share with him, too."

"Well, Sir," MacLeish continued, "This mornin', w'd y' see two o' th' men wit' 'ospital fever? They're not doin' good a'tall, 'n' then, Sir, when ya' were in Bruns'k, I 'ad a...uh... unexpect'd visit from a Q-master off'cer."

Knowing his mate as trustworthy, Walker's ears perked up. "Let's get some tea while you tell Dr. Grant and me about this visit."

After hearing the account of a quartermaster major coming into the hospital, completely unannounced, exactly when he was in Brunswick, Dr. Walker was immediately suspicious. Then, the mate added critical pieces to the story. "Sirs," he recalled clearly, "As I was 'bout t' enter th' ward from th' basement, I saw th' QM major leavin' the 'pox room and placin' scrapin's from a scalpel in a vial in 'is case. I'm sure 'e didna' see me. I couldna' figure it out. Why'd 'e wan' th' scaprin's? I couldna' challenge 'im so I stepp'd quiet t' th' basemen' for a time. Then, I made loud footsteps 'n' came back t' th' ward."

Alex's mind was racing, "Scapings, you say? Do you know where they came from? And did you get a good look at the quartermaster major? Can you describe him?"

"The scrapin's—I figure they mus' be from one o' th' 'nfected lads. And oh, yeah, I recall 'im alright. 'E's one o' them look down y'r nose off'cers—'bout Dr. Walker's 'eight, but on th' plump side 'n' gettin' gray 'air under 'is tricorn 'at."

Alex pressed, "Very good, MacLeish, very good, indeed. Could the scrapings have been from anything else, and are you certain of his rank? And anything else unusual about him?"

"Canna' think o' wha' else 'e was scrapin'. An' wit'out doubt, 'e's a major alright. Then come t' think 'bout 't, yeah, there's somethin' else: 'e wrote wit' 'is lef' hand." (1)

Alex's eyes brightened as he added, "Dr. Walker, I leave you two to see the lads with hospital fever. I've got to see Major Redmond upstairs."

Alex bounded up the stairs two at a time and found Red Jack finishing his breakfast. Red Jack greeted Alex, "Well, I might have died before you came to see me again! And you dashed away so quickly the last time."

"I knew that arm of yours would be fine, Major Redmond. Let me take one more look. Then, I've got a curious question for you."

"Dr. Grant, you saved my arm. I'll go to the end of the earth to answer any question you ask me," beamed Red Jack.

"Well, your arm is doing so well, I'll get you back to your engineers in a couple more days. Here's my question. I can't get into details, but Dr. Walker and I would like to find out the identity of a quartermaster major—on the heavy side, with graying hair. Do you know him?"

Red Jack shook his head, replying, "Dr. Grant, the artillery, cavalry, and foot officers have their social circles, and the engineers, quartermaster, commissary—well, we have our own. You doctors are off by yourselves. After all my years in New York, I know all the officers in my circle, and there is no major—fat or thin—in the quartermaster corps. There's a colonel, a few captains, and junior officers—but definitely no major now. There was one major, but he sailed home in November! What's this all about?"

As Alex darted downstairs, he called back, "Major Redmond, thank you, and I'll tell you when I know more later!"

Alex caught up with Walker just as he was leaving the fever ward. Suppressing his new intelligence, Alex asked innocently, "What do you make of Mate MacLeish's encounter with the quartermaster major?"

"I'm no detective, Dr. Grant, but I think there's something devious afoot. The timing of the major's visit and his sneaking into the smallpox ward—Good Lord, that stinks with suspicion."

Then Alex dropped, "And what would you think if I told you there is no quartermaster major?"

"What?" Walker shot back incredulously.

"I have it from Major Redmond, who knows all the officers in the auxiliary corps, that there was one quartermaster major, but he sailed to England in November. Good heavens, Dr. Walker, I fear there's a bloody plot of some sort right under our noses. Can you report this to General Howe?"

"Maybe in your army, Dr. Grant, but in His Majesty's Forces, there's no way, not with what little intelligence we have. We have no firm evidence. Just the word of a lowly surgeon's mate and suspicious circumstances. Dr. Grant, I'm just a doctor in the British Army. I have no position in the chain of command. I'm afraid, my trusted friend, we'll need a lot more before going to the commander in chief."

****

Alex, Walker and Mate Archibald MacLeish were not the only ones harboring suspicions about the alleged quartermaster major. The young quartermaster lieutenant at the Brunswick storehouse had been stewing for days over his own encounter with the quartermaster major. He thought to himself, "What would the quartermaster major really do with so large an order for blankets, and why was he so threatening to me?" Though new to his rank and position, the lieutenant was not easily bullied for he had connections in the army. His name was Martin Walker, grandson of a retired major general who had fought with distinction in the French and Indian War as well as being the favorite nephew of the Director of the His Majesty's Main General Hospital in New York, Dr. Timothy Walker.

Lieutenant Martin Walker's immediate superior was a quartermaster captain who had risen to his rank almost invisibly. The captain came from a wealthy family but was dull and lethargic. On several occasions, the captain told Martin, "Lieutenant, the way to get ahead in this army is to avoid sticking your neck out. Just keep things running smoothly." Indeed, when Martin went to him about the blankets, the captain dispensed with any involvement in the problem saying, "Well, Lieutenant, you know the system. If a superior officer requisitions them, damn it, just find them."

By scrounging through the recesses of the giant storehouse, Martin Walker's sergeant found a stash of old, moth-eaten blankets, amounting to about two-thirds of the order. He had the sergeant place these in the bottom of the shipping chests and added a few new blankets on the top of each chest. "At least," Martin thought, "I've got the appearance of a complete order."

But he still fumed at his treatment and finally decided to confide in his uncle, Dr. Timothy Walker. Not knowing when his uncle would next visit Brunswick, Martin decided to write him a letter at His Majesty's Main General Hospital in New York City. It read:

February 12, 1777
Dear Sir,

I hope you are doing well since your inspection visit to Brunswick a few weeks ago.

I am now asking for your advice on a personal matter. I have reported this incident to my captain, but he simply dismissed my concerns. Two days ago, a quartermaster major came into our storehouse in Brunswick and gave me a requisition for a huge amount of winter supplies including great coats and blankets. The major was heavy and graying. These supplies were to be shipped in ten days—on the 20th of February--to a post on the western frontier of our lines. The quartermaster major told me that civilian teamsters would receive and deliver the supplies. The teamsters will certainly be Charles and William Williamson. They're the only civilian contractors the army has in Brunswick. When I told the major, we did not have this number of blankets available, he berated me openly and threatened to remove me from my post. My sergeant and I have managed to find a supply of tattered old blankets, just to comply, and put them in the bottom of the chests for shipment. I have never witnessed such high-handed treatment of an officer as I experienced from this major. One other observation has raised my suspicion. The requisition was written with the left hand whilst all others I have received were by a right-handed clerk. With my captain so aloof, I am asking your advice in view of your many years in His Majesty's Service.

Your most obedient servant, and nephew,
M. Walker, Lt, Quartermaster, Brunswick New Jersey

Martin Walker placed the letter in an official pouch and addressed it to:
Mr. T. Walker
British General Hospital, New York City

With regular dispatches carried twice daily between Brunswick and New York City, Martin expected to have a reply quickly. As he walked back from the postal station, he had no idea how his letter might unveil the brewing plot.

---

(1) In 18th Century England, left-handedness was uncommon. Indeed, because using one's left hand was considered awkward or threatening or the work of the devil or clumsy (well into the 20th Century), children of wealthy families were often forced to write with their right hands.

Chapter 12-The Setback
Friday, January 31 to Saturday, February 1, 1777
Morristown and British Headquarters, New York City

A mid-winter blizzard dropped two feet of heavy snow on Morristown, delaying Hobbs' departure for New York. Hobbs was eager to get going, but the engineers could not clear the pass east of the encampment for four days. Then, on a bright, frigid morning, Tench Tilghman and four Life Guards escorted Leffingwell and Hobbs east toward the British lines. Leffingwell's scarlet uniform could be spotted from a mile away against the freshly fallen snow. Through his telescope, a British cavalry officer took in the curious entourage of a British officer leading Americans eastward. He positioned his cavalry squadron in the woods along the road, well ahead of Leffingwell and the Life Guards. But Tench easily made out the British movements through his own telescope. Fearing an attempted ambush, Tench parlayed with Leffingwell. "Major, your cavalry must suspect some trickery on our part. May I suggest you ride up the road, call them out and present them with General Howe's letter of passage?"

"Delighted!" Leffingwell replied, and he slowly rode ahead. A moment later, Tench heard Leffingwell's high pitched voice, calling the British cavalry, "I say, chaps, Major Richard Leffingwell here, Senior Aide to General Howe. If you'll come out of the woods, I'll explain everything."

The squadron dashed from the trees and surrounded Leffingwell. The cavalry officer had a grand smile on his face and said, "Major, I recognized your voice and knew this could not be an American trick." After Leffingwell handed the squadron leader Howe's letter of passage, Tench and the Life Guards rode to bring Hobbs to meet the British cavalry.

Tench addressed Leffingwell, "Major, in all our days, I

suspect we'll never have another encounter quite like this one!" Recognizing their humanitarian mission, the British squadron leader responded in kind. "Dr. Hobbs, if you're ready, it will be my honor to escort you to Manhattan. On behalf of my commander, may I offer our heartfelt gratitude to you for coming?"

Hobbs agreed, "Well, then, gentlemen, it's darned cold out here. I can't wait to get to Manhattan!"

Tench bade a farewell, "Good journey, Dr. Hobbs. Return safely." Then Tench and the Life Guards turned westward toward Morristown. The others rode east. At dusk, Leffingwell and Hobbs, fatigued and half frozen, dismounted and entered the Main British General Hospital in New York City. There, they found Dr. Walker at the bedside of wounded soldiers. Leffingwell cleared his throat to get Walker's attention and said, "May I present Dr. Grant's colleague, Dr. John Hobbs?"

Walker exclaimed, "Thank heavens! We had given you up for lost, and I am glad you're here. We've been nearly overwhelmed. But, of course, you must want to see Dr. Grant. He's been through a great deal. My surgeon's mate will fetch him."

From a quarantine room, Alex entered the main ward. Hobbs clutched his hands. "Dr. Grant, I haven't seen you in over two months. Thank goodness you're looking fine, but you could certainly use a little meat on your bones!" Over Alex's shoulder, Hobbs saw Jesse enter the ward. He greeted her affectionately, "And, Jesse, I am delighted to see you thriving as well. Now I know why Dr. Grant has recuperated so nicely." Then catching himself, he added sheepishly, "...because of Dr. Walker's care and yours."

Walker welcomed them to warm themselves by the fireplace while Jesse brought tea for all. Alex asked, "Tell us, what took so long?"

Hobbs replied playfully, "Why, Mother Nature herself who sent a winter storm at a particularly inopportune moment! But we're here now, and I brought your special instruments. Pray, what have you been up to?"

Walker began, "Dr. Hobbs, five days ago very early in the morning, General Howe called me urgently to headquarters. It turns out that a woman of his military household was having severe abdominal pain. To be brief, she developed a large ovarian cyst which was bleeding and rupturing. Knowing from our medical discussions that Dr. Grant had unique experience with abdominal surgery, I convinced General Howe that Dr. Grant was her only chance for survival."

Alex added modestly, "Dr. Walker, Jesse, and two mates made the surgery go exceedingly well. For the first few days, her abdomen was markedly distended, but just giving her tea and other liquids, she's done much better. She's a brave one, all right. I'd like to take you to see her—just as soon as you've warmed yourself."

"And whom are we going to see?" asked Hobbs fully anticipating the answer.

Twenty minutes later, Alex introduced Hobbs to Elizabeth Loring. Not waiting for an introduction, she quipped, "Dr. Hobbs, why have you kept me waiting so long to meet you? Dr. Grant has been praising your skills and experience."

Hobbs knew he was being charmed and responded fittingly, "If Major Leffingwell had told me how gracious and delightful you are, I should have crawled through the storm."

When the laughter quieted down, Alex queried, "And how are you feeling this evening, Mrs. Loring?"

"Overall, I feel better and managed to walk around the room even though you advised complete bed rest, but I have noted a chill every so often. And then, where the dressing is over my belly, I do feel a bit more pain than yesterday."

Despite her brave efforts, Elizabeth writhed momentarily and held her lower abdomen when a spasm overcame her. Alex was concerned. "Now, then, it's been five days since the operation. It would be safe now to inspect the incision."

Alex washed his hands with soap and then rinsed with carbolic acid. After he carefully removed the dressing, what he saw, even in the dim light of the room, raised his concern. "Mrs. Loring, around the edges of the incision I notice some redness, but I don't see any laudable pus now. (1) I'm going to redress your belly. We'll apply warm towels to it and check in the morning when we have good light. I'll have Nurse Jesse stay beside you tonight in case you need anything." Elizabeth gave the doctors a worried half smile and grabbed Jesse's hand as she felt another spasm of pain.

At six o'clock the next morning, Jesse ran to Alex, "Please come see Mrs. Loring right away. I fear she has burst her wound!"

Elizabeth looked drained as she whispered, "Dr. Grant, I feel so terribly weak. I don't believe I can get out of bed."

When Alex pulled back the covers, his eyes widened, and his head flinched back. To Jesse, he described, "The dressing is soaked with foul pus." He removed the dressing with thumb forceps and added, "The redness has spread two inches on each side, and now there is yellowish pus seeping from the middle of the incision. See, you are correct. She has burst open her wound."

Hobbs and Walker walked to the bedside and sensed the

concern. Looking at a worried Elizabeth Loring, Walker advised, "Perhaps we should step outside to discuss this."

In the foyer, Alex added, "When the wound has suppurated like this, the result can be deadly."

"My Lord, it looks like the flesh is being eaten away," Walker observed.

Rubbing his forehead, Alex summarized concisely, "If we don't control the wound suppuration, Mrs. Loring will follow the course of the others we've seen previously. Time is of the essence. Dr. Walker, would you please have General Howe come over to the hospital right away? Jesse, please give Mrs. Loring a dose of laudanum and wash her abdomen with the soap and then carbolic acid solution. I'll be in to see her in a minute. Dr. Hobbs, would you please prepare the operating theater for a revision of her wound? And everyone, make it fast!"

As Jesse was finishing the abdominal washing, Alex came to the bedside. General Howe rushed in accompanied by Dr. Walker. The general appeared distraught, beginning, "Dr. Grant, what has gone wrong here?"

"General Howe, as you know from your military experience, most wounds heal by showing laudable pus. But in Mrs. Loring's case, after the operation on her abdomen, she has developed serious wound suppuration. We have a chance to control it by removing the dead tissue. If we don't, I'm afraid this could be fatal."

"See here, Dr. Grant, I trusted you when there was a tumor in her abdomen, but you didn't tell me about such complications as this."

His patience wearing thin, Alex continued, "Sir, I beg your

understanding. Mrs. Loring has faced two life-threatening problems. We had to remove the ovarian tumor, or she would have died from hemorrhage. Now, her course is complicated by severe wound suppuration. We must proceed immediately. Dr. Walker, do you wish to add anything?"

"Your Excellency," Dr. Walker added calmly to General Howe, "I agree entirely with Dr. Grant in that surgical removal of the suppuration is the only course, but even so we may not be able to control the complication."

"And exactly what will that mean?" asked the now pasty-looking general.

Alex replied, "General, Sir, I'd estimate that our chance of saving her is no better than one in three."

Momentarily stunned by the terrifying assessment, Howe paused but then responded bitterly, "If she doesn't survive, Dr. Grant, the consequences will be severe!" He then stormed off.

Even the ever-cheerful Dr. Hobbs looked gloomy. "Your commander in chief is not a very gracious fellow, is he, Dr. Walker? Lads, let's do our best."

In the operating theatre, Alex strapped Elizabeth to the table, marked the margins of her abdominal redness, and did a final carbolic acid rinse. At the head of the table, the surgeon's mate noted that Elizabeth was heavily sedated as he placed a wooden rod between her teeth. With Hobbs assisting him from across the table, Alex opened the incision fully. Copious volumes of foul brownish-yellow pus streamed out. Elizabeth bit down hard on the rod, writhed in pain, and then mercifully lost consciousness.

"We had better move quickly," said Alex as he cut away the

blackened skin and fatty tissue with his own large surgical scissors. Hobbs used clawed-end retractors to hold the wound edges apart and observed, "We are here just in the nick of time. The dead tissue is superficial. Fortunately, the abdominal tendons remain pearly white and healthy."

Within minutes, Alex and Hobbs completed the excision, clamped multiple small bleeding vessels with Alex's delicate instruments, and ligated the vessels with fine silk thread. Hobbs volunteered, "Dr. Grant, having your special instruments here has made our case go more smoothly, hasn't it?"

Alex inspected the operating field. "In part, yes, but having you here knowing all the surgical procedures is still more important. Well, Dr. Hobbs, we'll leave the skin and subcutaneous tissue to heal by itself, from the bottom up. Especially with a slender person like our patient, it'll take about three weeks. (2) We'll see healthy pink tissue beginning in a couple of days. I think we've truly gotten control of the suppuration today. Dr. Walker, when we've finished here, would you please see if you can inform General Howe?"

When Walker returned with the British commander in chief, Mrs. Loring was already awakening from the effects of the surgery and laudanum. General Howe glanced at her lying neatly covered by fresh sheets and blankets, her color already appearing better. General Howe placed his right hand tenderly on her forehead as he whispered, "Darling, I'm here with you. Is there anything I can get you?"

Though still groggy, she smiled at him and said, "Yes, General, I'd like some cherry pie!" At that moment, Howe knew his lover was going to be all right. He sighed and uttered, "That's my Elizabeth!"

A much-relieved General Howe expressed his gratitude to

Drs. Grant, Hobbs and Walker. As commander in chief, Howe could not bring himself to apologize for his threats to Alex before the surgery, but Alex read the contrition in Howe's face.

That evening after General Howe left, Alex made one more visit to Elizabeth's bedside by himself. He was about to find out there was much more to Elizabeth Loring than he could ever have expected. Certain that no one else was within earshot, she quietly expressed her heartfelt feelings, "Dr. Grant, I am indebted to you for saving my life, not once, but twice. And as I was spiraling downhill, I feared that I was headed to my grave before I could disclose to you a serious and devious threat."

---

(1) Elizabeth Loring's surgery took place long before the widespread introduction of effective antiseptic techniques in the late Nineteenth Century. As a result, virtually all wounds became infected. Indeed, the presence of pus was so common that surgeons thought it was part of the normal healing process, and they referred to it as "laudable pus."

(2) Leaving Elizabeth's wound open and allowing it to heal from the bottom up was another of Alex's surgical innovations. This approach is still used today in dealing with wounds of an infected site since it avoids the high re-infection rate of suturing the wound closed. Alex's projection was correct in that it would take several weeks for the healing to be completed.

Chapter 13 - An Unexpected Source
Thursday, February 13 to Friday, February 14, 1777
New York

When Lieutenant Martin Walker's letter to his uncle, Dr. Timothy Walker, arrived at the New York military post office, the private who was sorting the military mail was already annoyed. That afternoon, the dispatch rider from Brunswick handed him a heavy canvas bag which was soaked from the downpour earlier in the day. The private thought, "There must be hundreds of dispatches and letters in the bag. If I open it now, they'll all get wet, and all the bloody ink will blur. I've got no rush to lug the wet mail sack around. "

He placed the bag near the fireplace to let it dry and took his afternoon tea in the café across the road. He returned much later and dumped the bag's contents onto his sorting table. Pleased with himself that the letters on the table were dry, he then looked in the sack and retrieved one letter that was still stuck to the canvas. He carefully removed it and squinted at the address. With the ink smudged from the rain, the best he could make out was:

__ T. Wa_____ Bri___ General
H_____ New Yor____

Puzzled by the incomplete words, he placed the letter aside and closed the post office for the night. The next afternoon, he showed it to his lieutenant who replied, "Very good of you to save this one, Private. I'd wager this was intended to a Brigadier General whose surname begins with the letters WA and his first initial with T. The letter H must be the beginning of his unit, probably Highlanders. This blasted rain! Consult the Army List to find out who the recipient is and report to me. Our duty is to get it the letter to him."

After searching the list for just a few minutes, the private found a single match. To the postal lieutenant, he proudly reported, "Sir, I have this figured out. The only brigadier fitting the address is Brigadier General Thomas Watson of the Highlanders—the 71st. They're stationed down at Fort George. My billet is nearby. I can personally deliver it this evening."

"Excellent, my good man. Do just that. It looks like more rain is coming this evening. You may close the post office and leave for Fort George as soon as you can. Well done!"

At the entry to Fort George, built years before on the southernmost tip of Manhattan, a sentry directed the postal service private to the Highlanders' Headquarters. He announced to the captain on duty, "Sir, beggin' your pardon. I've a dispatch for Brigadier Watson. It's from Brunswick."

"Private," the captain of the Highlanders began, rolling his r's in a heavy Scots accent, "Very good of you to make it down here on so dreadful a night, but Brigadier Watson sailed for Scotland last month on an urgent family matter. We don't expect him to return for two months or so. I'll be sure he gets it upon his return." The captain tossed the letter into a basket, marked "No Action Necessary."

****

While Martin Walker's letter to Dr. Walker got misrouted, Alex Grant was about to get critical intelligence from a totally unexpected source. At Elizabeth Loring's bedside, Alex leaned forward to hear her solemn, soft-spoken words. She continued, "Dr. Grant, several weeks ago I overheard a chilling conversation between General Howe and the American prisoner, General Charles Lee, about a dreadful plot against the American Army. I have had to hold onto this until I could put it to proper use, but I remember every word of the conversation as if it were yesterday."

Stunned by her opening disclosure, Alex whispered, "With your...relationship to General Howe, why are you telling me this?"

"You see, Dr. Grant, for my own safety, it has been known solely to General Washington that I have been placed here in highest British circles as an American agent. I have awaited critical intelligence before potentially exposing myself, but now I have such information...about a heinous plan. And you must get it to General Washington."

"Just a moment," a flabbergasted Alex queried, "But what would be my role?"

"I think you'll understand how you can help once I tell you the parts that I overheard—without General Howe's knowledge. General Lee rushed to see General Howe. Lee was very excited, and his voice was loud and carried through the walls. He revealed that a dragoon officer was at work on a plot to, as he said, *decimate* the American Army before the spring campaign begins. Understandably, General Howe did not allow Lee to tell him the plot's details. General Howe wanted to be able to distance himself from such a scheme and to say he did not know of it. Commanders must play such games, but Lee told him the name of the dragoon officer. Lee's voice softened when he stated his name. I regret that I could not hear it nor do I know the timetable for the plot."

"This is appalling. How can we stop this?"

"My dear Dr. Grant, as an expression of my gratitude to you for saving my life, I have pressed General Howe—as much as I reasonably could without raising suspicion—to expedite your parole. You see, the documents are already being prepared, and with good fortune you might just be able to deliver word to

General Washington before it is too late to stop the plot. General Howe must exchange documents with General Washington. I pray that this doesn't take long."

"Mrs. Loring, I hope your intelligence will help foil this plot, but I must get other intelligence to inform General Washington. You must be very careful. No matter how much General Howe cares for you, when things get…embarrassing for him, there's no telling what the consequences might be."

With this new information, Alex rushed back to the hospital ward where Dr. Walker was finishing his rounds. "Dr. Walker, may we meet in your office? I'd like to bring in Hobbs and Jesse, too."

Alex ushered his trusted medical colleagues into Walker's office and leaned against the door. Hobbs began, "Alex, you look alarmed. What's the matter?"

"I'm going to share critical intelligence with you. I need your advice. I don't believe I'm exaggerating when I tell you this involves the highest circles of British Headquarters and the fate of the American Army!"

Jesse and Hobbs looked at Alex with rapt attention. Hobbs quipped, "Alright, Alex, you've piqued our interest."

"Dr. Walker knows part of the story but not what I just learned. I cannot reveal my latest source, but here are the points. First, a British dragoon officer is plotting to decimate the American army in Morristown. Second, while Dr. Walker was on inspection in New Jersey, a British quartermaster major came into this very hospital, entered the smallpox isolation ward, and collected several tubes of smallpox debris from our most severely afflicted men. Third, that individual was surely an imposter because *there is no major in the quartermaster department* here in New York. Fourth, the imposter was left-handed, whereas nearly every educated Englishman is right-handed. My dear colleagues, what do you make of all this?"

Walker did not know of the first point but leaned forward to get Hobbs's and Jesse's reactions as they were hearing the story for the first time. John Hobbs hit the nail on the head. "That scoundrel's most likely acting alone, a rogue seeking to settle a score of some sort. I'll bet he's planning to spread smallpox into Morristown!"

"Agreed," Dr. Walker added quickly, "the disguised quartermaster major was most likely the British dragoon officer who had a twisted reason to spread disease among your troops. As a doctor, I would never condone any such plot to spread smallpox and I will actively work to thwart it. As a young doctor, during the French and Indian War, I heard that British commanders approved the spread of smallpox among enemy Indian tribes. With several senior doctors, I spoke out against these practices as they are inhumane."

Alex replied, "Dr. Walker, this is good to know. You will be essential."

Hobbs added, "That's exactly my analysis too, but we are still missing some key intelligence: his identity, his schedule, and his means for getting the pox into Morristown."

Hobbs then queried, "Dr. Walker, surely there is enough information to go to General Howe or his chief of intelligence, isn't there?"

Before Walker could reply, Alex remarked, "Sadly, my friends, I believe General Howe already knows of the dragoon officer's plot, but he does not know its specifics. I suspect he will choose to look the other way."

"Dr. Grant," asked Hobbs, "How exactly did General Howe find out about the plot?"

"My source told me it was none other than General Charles Lee."

Hobbs rose to his feet. "That bloody traitor! I'll hang him myself."

"Hold on, everyone," Alex begged. "I don't know what Lee's role is. A plotter or a messenger? But we'll have to find out. And I have one more question: can the rogue be stopped in time?"

Chapter 14 - The Parole
Friday, February 14 to Tuesday, February 18, 1777
New York City and Northern New Jersey

Lieutenant Edmund Pike, British Military Postal Service, was worried. His throat was sore, and he had spasms of coughing and bone-rattling chills. Since childhood, he had numerous episodes of wheezing, some of which caused him to be dreadfully short of breath. Doctors had told him to stay indoors during cold damp weather, but he was not able to adhere to this advice as an officer in New York. He went to the postal sorting table and said, "Private, I'm feeling rather poorly and am going to the General Hospital about my breathing."

There, he was greeted promptly by the Scottish Surgeon's Mate. "G'd day, Sir. What brings y' by?"

The mate gave Lieutenant Pike an elixir for his cough and advised him to rest in bed for the next few days since the cloud formations heralded damp and cold days ahead. As Pike buttoned his great coat, his eye caught the sign above the mate's desk.

British General Hospital New York City
Mr. T. Walker
Surgeon and Director

"Is Surgeon Walker still the director of this hospital?" he asked the mate nervously.

" 'e most certainly is! 'n 'e's the best in the whole bleedin' army!" replied the mate proudly.

"Oh, just curiosity," said Pike to the mate. Rushing out the door, Pike thought to himself, "I've got to get back to the post station. Good Lord, my service delivered the dispatch from

Brunswick to the wrong officer. We delivered it to General Watson. It must have been intended for Surgeon Walker. I fear the delay in delivery will be critical. There will be hell to pay for our error!"

****

The next day, a small party rode into the hamlet of Elizabeth, New Jersey from the east. At the head were six green-jacketed horsemen, their sabers slung from their hips, carbines attached to their saddles, and pistols encased in their holsters. Wearing red-plumed, black leather helmets with a skull-and-crossbones emblazoned on their facings, the distinctively uniformed horsemen were detached from the British 17th Light Dragoons. Their commanding officer held his carbine upright in his right hand, a white cloth affixed to the muzzle. Behind the dragoons rode a scarlet-uniformed officer, a blue-uniformed officer, and thin Black woman in a heavy gray, woolen coat. The party approached the village's main square to see seven blue-coated horsemen arrayed in a line to meet them. Each of these troopers wore a black cocked hat bedecked with black and white feathers. In their center, a lieutenant colonel held his saber high so that the dragoons could easily see his white cloth. He saluted and then bellowed, "Captain of 17th Light Dragoons, I am Lieutenant Colonel Tilghman of His Excellency, General Washington's Life Guards. I greet you and am prepared to receive Surgeon Alexander Grant. I am also ready to receive Surgeon John Hobbs and Nurse Jesse Jones under a special agreement between our respective commanders in chief."

In reply, the dragoon captain walked his horse half-way to the American line, returning the salute. "Lieutenant Colonel Tilghman, I have the honor to present to you the signed agreement executed two days ago by His Excellency, General Sir William Howe. There is one change, however. Surgeon Hobbs has chosen to remain in New York to provide care for the special patient. You see, Dr. Walker has been overwhelmed by other cases, and Dr. Hobbs has great experience in care of Mrs. Loring's wound problem. Surgeon Grant will vouch for Dr. Hobbs's volunteering to stay behind. I personally will escort Dr. Hobbs here safely whenever he's ready."

They exchanged the formal documents of Alex's parole. Tench declared, "Captain, as a gentleman and an officer, I accept your word on Surgeon Hobbs's decision. The parole papers for Surgeon Grant are in order, as agreed. Please bring Surgeon Grant and Nurse Jones to my line."

In the back of the dragoons' formation, Alex breathed deeply and spoke softly to Timothy Walker. "We do not know if we shall ever meet again, but it would be a great pleasure if we were to, under more collegial circumstances. I am forever grateful to you for saving my life and am most honored to know you as a trusted friend."

In the fading afternoon light, Walker responded, "After all, Dr. Grant, it is I who have the honor for all I have learned from you. I have such respect for you and I have enjoyed our collegiality. I will miss you as a kindred spirit."

Alex leaned forward in his saddle and whispered in Walker's ear, "Yet, our task is only half done. We must still stop this heinous rogue!"

Then, Alex removed his right glove and shook hands with Walker. Aloud he called out, "For the glory of the Almighty, may we meet again—in peace!"

Crossing the square to the Life Guards, Alex and Jesse received shouts from the Life Guards: "Huzzah! Huzzah! Huzzah!"

Alex waved in appreciation to his British escort as they galloped off.

Tench embraced Alex and whispered, "Is it true that Dr. Hobbs decided to remain in New York to take care of Howe's lover?"

"Yes, quite so. Mrs. Loring still needed our expert care, and I needed to get back to Morristown."

Tench understood, "Of course, you did. You've been a prisoner for so long."

Alex replied, "Colonel Tilghman, it's much more than that. You have no idea how timely my parole has been. May I have a word, just the two of us?"

They dismounted and led their horses to the far corner of the square. Alex began, "I have horrid news. A British rogue officer is plotting to spread smallpox in Morristown. And what's more, my friend, I believe he has a sole confidant: none other than General Charles Lee."

After Alex quickly summarized his intelligence, Tench concluded, "Curse the devils! Then we had better inform His Excellency tonight." With each party still having miles to go, they galloped, East and West, to their respective headquarters aiming to complete their journeys not long after nightfall. Tench's squadron led the way through the rolling New Jersey countryside toward Morristown. The roads were not well-marked, and by dusk the entire party was exhausted when Tench called a brief rest at a junction. He looked puzzled as he studied a worn, hand-drawn map from his pouch. "Any problem?" asked Alex.

"Blast it," Tench grunted. "Look at this map. There are two junctions shown along this road, but in this poor light, I can't tell where we are. If we are at the first, the road to the north swings back east...toward enemy lines. If we are at the second, the road north will take us to Morristown. With nightfall upon us, we had better make the right choice."

Sensing the confusion, Jesse approached Tench and Alex. "Gentlemen, I may be able to help," she offered softly. "You see, the family I worked for in New York had a country home nearby. When I was younger, I spent lots of time in these parts. If it's to Morristown we go, then ride a few miles farther along this road and take the road north." She smiled knowingly.

Alex nodded his head approvingly, now having even greater admiration for Jesse's many talents. Jesse led the party through the countryside, but they did not make it to Morristown until nearly eleven o'clock. The two Life Guards on duty outside Washington's Headquarters in the tavern saluted. Tilghman announced, "Sergeant, I must have a word with His Excellency."

"I'm afraid, Sir, His Excellency has retired for the night, seein' how late the hour is."

"Well then, please ask his valet to awaken him. And my party is cold and tired. I must get them inside also. Life Guards, job well done. Dis--missed!"

Tench ushered Alex and Jesse into the headquarters entryway, where they warmed themselves by the fire. From General Washington's room, a stout Black man walked out and welcomed them cheerfully. Billy Lee, Washington's trusted yet enslaved valet, said, "I see you've had a long journey. I'll add new logs to the fire, and there's hot tea in the kettle. His Excellency will be out shortly." Billy Lee turned and went back to Washington's sleeping quarters.

Inside his room, Washington received Billy Lee's news of

night visitors graciously. As commander, he was accustomed to receiving urgent matters at odd hours. Because Washington was always formal, Billy Lee helped him put on his full uniform even at this hour before greeting his guests. Entering the outer room, Washington extended a cordial welcome. "Dr. Grant, it is good to see you safe. You did have us worried for some time. And Nurse Jones, welcome back." Jesse was surprised that the commander remembered her from his visits to the wounded at the hospital. Washington continued, "I trust all went well, but where is Dr. Hobbs?"

Alex explained, "Dr. Hobbs is quite alright, Sir. We decided that Mrs. Loring still needed some American medical expertise. Dr. Hobbs, Sir, volunteered to remain in New York. I have General Howe's word that, when Dr. Hobbs is ready, he will be returned here safely."

"That is a bit unusual, but under the circumstances, I agree with the decision. Dr. Hobbs will be able to provide immediate expert care if she develops any new problems, and he can assist with any additional intelligence. Now, Colonel Tilghman, let's all move to my office, and please tell me about the urgent matter you have brought from New York."

Washington was a master of self-control, but as Alex gave his detailed intelligence report, the commander in chief's face twitched repeatedly. Washington keenly sized up the approaching threat. His rage barely concealed, he hissed, "Now then, what you *believe* is that a British officer—a dragoon, mainly acting alone—is plotting to spread smallpox into our camp. The rogue has the uncommon characteristic of being left-handed. You also believe that General Howe may already be aware of a devilish plot of some sort but has elected to do nothing to cut it off."

Washington continued, "And His Majesty's commander in chief has been informed by his prisoner of war, General Lee! Dr.

Grant, if that's all, please summarize what we do not yet know."

"Your Excellency, I have listed these missing points in my logbook: first, the rogue's identity; second, his means of spreading the pox; third, his shipping point; and fourth, his timetable."

Washington's anger had abated somewhat as he replied, "Colonel Tilghman, would you kindly take notes of this meeting? Dr. Grant, because this is such critical intelligence, I am compelled to ask about the reliability of your sources."

Alex replied, "Sir, I learned from Dr. Walker, Director of the Main British General Hospital, of the rogue officer collecting the smallpox debris. In turn, Dr. Walker's source was a direct observation by his surgeon's mate. May I have a word with you, Sir, about my chief source?"

Washington and Alex stepped into the entryway for two minutes. Upon their return, the commander in chief declared, "We have the intelligence from a most trusted source. Dr. Grant, please continue with your analysis of what intelligence we are missing."

Alex stepped to the Northern New Jersey and New York map pinned on Washington's wall. "Since I learned of the plot, I've tried almost constantly to find these missing pieces. As for the shipping point, the only two possibilities are New York and Brunswick. The rogue gathered the smallpox debris from the General Hospital in New York, but he'd probably not use New York as the shipping point... too many quartermaster staff around and a more difficult journey across the bay to New Jersey and Morristown. Brunswick is more likely. It's a large post, with a huge storehouse and with proximity to here. Any questions?"

Seeing the grandfather clock showed midnight,

Washington interjected, "Outstanding analysis, Dr. Grant. Please continue. I hope we can go on a bit longer."

As the others nodded in approval, Alex continued, "As for the means of shipping, he'd probably conceal the pox debris in a shipment. He'd have to use wagons, but I can't anticipate how he planned to get British Army supplies into Morristown."

Tench replied, "Look, he's a devious scoundrel all right. Perhaps he's bribed army teamsters to drop the wagons near Morristown. But our cavalry scouts report that the British Army has been using civilian teamsters for much of their hauling, especially from Brunswick. That would make it even easier for him to arrange a bribe...and he could have prepared a false requisition with no trouble at all."

"Well then," summarized Washington, "we're focusing on wagons loaded with a smallpox infested shipment of some sort on route from Brunswick to Morristown. We will not eliminate other possibilities yet, but this is an excellent start. Thank you, everyone. You've had a grueling day. Let's get to sleep and reconvene at ten o'clock tomorrow. Colonel Tilghman, please arrange a full Council of War and have the Captain Commandant of the Life Guards, Colonel Gibbs, join us. We'll have to formulate a response to this threat even without a complete picture. In the meantime, Colonel Tilghman, inform all the sentries to be sharply looking for any wagonloads, especially driven by civilians, that might contain the 'pox. The sentries must stop them, and I'll want to know of any such wagons immediately. Dr. Grant, tomorrow please give us a report on the smallpox cases we already have in camp. I thank you for your exceptional service. By God, we must head off this plot."

****

Lieutenant Edmund Pike felt his breaths becoming tighter

as he rode through the cold air back to the British postal station. His private helped him from the saddle and sat him beside the fireplace. "Sir, if you don't mind my saying so, you look like a ghost. Why aren't you in bed?"

Pike wheezed, "To hell....private...the letter...you took...to Fort George...damn, it was... not for...Brigadier General Watson...of the Highlanders...I'm sure we misread...the smudged address...but I recall...the third letter...in his last name...did not look like a "t"...I'm certain...it was an "l"...the letter is not for Brigadier Watson , but for... for...British General...Hospital...Mr. T...Walker...Surgeon and Director...I don't care...what you'll...have to do...Just get...that letter back...and deliver it...to the General Hospital...Now, get moving...the consequences of our mistake could be immense...I pray there's...no life lost."

At Fort George, Lieutenant Pike's private found the letter still in the "No Action Needed" basket and, pocketing it, galloped north up Broad Way. Rushing into the General Hospital, he called to the surgeon's mate, "I have an urgent dispatch for Surgeon Walker."

"Just a moment Private. Dr. Walker is on rounds. I'll be glad to give him the letter."

The private replied anxiously, "I'm afraid I owe him an explanation. I'd prefer to wait."

"Your choice," responded the mate casually.

An hour later, the private handed the letter to Dr. Walker, who scanned it curiously. "How on earth did you ever decode this smudged address and get it to me? It's from Brunswick."

Walker quickly opened his nephew Martin's letter. "My Lord," he thought, "This letter was written on February 12th.

Today is the 18th. The pox-laden shipment goes in two days. My nephew Martin has filled in the puzzle. How can I get this new intelligence to Dr. Grant?" And then he had the solution. Concluding, Dr. Walker thanked Pike's private, "Please give my compliments to your postal officer. Good day to you and my gracious thanks."

Much relieved, the private took a deep breath and rode to the tavern just down Broad Way. "Lieutenant Pike will be glad to know about the surgeon's greeting," he thought. "As for right now, I could use a pint or two!"

Chapter 15 - The Calcutta Inoculation
Monday, February 17 to Wednesday, February 19, 1777
Morristown and New York

As the grandfather clock struck its tenth chime, General George Washington stepped from his quarters to the entryway, now set up for a formal Council of War. Around the long table, his senior generals were already seated. They rose in unison as he entered. Washington took the middle seat, facing the door, and motioned with his right hand for all to sit. "Gentlemen, thank you for attending on such short notice. We are delighted that Dr. Grant has been returned safely after being a prisoner for six weeks. Dr. Grant, please stand so that we may recognize your return. He was granted a parole by General Howe because of his care to one member of the British commander's military household." Even though Washington politely used this vague reference, the council was fully aware that Alex had saved Elizabeth Loring's life. A few generals snickered at the reference to Howe's lover.

From his seat in the corner, Alex rose and saluted the council members, each of whom applauded him enthusiastically. Embarrassed by the adulation, Alex sat down quickly.

"Not only has Dr. Grant returned safely, but he has also brought critical intelligence about a contemptible plot intended to incapacitate our army," Washington announced. The commander in chief then explained the smallpox scheme in detail. When he finished, the council was outraged not only by the rogue's scheme but also by Lee's complicity and Howe's apparent acquiescence.

Major General Greene, responded vitriolically, "Gentlemen, we may now dispense with any belief that General Howe adheres to the code of conduct among civilized officers, but my still greater anger is reserved for Charles Lee. From the account we've heard, Lee may have been only a messenger to Howe, but I'd wager that he advised the plotter."

The other council members rapped on the table in agreement. Brigadier General Knox's voice boomed through the room. In his Boston accent, Washington's stout Chief of Artillery began, "My brother officers, I am affronted by the enemy's duplicity, but immediately I have a question for Doctor Grant. Sir, how vulnerable are our troops to the smallpox, if we assume that the infested wagons somehow arrive in our camp undetected?"

"Thank you, General Knox, for so pertinent a question. With most of our soldiers coming from small villages and farms, not cities, few have had the natural pox. Similarly, even fewer would have had inoculation prior to entering the army. Last winter, there was an outbreak among our troops surrounding Boston, but few of our current regiments were even present then. Then, when a few cases broke out in New York and New Jersey regiments last month, General Washington recommended quarantining, but not inoculations. You see, nearly all the lads know of someone who either died or got very sick after inoculation. When someone gets the natural smallpox, they think of it as God's will. Despite the medical fact that inoculation is much safer than natural smallpox, the rank and file—and often some officers too—have an abiding fear of the current inoculation procedure. Finally, there's also an unanticipated belief some soldiers have. They are fighting the British to achieve not only governmental freedoms, but personal freedoms as well. Strange as it seems, these men say they will not give up their freedom to decide for themselves about getting an inoculation, even though the incidence of death from the inoculation is only one in one hundred. As for the outbreak in January among the New York and New Jersey regiments, we were most fortunate in that the cases were caught very early, thanks to Dr. Hobbs and the regimental surgeons. Quarantining alone limited the number of cases.

Pardon the long answer, but my judgement is that because of our army's low rate of both natural smallpox and of inoculation, we have a great deal at stake if smallpox debris gets spread widely into camp. It would mean affliction of all those vulnerable and a death rate of 15 to 30 percent of those infected. We face an ominous situation, indeed."

The generals absorbed Alex's frank assessment soberly, and then another New Englander, fiery General Israel Putnam, erupted, "But, Dr. Grant, from what you just reported, why won't you be able to control an outbreak by quarantining, just as you did last month and as we used in the previous war?" Putnam had just returned from Philadelphia, where he was Military Governor.

Alex knew Putnam's reputation well. At fifty-eight years old, he was blustery and intimidating, but he was good hearted and brave, his military leadership going back to the French and Indian War. Alex responded respectfully, "General Putnam, in theory, quarantining works, if it can be initiated early and strictly adhered to, but soldiers quarantined because of exposure often slip away to have rum with their mates. Others will visit their favorite camp followers. Accordingly, Sir, in practice, as in the last war, quarantining often proves very limited among men incubating the pox. With the cases here in January, we were lucky that we caught it very early."

Washington took in the reactions of his council and recognized Major General Sullivan, a veteran of every campaign of the war. "General Sullivan, you were at the Siege of Boston. What comments do you wish to make?"

Courageous and aggressive sometimes to the point of overconfidence, Sullivan urged, "Now, look, we believe the smallpox will be shipped in wagons loaded with supplies. I say, starting immediately, we put out cavalry scouts on all approaches from Brunswick, day and night, to intercept the wagons! We do not know exactly where in the wagons the smallpox is stashed. Blankets have been used when spreading to the native tribes. I say, it doesn't matter. When we intercept the wagons, we burn them!"

Washington turned to Lieutenant Colonel Caleb Gibbs of the Life Guards, who was seated behind him, and asked, "Captain Commandant, we welcome you back from Philadelphia. I extend my deepest appreciation for being my liaison to Congress for the past two months. Your diplomatic skills and military knowledge have been of inestimable value to me in our dealings with President Hancock. Now, to get our preparations in order, are you able to set up such a set of patrols?"

Gibbs, another New Englander, had earned a reputation for organization and bravery. Genial and quick witted, he was popular with other officers and the rank and file. He was appointed Captain Commandant when Washington's Life Guards were formed in August 1776. He vowed never to fail Washington. Gibbs replied, "Yes, Your Excellency, I will see to it this afternoon. Good to be back from Philadelphia, Sir!"

But Gibbs was already having his doubts and nodded to his immediate junior, Tench Tilghman, who immediately knew that Caleb needed to talk about this plan.

When Washington called for other comments, Greene signaled his desire. "Gentlemen, I am concerned that putting out scouts is not enough. Perhaps the rogue's teamsters know a back road. Perhaps the rogue will find out that we are onto his use of wagons. Will we be ready if he changes the mode of shipping? Perhaps he will even change from an infected shipment— to even infected civilians. What will we do then?"

Alex rose, "Gentlemen, in view of General Greene's cogent points, I believe we need a second line of defense, so to speak.

We ought to inoculate the whole..."

Before Alex could complete his sentence, General Israel Putman interrupted, "But you just told us that there is too much resistance to inoculation among the men! Well, exactly what is your advice, doctor?"

Alex was ready. "General Putnam, the men's fear of inoculation centers on the need for cutting the skin, using pus from often a fatal case, the ensuing illness, and finally, a small, but recognized fatality rate. I acknowledge these are all real problems. The response would be different if we had a simpler technique employing a smaller inoculum from a sporadic, mild case. And if this technique proved safer, faster, and highly protective, I think we will win over the lads."

Earlier, Alex had briefed Washington on this proposed intervention to gain the commander's support. Washington chimed in, "Dr. Grant, please describe your new technique."

"Thank you, Your Excellency. I'm afraid I cannot quite take credit for these modifications because they have been used in India for some time. I have read about them in an article by British doctors who served in Calcutta. They wrote of much faster onset of protection, much milder and much shorter illness after this type of inoculation, and a very strong protective effect. You see, rather than placing the inoculum in a skin incision, we mimic the likely natural way of spread by placing the inoculum in the nose. This inoculation method is faster and easier. It's been called the Calcutta method as opposed to the English method. Yet, despite its advantages, it has not been recognized in British Army medical circles and has not been adopted." (1)

Always thoughtful, General Greene queried, "Although the Calcutta method appears to have clear advantages, do you have anyway of convincing dubious soldiers?"

Alex answered confidently, "Indeed, I do and will get right on it."

* * * * * * * * * *

Walker ran up the Main General Hospital staircase and found Hobbs at Elizabeth Loring's bedside. Walker called out ebulliently, "Good day, Mrs. Loring. And Dr. Hobbs, how is the wound of our prized patient looking?"

Elizabeth beamed at both doctors. "Gentlemen, I am clearly not the prized one here. It's the two of you with your endless doctoring skills."

Hobbs smiled playfully. "Dr. Walker, I was just telling Mrs. Loring that the healing is progressing well. The pus is gone, and the edges are beginning to close. There are some areas of debris which I was just about to excise. Care to help?"

After Hobbs completed the debridement with scissors and scalpel, which were cleaned with carbolic acid, Walker noted, "That's an impressive technique for cleaning the wound. I'm glad you demonstrated it to me. That's completed so let's go to the kitchen for tea. Mrs. Loring, we'll bring some back for you."

As they walked to the quiet kitchen, Walker's countenance changed abruptly. "Dr. Hobbs, I've just gotten new intelligence about the plot. It came from Brunswick by way of, strangely enough, my nephew who is a quartermaster lieutenant at the big warehouse there."

"Can you use that information to finally identify the plotter and have him arrested?"

Walker thought for a minute before replying, "I'm afraid

not. General Howe already knows and might just protect him. No, Dr. Hobbs, you've got to take the intelligence to General Washington in Morristown. And as an officer in His Majesty's Army, I cannot officially transmit this intelligence to you. We'll have to keep our communications mum, right?"

"Dr. Walker, my friend, I'm no intelligence officer. I'm just a plain old doctor. I don't think I can do this."

"Well, can you think of anyone else who has a legitimate reason to go to Morristown— and very soon at that? Time is of the essence."

Hobbs knew he was trapped and good-naturedly gave in. "Right you are. Mrs. Loring's wound is healing well enough that I can safely leave, especially now that you can do any further necessary debridement. That leaves two questions: how do we arrange my departure, and will it be in enough time to head off the plot?"

"There was an unfortunate delay in getting this intelligence because of an unforeseen error in the delivery of my nephew's letter, but we can only do our best now. Let's go over the letter one more time. You must conceal it perfectly if somehow you were to be searched on route to Morristown."

That evening, Walker ran into the hospital and called Hobbs to the corner. "Better pack your bag. You're leaving tomorrow morning for Morristown. I'll ride with you, and you'll have an escort of dragoons as far as Elizabethtown. It was rather easy to arrange really. The route will be the same one we used for Dr. Grant's parole, and General Howe was so pleased with Mrs. Loring's recovery that he signed your letter of passage immediately."

Hobbs then made his way to Elizabeth's bedside to explain

156

his departure in the morning. Genuinely moved, Elizabeth whispered, "I realize that staying here to take care of me was a huge imposition, Dr. Hobbs, and I do express my heartfelt gratitude. I wish you all success. When you get to Morristown, please extend my appreciation once more to Dr. Grant." She motioned for Hobbs to come closer. As he leaned in, she gave him a thankful peck on the cheek and said ever so softly, "And give General Washington my regards."

Hobbs looked perplexed. She nodded, "He'll know."

---

(1) A nasal route for smallpox vaccination had, indeed, been used in Asia for centuries, but in 1777 it was not employed in Europe or the Americas. Nevertheless, it is plausible that word of this innovation could have made its way to a well-read doctor, like Alexander Grant. Today, nasal vaccinations are used for protection against some respiratory infections such as influenza in some groups, but seniors still require the shot.

Chapter 16 - The Demonstration
Monday, February 17 to Friday, February 21, 1777
Morristown

Alex reasoned that he had to convince the rank-and-file that the Calcutta method was safe. Right after Washington's council was adjourned, Alex arranged an extraordinary demonstration on the General Hospital's lawn. On that sunny, still afternoon, a large group of hospital staff and ordinary soldiers turned out to watch. Alex, who had natural smallpox long ago, had collected pustular debris from a sergeant with a sporadic, mild case and placed the pus on a glass plate. Jesse also had natural smallpox as a child, and with her assistance Alex prepared the inoculum by mixing the pus with a few drops of a dilute salt solution in a glass vial. Two chairs and a wooden table were arrayed in front. Alex sat in one and spoke to Jesse loudly enough for all to hear, "This afternoon, I wish to show you an easier and, indeed, safer method for inoculation—for protection from smallpox." He made no mention of the potential threat from the rogue's plot; there was no advantage in spreading that fear at this time.

Jesse then responded with her rehearsed lines. "How easy is the Calcutta method is to inoculate? How safe is it, and how fast does it give protection?"

Taking in the crowd's rapt attention, Alex explained, "I am so confident about the method that I have recruited an officer, admired by all, to take this inoculation. I am proud to introduce my esteemed colleague and Adjutant General...,"

There was stunned silence in the crowd as a short, brown-haired senior officer walked from the hospital door to the other chair on the lawn. Alex continued, "...Colonel Joseph Reed."

At age 35 years, Reed had already established himself for his intellect and bravery. An accomplished attorney, he had served on Washington's staff in 1775 and 1776. After seeing action at The Battle of Princeton, he took a few weeks leave to attend to urgent matters in his legal practice and had just returned to camp.

"Colonel Reed, how are you feeling today?"

"Perfectly fine, Dr. Grant."

Alex continued to gather Reed's medical history. "And have you ever had the natural smallpox or the typical inoculation?"

"No, Dr. Grant, I haven't."

"And, Colonel Reed, why is that?"

"I grew up nearby, in a small village outside Trenton. We did not see the smallpox there. Then, when the inoculations were offered by the army, I was on leave and missed my chance."

Alex concluded, "Colonel Reed, do you now volunteer of your own free will to take the Calcutta inoculation method?"

"Indeed, I do, Dr. Grant."

Jesse took a swab from a vial and twirled it in Reed's right nostril. Loud enough for all to hear, Alex said, "That's all there's to the Calcutta method. Please note there is no incision, no cutting of the skin. So that we may record any fever or rash and to prevent spread to others, I will observe you in the General Hospital, as we previously agreed."

A barrel-chested sergeant from the Maryland Continental Regiment called out, "Dr. Grant, I also missed the inoculation.

Would I be able to get the Calicut..er, Calcutta inoculation today, too?"

Spontaneously, four of the sergeant's men stepped forward also to volunteer. Alex flashed them a gratifying smile and thought to himself, "I know these brave men. They fought in every major battle in 1776. At Long Island, they carried out a valiant rearguard action which allowed hundreds to escape a British trap. Many already were calling them 'The Immortals.'" Alex then said aloud, "We have indeed prepared enough of the inoculum for the five of you. Please come to the table where we'll get a bit more information and provide the inoculum."

Knowing of the faster effect of the Calcutta method, Alex carefully examined Colonel Reed and the five Marylanders closely over the next three days. Each developed only a slight fever and a few small nasal pustules for a single day. By the third morning, the pustules were healed, and the men felt well. Alex gathered the volunteers. "Gentlemen, I am delighted that you each had only the mildest of reactions for a very short time." He had demonstrated that the Calcutta method was safe among the tested men and led to the quick onset of a short illness. But he had one persisting concern about the method, and he needed to get advice from Hobbs. To the Maryland men, he added, "I thank you for volunteering. In the next day or so, I may ask you to volunteer once more. For now, please enjoy returning to your honored regiment. Colonel Reed, please come with me."

Reed and Alex ran to the upstairs ward where Hobbs was preparing a captain of the engineers for return to his unit after recovering from dysentery. "Good day to you both," beamed Alex.

Hobbs replied, "Dr. Grant, you look like you're about to burst with excitement. What news do you have?"

Alex showed him his medical journal. "I've carefully recorded the results of my work on the Calcutta inoculation. See the first note where I record that I gave the Calcutta inoculation to six volunteers who previously had neither natural smallpox nor the English inoculation. One volunteer is Colonel Reed. The others are a Maryland sergeant and four of his men. See here that each had fever for only a day and a few small, nasal red spots that turned to pustules. By three days, these crusted over, and all the volunteers were fine."

Hobbs was ecstatic. "Dr. Grant, why, that confirms that the Calcutta inoculation has far fewer reactions than the English method, and it has a much faster course. This is, indeed, a major advance." (1)

The captain of the engineers had been listening intently. "Look, I'm certainly no doctor, but from my view, I find your results convincing. If you came to my engineers' unit, I'd bet the susceptible men would jump at the chance to get the Calcutta inoculation."

Alex responded, "We must get these results to General Washington. Assuming he agrees to begin inoculations throughout the army, I'd like to begin with the engineers' unit. What do you think, captain?"

The officer nodded affirmatively. Alex called to Reed, "It will be better for you to be there as we report to General Washington. Nothing like having living proof of a senior officer as part of the explanation!"

"Before we walk over, gentlemen, may I have a word?" Alex confided his concern to Hobbs and Reed. "I now feel confident about the safety of the Calcutta method, and the mild illness it produces mimics natural smallpox. The article from India records that it provides life-long protection. Here in camp, we face an urgent need for protection, but I am torn whether we should test its protective effect on our men before beginning the inoculations."

Hobbs nodded in acknowledgement of the dilemma and advised, "Dr. Grant, if we test the Calcutta method's protection first, that will mean a delay of up to two weeks or possibly more. Based on the arguments you just made, I clearly favor beginning the inoculations while we conduct a test to confirm its protection." (2)

"Very well, Hobbs, that balances our responsibility to science as well as to our men. Now we will have to convince the general." Joseph Reed added, "Doctors, you present cogent reasons for your proposed approach. I know General Washington as an excellent listener and a clear thinker. He will undoubtedly approve your plan."

The headquarters sentry recognized Reed, Alex and Hobbs and escorted them into the entryway. Reed asked the junior Life Guard at the desk, "Major Grayson, where is Colonel Gibbs?"

"He's on patrol somewhere south, toward Brunswick. What do you need?"

I believe you know Drs. Grant and Hobbs. The three of us would like to see His Excellency as soon as possible regarding the Calcutta inoculation. He'll know."

Major Grayson knocked softly on Washington's door, entered, and returned in a few seconds. "His Excellency will see you promptly."

Washington rose from behind his desk. A few letters were neatly placed along its right side. Three straight backed chairs faced the desk. A map of the Northern Jersey and New York area was pinned to the wall beside the desk. On a table by the window was an unrolled copy of a detailed New York City map, engraved in London. On his desk was a framed silhouette of a woman's head. Alex presumed it was Mrs. Washington. Otherwise, the room was bare. Alex thought the commander looked drawn and pale. Yet, Washington welcomed them heartily, "Gentlemen, very good to see you. What's this urgent news that you bring?"

Alex began, "Your Excellency, we bring news about the Calcutta inoculation method." After he showed Washington the results in his journal, Alex concluded, "Sir, this method is simple and fast. It produces far less illness than the English inoculation method, and it provides a shorter illness."

Alex then presented the reasons for their approach. He concluded, "Sir, if you agree, we propose to begin inoculating the susceptible troops while we test its protection on the men of the Maryland regiment."

Washington responded, "Dr. Grant, Dr. Hobbs, I have great respect for your medical analysis and will accept your two-part solution. I'll leave it to you to work with the Marylanders. As for general inoculation, I am keenly aware of my soldiers' fears about at least the English method. Gentlemen, I will prepare an order, but we must gain the confidence of our rank and file. Will those men inoculated need to be quarantined? We must keep up our troop strength."

Alex responded, "Yes, Sir, quarantine would be in order, but only for three to six days. We estimate that over half the men will need the Calcutta inoculation. To win the lads over, I propose we bring along Colonel Reed and one or two of the Marylanders to tell their story. Dr. Hobbs, Jesse and I will prepare a schedule for the inoculation so that our troop strength remains adequate. Sir, is there anything else?"

"Major Grayson," Washington asked, "Would you kindly inquire of Commissary General about our number of cattle? I'd like to give each regiment that gets the Calcutta Method a supper of fresh beef."

Grayson responded crisply, "I'll see to it, Sir. Nothing motivates the lads better than a full belly! And, Sir, I'll draft the order."

"Tomorrow morning, I have my regular Council of War. Colonel Tilghman will make the first item on the agenda the general order for the inoculations, including the schedule. To answer any questions from the Council, Drs. Grant and Hobbs, would you both kindly attend? Colonels Reed and Tilghman will be there as a matter of course. Good day, and I extend my most heartfelt gratitude for your successes with the Calcutta inoculation method."

The next morning at precisely nine o'clock, Commander in Chief Washington called the council to order and provided his senior officers with the background of the new General Orders. He then polled the council on required troop strength. "Gentlemen, we face a double hazard: first, the spread of a possible smallpox infestation and second, the need to counter any British move. How many men will we need fit for duty?"

General Henry Knox boomed, "My colleagues, our total strength in mid-February was down to only three thousand, but new recruits have been increasing week by week. Our present strength is five thousand, and I project almost nine thousand by the time the campaigning season begins. I doubt Howe would attack us in this stronghold, especially if we are in the middle of an outbreak, but he's crafty enough to strike at Philadelphia. However, our agents in New York indicate the redcoats are simply enjoying themselves and have begun no preparations to go into the field. Because it would take Howe weeks to begin a march on the capital, I believe this is a favorable time to give the susceptible men the Calcutta inoculation as quickly as possible."

Washington then recognized his second in command. Greene rose to ask his questions. "Dr. Grant, General Howe has a far larger force at his disposal, probably about eighteen thousand men total. Nevertheless, I support General Knox's proposal for prompt inoculation with the Calcutta method. The timing now is better than later. But I have a few details to ask about. How long will it take you and the hospital staff to complete the Calcutta inoculations? From your description, it would seem the regimental surgeons or even their mates could administer the method, once you show them how it's done. And would you recommend that the camp followers get inoculated, too? I congratulate you on knowing of and testing the Calcutta method. Our lads will be fit for duty much faster. I thank you wholeheartedly."

Alex stepped forward to address Washington's senior officers. "I am most grateful that the council favors prompt inoculation with the Calcutta method. To General Greene's questions, yes, we will be able to enlist the assistance of regimental surgeons and mates in the Calcutta inoculation, according to a rotating schedule we have prepared. Also, it is necessary to have the camp followers inoculated to prevent spread of the natural pox."

When Alex finished, Washington nodded to Lieutenant Colonel Gibbs, who distributed a draft of the General Orders. Solemnly and deliberately, the commander read them aloud.

"GENERAL ORDERS, 21 February 1777

With the threat of smallpox now judged to be great, His Excellency General Washington expressly orders that each Regiment prepare a list of officers and men who have had neither the natural smallpox nor previous inoculation. Director of the General Hospital Dr. Alexander Grant and his staff have demonstrated in this encampment the ease and safety of an alternative preventative method, called the Calcutta inoculation, and this method has been used in India for decades. Dr. Grant and staff are to demonstrate this method tomorrow morning at the camp of the Engineers. Dr. Grant and staff are then to provide necessary training and supervision for all Regimental Surgeons to complete the Calcutta inoculations for their soldiers who would be subject to the natural smallpox. All men and camp followers who receive this inoculation are to remain quarantined in huts for six days. The General assures the officers and men of the safety of the Calcutta method. Therefore, any soldier who does not turn out for the inoculation or does not follow the six days of quarantining will be punished. The General is resolved, for the Honor and Safety of the Army, to see that this order is fully enforced. Protecting our Soldiers through inoculation will assure that the Continental Army has adequate forces to thwart the enemy. Courage in battling the dread smallpox is equally essential to battling the Enemy Soldiers.

The time will be soon at hand when the Army will, once more, face the Cruel and Unrelenting Enemy. The coming campaign will determine whether Americans are to be Free, and the fate of unborn Millions will now depend, under God, on the Courage and Conduct of this Army. We place our confidence in the goodness of the Cause and the aid of the Supreme Being. The Eyes of all our Countrymen will be upon us. Let us animate and encourage each other, and show the whole world, that Freemen contending for Liberty on their home ground will surely have Victory over the slavish King's Forces and His Mercenaries."

Washington's words moved the council. His five division commanders rapped on the table. Henry Knox shouted, "Your Excellency, that'll motivate the lads! Huzzah!"

The commander in chief summarized, "Dr. Grant, these General Orders will be posted immediately. You and your staff had better get going. It will be a demanding time for you. Thank you on behalf of the Army. The Council will please remain to take up our other business."

****

With their British Dragoon escort, Drs. Hobbs and Walker crossed the Hudson River on the military ferry and rode westward to Elizabethtown, the same village where Alex had previously been transferred to the Life Guards. On this day, they saw no Americans. The dragoon captain was clearly anxious, "Dr. Hobbs, my orders are to bring you here and no further west. You have the letter of passage from General Howe, and you have your American uniform and credentials."

Hobbs replied, "No problem at all, Captain. I know the rest of the way very well, and your dragoons need to return before dark. Just let me have a word with Dr. Walker."

Hobbs and Walker dismounted and walked to the far corner of the square. Hobbs began, "Dr. Walker, I'd like to think we'll meet again. War time is so unpredictable. I'm sure Ms. Loring will have a full recovery. In the meantime, look after yourself. I will miss seeing you."

Walker grabbed Hobbs by the shoulder, recalling that Hobbs attended medical school in Edinburgh and served in the king's army during the French and Indian War in upstate New York. "Yes, it is our loss that you didn't stay in the British Army after the last war. We could have been life-long friends."

"I was having another thought—it's too bad your parents didn't come to America!" quipped Hobbs with his endearing smile.

As Walker and the dragoons retraced their journey on the road back to New York, Hobbs followed it west toward Morristown. He had just gotten out of sight of the dragoons when two American cavalry scouts dashed down the hill toward him. The cavalry lieutenant recognized him. "Dr. Hobbs, you took care of a pistol shot in my leg last year. We're here to escort you to headquarters. You and the dragoons arrived at Elizabethtown sooner than we expected."

Hobbs was flattered. "It's a good thing I fixed up your wound alright, isn't it? Now, will you escort me to General Washington. I have a matter of great importance."

"With pleasure," the cavalry lieutenant called out as they galloped west.

Hobbs and the cavalry troop pulled up in front of Washington's Headquarters well after dark, but lamps were shining in the windows. The sentry admitted Hobbs to the entryway where General Washington was bent over a map of New Jersey. Beside him was Caleb Gibbs.

Washington bid Hobbs a warm welcome. "Dr. Hobbs, welcome back. I was expecting you as I had a dispatch from General Howe about your return. I gather his... household member... has recovered."

Hobbs was exhausted from the ride. "Your Excellency, yes, she is, but my return is earlier than expected for another reason: intelligence that I bring."

Noting Hobbs's fatigue, Washington added, "Colonel

Gibbs, let's sit down in the kitchen. There's hot soup still on the fire for Dr. Hobbs, and he can nourish himself and shake off the chill. Then, I want to hear about his intelligence."

John Hobbs gulped the beef and barley soup lustily and retrieved Lieutenant Martin Walker's letter from a pouch hung around his neck. He handed it to Washington. As the general read the note aloud, his eyes widened. He concluded, "Gentlemen, Lieutenant Martin Walker's letter informs us that the civilian teamsters are the Williamson brothers and that they will, in fact, be transporting smallpox in a shipment of blankets, coming from Brunswick. And more, the rogue officer is left-handed, indeed. Now we have the exact date of shipment: February 20th. Gentlemen, that's tomorrow! Good Lord, if we had only gotten this letter earlier. Colonel Gibbs, is there time to respond?"

Yet, Caleb Gibbs was dubious and first asked, "Could this be a plant, a ruse, to throw us off the real route?"

"Good question," responded Hobbs, "but I'm certain it is legitimate. Lieutenant Walker of the British Quartermaster Department is the officer at the Brunswick warehouse. His uncle is Dr. Timothy Walker, who is the Director of the Main British General Hospital in New York. Dr. Walker saved Dr. Grant's life in January. He's also an honorable gentleman and is horrified by the rogue's plot. He has been working discreetly with Dr. Grant and me to interrupt it."

"Very well, then," summarized Washington. "We have critical intelligence, and from all descriptions the plotter, disguised as a quartermaster major, is acting alone, except for advice from Charles Lee. Do we have the key points now?"

Caleb nodded, "Yes, Sir, excepting that we still do not have the rogue's identity, and he might change his plan. Sir, the letter from Lieutenant Walker arrived none too soon, but I believe we still have time to intercept the plot as we understand it."

Washington replied, "All right then, Colonel Gibbs. Concentrate your scouting patrols on the roads from Brunswick but keep watch on routes from New York in case of a change in the scheme. Civilian teamsters will be lightly armed; that's good. I don't know that we can find this rogue's identity, but we'll keep the new intelligence in mind. Excellent work, Dr Hobbs. I am most grateful. I wish that letter had gotten to Dr. Walker and therefore to us earlier. If we had received the letter even one more day earlier, our chance to interrupt the plot would have been much better. I bid you a good night."

---

(1) Dr. Alexander Grant, like Dr. Walker, was working at the dawn of clinical investigation. He was systematic in his approach and carefully documented his findings. Other physicians conducted noteworthy investigations in the 18th Century. In the late 1740s, British Naval Surgeon, James Lind, conducted what is often considered the first clinical trial in which he showed that fresh citrus fruits prevented scurvy, a potentially lethal disease due to vitamin C deficiency. A side effect of scurvy was impaired judgement which often led to poor decision making and consequent loss of life at sea. Scurvy afflicted sailors relying on the usual navy diet (devoid of fresh fruits and vegetables) after eight weeks or more at sea. In 1796, Dr. Edward Jenner, an English country physician, showed that vaccination with the mild virus, cowpox, provided protection from smallpox and was much safer than inoculation. These pioneering physicians set the stage for modern medical investigations.

(2) Dr. Alex Grant and colleagues faced an ethical dilemma, still relevant today. Their solution was to proceed with

the Calcutta inoculation even before they had their own evidence of its protective effect. They were comforted by their data, though limited by modern standards, on its safety and by citations from India about its effectiveness. During the COVID-19 pandemic, The United States Food and Drug Administration recognized its obligations to both science and the public good when it provided Emergency Use Authorization for new m-RNA vaccines. These novel vaccines were given approval in the face of a world-wide medical emergency even before the usual standards for effectiveness were met.

Chapter 17 - The Plot Unleashed
Monday, February 17 to Thursday, February 20, 1777
Morristown and Brunswick

Banastre Tarleton's head ached when he awakened in Kate's bed. His clothes were strewn around the brothel room, but she was no longer there. As he washed his face in the basin and dressed, he mused about his nighttime conquest. He had long fantasized about bedding Kate. He recalled having several whiskeys with her even into the wee hours, speaking softly to her, and then retiring to her bed after everyone else had left the establishment. Tarleton found Kate in the kitchen preparing breakfast of eggs, ham, and coffee. "Ban," she murmured, "Do ya' have t' leave this mornin'? I'm wishin' ya' could stay a while, after breakfast, ya' bein' a fine lover 'n' all."

"Ah, Kate, you excite me so," he whispered into her right ear. "For you, I have all day."

There was more to Kate's motive than she let on. During their drinking the previous night, Tarleton's tongue loosened. Kate was expert at exploiting such opportunities and recalled him saying that he was celebrating but did not say why. When they made it to her chamber, Kate enticed him by slowly removing her gown and then unbuttoning his shirt and trousers. Rather innocently, she had asked, "And what's m' big Ban celebratin' anyway?"

As she fondled him, he blurted, "I cannot tell you, but this week, I'll bring this rebellion to an end."

Tarleton was often full of himself, but Kate sensed he had a lot more to tell about his celebration. She flattered him, "'ow brave! And 'ow could ya' be doin' that?"

"Ah, my dear Kate, I'll have to tell you when it's accomplished. Come, let's go back to bed."

Kate serviced Banastre to his full pleasure—and to hers. Afterwards, he fell soundly back to sleep. Kate crossed the room to a sofa, took out a small notebook from under the cushion, and entered a page of notes, written in her own code. Later, when Banastre woke, he gave Kate one final embrace and added. "I won't see you for a while. I'm off to Brunswick Wednesday morning." Tarleton dressed and rode back to his quarters. "There's still much I have to do," he thought.

Kate tried to put her new information together. She reasoned that Tarleton was heading up a plot of some sort. She guessed it might be to assassinate or capture a high-ranking American officer. She deduced that it would begin soon, even in three or four days in Brunswick, New Jersey. "If that's so," she thought to herself, "this'll bring m' a nice gold reward from m' American agent."

That gray, cloudy afternoon, she walked two blocks up Broadway to French Church Street. On the far-right corner stood a three-story home. She used the large pineapple-shaped door knocker, but there was no reply. "Damn," she muttered to herself. I mus' 'ave just missed 'im. I canna' go to 'is shop. I'll 'ave t' return t'morrow." Early the next morning, a swarthy, graying man responded to Kate's knocking and gave her a gracious welcome. "*Ma chère* Kate, how good to see you again," he said in a French accent with a Caribbean lilt. He peeked down the street but saw no one. Switching back to his native language, he continued, "*Entrez, s'il-vous-plâit.*"

Looking harried, Kate stepped quickly into the house. The dark-complexioned gentleman took one more glance into the intersection and shut the door. Kate whispered, "I've go' li'le time, but I 'ave 'ntelligence for General Washington, if ya' 'ave m' usual payment."

"*Mais oui*, Kate, but no need to whisper. I'm the only one in the house. *S'il-vous-plâit,* have a seat by the fire. *Maintenant, dites moi.*"

After Kate revealed her information, the agent summarized, "May I see if I have this correct? A British *officier*—a regular frequenter of your establishment— is involved in a plot of some sort. You suspect it may be to assassinate or capture a senior American officer, *n'est-ce pas*?"

Kate nodded nervously.

"*Et l'officier*, he's going to Brunswick this week, you think, to unleash the plot." Kate nodded once more.

"Does he have, eh...*conspirateurs*?"

"I donna' know, *Monsieur*, but 'e didna' talk 'bout others."

"*Et, très bien*, and could you describe him, or would you happen to know the plotter's identity?"

"*Monsieur*, I come by m' 'nformation...erm, discreetly, 'n' I make it a practice not t' tell m' sources. If I did, that'd be th' end o' m'...erm, help to ya'."

The agent continued, "Kate, ma chèrie, you have always provided me with reliable intelligence. You can get it in ways no one else can, of course. I fully understand your need for...uhm, confidentiality, but if this is a plot to kill an American senior officer, I beseech you to make an exception." He sensed he was convincing Kate and then added, "Would it help if I tripled your usual fee?"

Kate's eyes widened. "Yeah! *Monsieur*, 'ow about if I tell ya' this? 'e's a 'andsome, red-'eaded dragoon lieutenant colonel. Now, I 'aven't given ya' 'is name, but you'll be able to narrow it down. 'ow's that?"

"You have kept to your business practices, and I'll keep mine. Just give me a moment," responded the agent. The aging gentleman left the parlor and returned to hand Kate a small silk purse. "Please check the amount. I'm sure you'll find your usual payment there...multiplied by three."

She confirmed the amount in gold coin, placed the purse in her money belt, and bade him goodbye, "*Merci, Monsieur Fraunces*. I'll keep on th' alert. I 'ope ya' can stop th' plot."

Samuel Fraunces, who was French by family background and had grown up in the West Indies, was a successful merchant and moved in elite New York circles. As the owner of Queen's Head Tavern on Pearl Street in New York (1), he met men of all stations. And plied with his abundant whiskeys, wines, and beers, the men loosened their tongues and revealed to Fraunces all sorts of information. In the past year, he had served as an unsuspected conduit of intelligence to George Washington.

From Kate's description of the plotter, Fraunces immediately suspected his identity but prudently kept that to himself. One man fit her description, and he was a well-known visitor at the tavern where he drank heavily and ate expensive meals. Fraunces recalled that within the last week the officer had to write a note of promise to cover his bill since he had insufficient coins. But Fraunces could not recall the officer's name. "What in heaven's name did I do with it?" Then, snapping his fingers, he remembered. From his desk off the parlor, Fraunces pulled out a stack of hand-written notes. Halfway through the stack, he found what he was looking for: a promissory note written with a left-handed slant. It was signed, "B. Tarleton, Lt Col, 16th Light

Dragoons, New York City."

Fraunces took out a small, worn notebook from the desk's cubby and started to encode a letter. By his usual practice, he started with a recent letter from family in the Caribbean and then wrote his message in lemon juice at a perpendicular angle. Washington and his aides knew to heat the letter to read the encoded message, but to anyone else, it looked completely innocent. Fraunces wrote:

Tuesday, February 18th, 1777
Your Excellency,

I have the duty of reporting essential intelligence, obtained today from a most reliable source. A British officer is about to carry out a plot which will originate in Brunswick within the next two days. My source could not discern the exact nature of the plot but suspects it is to assassinate a high-ranking American officer. My source provided me sufficient information so that I was able to identify the plotter. He is Lieutenant Colonel Banastre Tarleton of the 16th Dragoons. Your intelligence service is likely to be familiar with him and know him as a cunning and ruthless man. I wish you every success in intercepting him.

I have the honor to be your obedient servant,
Samuel Fraunces, Sr.

As he completed his meticulous letter, a young man unlocked the front door and entered the parlor. Fraunces called, "Samuel, my son, hurry into my office."

Samuel Fraunces, Sr. handed his son the folded letter. "*Mon fils*, it's better if you don't know the background of this secret letter, but it is urgent you get this to General Washington in Morristown. Place the letter in your boot. It cannot fall into the hands of the British, even if you must destroy it in case you are about to be intercepted. The ferry is too risky. Tonight, take our skiff to cross the Hudson. That will be safer. You'll get a horse at our usual agent's house at Paulus Hook. Spend the night there and leave by dawn tomorrow for Morristown.

The younger Fraunces followed his father's instructions in detail, and by sunrise on February 19th he was riding through a light fog along the main road toward Morristown. His heartbeat quickened as he peered ahead at two shadowy, mounted figures ahead. "Halt, in the name of the king," one shouted at him. Samuel raced back up the road as two British cavalrymen pursued him. Fearing the pursuers were overtaking him, Samuel wisely reached into his boot and crumpled the letter. As he took a sharp turn on the road, his pursuers could not see him momentarily, and he threw the crumpled letter deep into the dense woods. The letter landed in a pile of leaves, completely unseen by anyone passing on the road. Knowing the road well, Fraunces spurred the horse onward, back toward Paulus Hook. As he raced closer to the Hudson, the fog thickened. Now, he was able to get ahead of the cavalrymen and dashed onto an overgrown, narrow side trail. He heard them race by his hiding point. Several minutes later, the British cavalrymen doubled back searching for a trace of him. In the fog, they missed the concealed opening to his trail. One muttered, "That bloody rider has escaped. We had better resume our position on the road in case he tries to get past us."

Once Fraunces felt it was safe, he quietly walked his horse back to the main road. Although there was no sign of a British patrol, he thought, "I must avoid the main road. Damn, I have no idea where in the woods the letter landed. My mission to Morristown is ruined!" He took trails, known only to locals, back to the agent's house at Paulus Hook. There, he hid the rest of the day and that night planned to re-cross the Hudson to report to his father. But as he looked from the house, he saw sentries guarding the river front, and the Royal Navy now had the *HMS Asia*, a ship of the line, stationed in mid-channel. Two of its long boats patrolled the river. Fraunces presumed that the cavalrymen pursuing him had alerted their superiors. He thought to himself, "Drat, now I am left marooned here. My father does not know what's happened, and the intelligence letter is lost deep in the woods. Father did not tell me of its message. There's not even a purpose of my trying to get to Morristown once more. What a failure! I have no choice but to remain in here. Fortunately, there is a secret cellar in case any redcoats come searching the house." (2)

****

On Wednesday, February 19th, Tarleton packed his satchel for Brunswick. In the bottom of the bag, he placed his disguise as the rotund quartermaster major and then layered a fresh dragoon uniform on top. In his dispatch pouch, he carefully placed the glass vials into a wooden rack. Each vial contained the now dried smallpox debris.

"The sky is clear, and the day pleasant—good omens as I start for Brunswick," he thought while he rode to the military ferry dock. As he crossed the Hudson River, he admired the palisades, to the north, rising majestically three hundred feet from the river's bank and directly ahead the lush green, rolling hills. "What wondrous, pristine country this is. When the rebellion is put down, I could be very comfortable here." He disembarked at the Amboy pier and rode another dozen miles just to the north of Brunswick. There, he took a side road and behind a thicket changed into his disguise. By dusk, he had checked into the Brunswick Tavern and ordered dinner with a bottle of Bordeaux in his room.

Full of excitement, he slept only fitfully. By six o'clock on

February 20th, even before the tavern keeper was awake, Tarleton was once more in his disguise, left payment for his room at the desk, and rode onto the lane. He took coffee and a leisurely breakfast at a roadside tavern and before nine o'clock, he arrived at the Brunswick military storehouse. Minutes later, the Williamson brothers pulled their two empty wagons into the front clearing. Tarleton called out, "Good morning, gentlemen. Please wait here while I see the quartermaster officer."

Charles Williamson replied, "Good mornin', Sir. Just call when you need us to load the wagons."

Entering the storehouse, Tarleton greeted Martin Walker much more cordially. "Good morning, lieutenant. Perfect morning, isn't it? And were you able to fill my requisition? I recall you anticipated possible shortages of blankets."

Still suspicious, Martin responded cautiously. "Yes, Sir, we had to search all over but were able to find all the required blankets plus the other supplies. Everything is in those chests by the door. I have ticked off the items on my copy of the requisition. May I please have your countersignature?"

"Of course, but do you mind if I first check the chests?"

Martin's heart raced thinking that the quartermaster major would find the tattered, moth-eaten blankets in the bottom of the chests, but Tarleton's inspection was cursory. After opening just three chests and inspecting only the top items, he declared, "All seems in order, lieutenant. Excellent resourcefulness. I'll have to give the Quartermaster General a glowing report. Now, hand me the form to countersign. Would your men kindly help my teamsters load the chests onto the wagons?" With his left hand, Tarleton scribbled an illegible signature.

While the wagons were being loaded, Tarleton took

Charles Williamson aside. "Here is your voucher to claim payment when the job is done, and here are detailed directions to the outpost. You see, I have pressing business in New York and won't be able to accompany you. For your extra effort, here is an additional ten pounds in gold coin, a bonus for getting the shipment there safely."

Williamson put the coins in his leather bag and entered the storehouse to get the last few chests. With no one else by the wagons, Tarleton took out his glass vials of smallpox debris and infested the blankets already in chests aboard the wagons. As he was about to empty the last vial, one of the teamsters' horses got startled, brayed loudly, and jolted the wagon. The sudden thrust knocked several vials to the ground. Worrying that the braying would bring the Williamsons right outside, Tarleton quickly wrapped the contaminated shards in his handkerchief and tossed it into a trash barrel next to the wagon. Tarleton was relieved that it was another five minutes before the Williamsons exited the warehouse.

The Williamson brothers, unknowing accomplices in Tarleton's scheme, secured the last chest on board and headed on the road west to the 42nd Regiment's outpost. They passed the last British cavalry station, but it was empty. Williamson presumed the troopers were on patrol.

Still disguised as the quartermaster major, Tarleton took the main road a short distance northeast toward New York, but he thought, "I surely do not intend for my whole plot to rest with those two bumpkin teamsters. To be sure they do not waver, it's time to follow them. They're going into contested territory, but I'll stay out of sight and off the road." Tarleton took off his scarlet quartermaster coat and tricorn hat and replaced them with his green dragoon's jacket and skull and crossbones helmet.

But there was suspicion on both sides of the contract. Less

than five miles from Brunswick, Charles Williamson called over to the adjacent wagon, "Brother, what do ya' make of that quartermaster major? I've spent a lot of time around British Army circles and even worked in Howe's informant ring. There's somethin' shady about his story, but I can't quite figure it out."

His younger brother responded, "Well, I dinna' like him either, too haughty, too slippery for my taste. Can we just dump the chests in the ravine up the road and head for our nice warm beds?"

---

(1) This tavern later became known as Fraunces' Tavern, still located in lower Manhattan today. At the end of the Revolutionary War, it was here that Washington gave his powerful farewell address to his officers. The racial identity of Samuel Fraunces himself has been shrouded in debate. Born in 1722, Fraunces was often referred to as "Black Sam," but this was more likely an 18th Century expression noting his swarthy coloring than any Black or Negro lineage. Admiral Richard Howe, for example, was often referred to as "Black Dick." Accordingly, it is most likely that Samuel Fraunces was solely French, Western European, in origin.

(2) That the Fraunceses' mission to get Kate's intelligence to Morristown failed would have come as no surprise to spymasters of the day. Every mission was a high-stakes game pitting the skills and resources of Washington's agents against Howe's spies and soldiers or vice-versa. Accordingly, Washington had an extensive spy network with overlapping responsibilities.

Chapter 18 - Testing the Calcutta Method
Thursday, February 20 to Friday, February 21, 1777
Northern Jersey and Morristown

On the road west from Brunswick, Charles Williamson climbed down from his wagon to inspect a narrow ravine. "Ah, Will, as tempted as I am to dump the whole bleedin' load into the chasm, that wouldn't be very smart of us. Look, the ravine's rocky at the bottom, and the chests would be too easy to see. Besides, the major will quickly find out we've two-timed him. He'll come after us for his gold, maybe even throw us in jail, and we'll never get another contract. I don't like our position either, but we're bloody trapped. We've still got most of the twenty miles to go. We'll have to get the goods to the 42nd Regiment."

From a ridgeline one half mile away, Tarleton spotted the two wagons stopped along the road. Through his London-made telescope, he saw Charles Williamson amble to the ravine. When the wagons again lumbered along the road, Tarleton thought, "Good lads, now just get on with it!"

Another five miles west, the road descended slightly to a shallow crossing of the upper Passaic River. The banks on both sides were low and nearly flat. Charles alighted to inspect the crossing. Wading half-way across the frigid water, he called to Will, "It's no more than mid-thigh deep, but it's runnin' fast. Lots of stone in its bottom; that's good. Let's make it across. It's getting' on in the afternoon."

Charles drove the first wagon into the shallows, whipping his team to keep them moving. He crossed to the far bank and yelled to William, "Be sure to follow in my tracks!" William got his wagon less than half-way when his team stopped. He cursed them, but the horses wouldn't budge. Charles waded back into the river from the far side and grabbed the reins. "Will, they're gettin' as tired as we are. I'll pull the damn team. You crack the whip over 'em."

At last, the team lurched forward, but the current pushed the wagon downstream a few feet. Suddenly, the right front wheel clunked hard into a deep hole. The wagon tilted sharply, and several chests broke loose from their ropes, crashing into the flowing water. As one large chest slid off, it smashed into the front wheel and cracked it in half. With the wagon bed now leaning acutely, the remaining chests slid into the river.

Charles screamed, "Of all the bloody luck!"

"Bullocks!" shouted William. "What in hell will happen next?

Charles yelled, "Will, first, get those damn chests to the far bank. If water gets in 'em, they'll be too bloody heavy to move. In the meantime, get the damn team across. Those stupid beasts will freeze their legs."

Two hours of back-breaking work later, the Williamsons got all the chests from the river to the far bank. Charles opened several and replied, "At least these chests are watertight. The goods inside them are dry. Now let's get to the broken wheel."

Charles removed the spare from the undercarriage and replaced the cracked wheel. He looked skyward and said, "Will, we lost loads o' time there. It'll be dark in an hour. We can't make it to the outpost today. We'll make camp in the clearing just up ahead. It'll be cold tonight, but at least we've got plenty o' blankets!"

****

At the British warehouse in Brunswick, Lieutenant Martin

Walker fretted that he had not heard from his uncle. He thought, "It's been over a week since I wrote to him, but I suppose he's been very busy. Well, at least the quartermaster major was more gentlemanly on his visit today."

Lieutenant Walker's head storekeeper rolled a barrel in from outside. "Lieutenant, the barrel's just about full of trash. Shall I take the trash to the back to burn it?"

"Good idea, private. It's cold this afternoon, and we could use the fire."

The private upended the barrel and dumped most of the refuse into a pit. Looking into the barrel, he saw that twigs had jammed in the remainder. With his right hand, he reached in to remove the obstruction. Mixed in with the twigs was an old handkerchief. As he pulled on the twigs, he felt several cuts on his fingers. Reflexively, he pulled out his hand and stuck the fingers in his mouth. "What the devil cut me?" he asked himself. He finished burning the trash. When he returned to the storehouse, Martin asked, "What did you do to your hand? It's oozing blood."

"Oh, nothing much, Sir. When I dumped the trash, there were lots of thorns on some twigs. I must have stuck myself good, eh?"

"Well, get yourself to the infirmary, and get your hand bandaged. I don't want you bleeding all over our goods."

****

The next morning, Friday, February 21st, Alex met with the five Maryland soldiers at the General Hospital. "Gentlemen, once again, may I ask you to volunteer for your country? You have each received the Calcutta inoculation and demonstrated a mild illness. We believe that you now have life-long protection from serious disease if you are exposed to a natural case. I would like to show that your protection works. Would you be willing to help me? The results will be of great value to your fellow soldiers and our doctors."

The sergeant was first to reply. "Dr. Grant, I am proud to volunteer. The army must protect all the lads. The Calcutta method looks like the easiest way."

Following their sergeant's lead, each of the four other Marylanders stepped forward, saying, "Take me too."

"Very well, gentlemen, in the interest of the army, I thank you. We will arrange for the exposure this afternoon."

Joseph Reed entered the hospital room and drew Alex's attention by clearing his throat emphatically. "Dr. Grant, I'd like to volunteer also."

Alex responded carefully, "Thank you, Colonel Reed, but we had better check with General Washington to see if he can spare you from headquarters any longer. I suspect he'll be needing you there."

The Maryland sergeant scoffed, muttering softly to his men, "I'll wager a month's pay on it. We won't see any bleedin' high-rankin' officer back here for the exposure."

Late that afternoon, the five Marylanders marched smartly to the General Hospital's front lawn. The sergeant heard four chimes from the church bell. Turning to his men, he snarled, "See, what'd I tell you boys. No officer would do this work. As on the battlefield, it's hard duty; it's for the rank and file. The strength of the army is you men. Proud as hell, I am."

Jesse came to greet them. "Sergeant, I am glad to see you

and your volunteers all doing well this bright afternoon. Won't you come into the hospital? Dr. Grant will explain the process."

When the men marched into the hospital, Alex expressed his gratitude. "Now, may I call upon a *special guest.*"

From the rear ward stepped the commander in chief, resplendent in his elegant buff and blue uniform. The sergeant's mouth dropped for a second as he called out, "Men, Attennnnn....shunn! Salute!"

Although Washington had a reputation for being aloof to the rank and file, in personal instances like these, he was warm and, indeed, avuncular. "Gentlemen, I asked Dr. Grant if I might have a moment to express my personal appreciation to you individually. I know about smallpox since I survived a case when I sailed to Barbados with my brother many years ago. I admire the Maryland Regiment's courage in battle and now your personal courage in this task. I am honored to lead men such as you." He paused as his gracious words settled in. Washington continued, "You're wondering where Colonel Reed is, aren't you? Well, he's my adjutant general. I told him that I could not do without him."

The sergeant stifled a smug grin.

"But," the commander continued, "Colonel Reed maintained that he could not expect you men to volunteer if an officer would not. Gentlemen, the colonel will meet you in the smallpox ward.'

Once again, the sergeant's jaw dropped, his self-righteousness crushed. Inside the ward, there were three infected soldiers lying on clean straw pallets. Alex explained, "In some cases, smallpox is communicated by contact with the pustules. That's how the English inoculation was devised, but the pox is also be spread by breathing the same air. Gentlemen, Nurse

Jesse and I will be examining these three men. I want you to come and observe closely. That will give you sufficient exposure to test the Calcutta Method's effect. We'll be in the smallpox ward about a half hour."

Alex, Jesse, Joseph Reed and the Marylanders stepped to the pallet on the far-right side. Alex introduced the patient. "This is a private from New Jersey. He's been in hospital two weeks. Private, how are you this morning?"

"Feelin' better today, Sir, but I can't remember anything about my first week here. Now, I'm hungry as a bear after hibernatin'."

As Alex examined him, he showed the men, "See here, the private now has an array of healing pustules covering his body. At the worst point, he was covered with angry-looking sores. Most are now crusted, but these on his abdomen are still pus-filled." Alex scraped two pustules and noted, "They'll be healing soon. Very good, private, you've had a severe case, but we'll have you back with your regiment any day now."

Next to him lay a desperately ill lad from New York. He was covered head to foot with fresh pustules. His mouth was agape, his breathing high pitched and rapid. Reed had to turn his head because of the lad's foul breath. Alex called, "Private, can you hear me?"

There was no response. Alex noted, "Gentlemen, I'm afraid his hours are numbered. We will keep him clean and as comfortable as we can."

"Is that going to happen to any of us?" a frightened young Marylander asked.

Alex responded as comfortingly as possible. "Son, this

result happens to about one in six who get the natural smallpox but only in about one in a hundred who get the English inoculation. The reports from Calcutta say that your inoculation will be even safer and will protect you." And Alex added to himself, "For the sake of God, I hope so."

The third soldier in the smallpox ward greeted the medical entourage brightly. Alex asked, "Sergeant, would you please tell my colleagues how you've been doing?"

The sergeant enjoyed the company and stated, "I came down with the pox about ten days ago. I had chills, fever, and terrible headache. My body felt like it was being squeezed by a vice. Then the pustules started, first on my face, then spreading to my arms and everywhere. When I got here, I was bled...I'd say, about three times. That helped a lot. I have a few pustules left. See here on my belly. The doctors here in the General Hospital—they're the best."

Alex led the men from the smallpox ward. "Lads, you've had quite some exposure to smallpox cases. I am confident the Calcutta inoculation will protect you. As we agreed earlier, you'll be observed here in the hospital so that I may keep close watch on you. Nurse Jesse will show you to your quarters upstairs. I'll come by tomorrow. If you feel ill at all, let us know immediately."

For Colonel Joseph Reed's first day of observation in the hospital, he was bored and pleaded with Alex, "Good Lord, I'm fit as can be. Must I really take up one of your hospital beds? I can just check in with you each day."

While sympathetic to Reed's request, Alex nevertheless had his protocol to follow. "Colonel, I've got to keep you and the Marylanders quarantined. You've all had quite an exposure. If any untoward reaction develops, I must know without delay. General Washington agreed to have you stay here for observation."

As if Alex were prescient, that evening Reed began to feel unusually tired and fell asleep just after eight o'clock. A few hours later, he awoke with a chill. He shuffled to the window and closed it. "How stupid of me to leave the window open. No wonder I've had that chill," he rationalized. Reed grabbed an extra blanket and returned to bed. He felt the bed shake from his rigors. Later, his head and back began to throb, and he vomited twice. At dawn, Jesse rapped on his door. "Colonel Reed, how might you be feeling this morning?"

"Nurse Jesse," he responded faintly, "I'm afraid not too well."

When Jesse saw his condition, she immediately called Alex, who examined him and described his findings aloud. "You are feverish, Colonel, and your pulse is rapid—at 120. I see your face is flushed, but I don't see any rash. These findings together with your fever, aches and vomiting herald smallpox. Your case is having an extraordinarily rapid onset after your exposure. I am attributing that to the extent of your exposure and the severity of the cases you were exposed to. Reports from Calcutta said that illness occurred in perhaps one in ten following exposure to smallpox after the nasal inoculation, but those illnesses were typically a short, mild form of the disease. They never had to apply bleedings. I want to make sure you have enough laudanum for your head and back pains and take enough nourishment. I'll keep you on a light diet but with plenty of gruel and tea. For now, we'll quarantine you."

Reed smiled bravely. "Dr. Grant, sorry to let you down."

"I'll have no apologies from you. Well, let's see how things go. I am hopeful you'll have a truncated course. Jesse will see to your needs. I'm going to the ward to see how the Maryland boys are doing."

"Good morning, Dr. Grant," the Maryland sergeant said ebulliently when Alex entered their ward. "I've only got one complaint: where's our breakfast?" He joked, "Me and the boys, are you tryin' to starve us?"

"Sergeant, I'm delighted to hear that's your sole complaint. You see, last night, Colonel Reed had chills and other symptoms. I suppose he's got a brewing smallpox case after the exposure in the smallpox ward. That's to be expected even in some who've had the Calcutta inoculation. So, I'll put you lads on still closer watch. In the meantime, I'll order up a double serving of eggs and ham from the kitchen. We're fortunate in having a good food supply right now. Anything else?"

The sergeant bellowed, "Then double the coffee, too....eh, please, Sir."

Chapter 19 - Proving the Calcutta Method
Saturday, February 22 to Tuesday, February 25, 1777
Morristown, The American Encampment

Alex Grant rubbed his chin as he stood over Joseph Reed's bed. "Colonel, your aches have continued most of the day, but you've had no further chills or vomiting. I see a few red spots just below your right nostril, close to where I placed the inoculum. I emphasize how few these are. How are you feeling now?"

"Dr. Grant, much better. I'm even hungry. I'd like something more than gruel and tea."

Jesse added, "He looks just like his usual self."

Alex advised, "Colonel Reed, it's been less than twenty-four hours since you had the first chill. With natural smallpox, the course takes about four days after onset of chills for the spots to appear, typically on the forehead. Within the next day, new spots occur on the face and extremities. It takes another two days for fluid-filled vesicles to develop from the red spots and another two days for pustules to appear. When convalescence occurs, it begins about the tenth day. I'm very encouraged by what I'm seeing in you. The next day or two will tell us, but this looks like a very short course of illness. I'm going to check on the Maryland boys. For tonight, get plenty of rest."

In the Marylanders' ward, Alex found the men playing a game of faro. Sergeant, is the famine over?" teased Alex.

"Right you are, Dr. Grant. We're all now well fed. Thank you."

"Before you turn in, men, I'd like to examine you briefly. Colonel Reed had chills and aches today, but I'm delighted that he's already doing better this evening."

The sergeant jumped up to be examined first. Alex found no skin spots nor any back, belly or extremity tenderness.

"Sergeant," he chuckled, "You're a perfect specimen! Would the rest of you men kindly line up?"

After finding that the next three men normal, Alex stepped in front of the last soldier. The private rubbed his nose with right knuckles. "Anything bothering you, son?" asked Alex patiently.

"Not really, Sir. It's just my nose feels a bit sore."

Alex shined a large candle on the lad's face. "My God," Alex thought, "This private hasn't even started to shave. How old can he be?" Then to the boy, Alex asked, "Private, any chills, headache, backache, nausea, vomiting or rashes anywhere?"

"None at all, Sir, why do you ask?"

Alex was intent on being reassuring. "Well, son, you have three small red spots below your right nostril. Colonel Reed has the same, but he also has chills and aches. I'm very glad you do not so far. Would you lads return to your beds?"

Alex asked the sergeant to come to the corner of the ward. "One of your men—the last one I examined—probably has the beginning of smallpox, but I'm hoping it will be very mild. I'm going to put him in a separate room for now and keep a close watch on the rest of you. If anyone gets chills, pains, vomiting tonight, call for me immediately."

The sergeant's bearing became hostile. "Dr. Grant, you told us that the Calicut method was safe and would protect us. Now my youngest private has the smallpox. I put my faith in you, and now look what's happened!"

"Sergeant, please...please understand that you and your lads were vulnerable to the smallpox because you had neither the natural infection nor previous inoculation. Being in the army is a time when outbreaks of the pox are likely. I am at work to find a better way to protect all our men and am most thankful to you and the Maryland boys for volunteering. From the British doctors in India, the report was that the Calcutta method worked very well. But I must test it to see how it works here—what the inoculation would be like and how it protected. I am sorry if that was not clear, but I had no intention of misleading anyone nor of endangering anyone."

The sergeant's chin fell to his chest. He said softly, "Apologies, Dr. Grant. I'm worried about him. You see, the lad's my only son. He's just turned sixteen years."

Alex gently placed his hand on the sergeant's shoulder. "No apologies needed, sergeant. I want to keep your son quarantined until we see what happens, but I can arrange for you to be in his room to comfort him."

The next morning, Alex and Jesse got an ebullient greeting from Reed. "I slept fine. No chills. Aches gone. Come, see about those red spots."

Alex was ecstatic. "Hallelujah! The spots are gone. This is magnificent! Jesse, come with me. We must now go to see the Maryland boy."

When Alex and Jesse entered the quarantine room, the young lad greeted them with a smile. "Dr. Grant, the soreness in m' nose—it's gone." The sergeant added, "I looked at him myself this morning. I couldn't see any spots."

Next, Alex visited the sergeant's son and took the boy to the window to inspect his face in better light. "Son, do you have any other spots?" After the boy responded negatively, Alex inspected his face closely. "Sergeant, you're correct. The spots from his nostril have gone, indeed. Let's make sure there are no new ones elsewhere." Alex and Jesse inspected his arms, legs, trunk and abdomen. Alex clapped his hands together. To Jesse, he exclaimed "This is extraordinary. I want to report these findings to General Washington, but first, let's go see Hobbs."

Within the hour, Jesse, Hobbs and Alex were in Washington's office. From his journal, Alex showed the general the results: mild, short illnesses for Colonel Reed and the young soldier and the absence of any findings in the other four Marylanders. Washington nodded with gratification. "Dr. Grant, I congratulate you on these results. I am going to send a special dispatch to Philadelphia to Dr. John Morgan, currently the Director General of the Army Medical Department. I hope he will take full advantage of your observations. However, when Colonel Gibbs was in Philadelphia, he learned that Dr. Morgan was quarreling regularly with Congress. I do not know how much longer he will remain as director. It will be a pity if your results are lost amidst the furor. Your medical colleagues throughout the medical department should know of the Calcutta method and its protective effect. (1)

---

(1) Dr. John Morgan, a diligent, outstanding physician, was the first Director-General of the Continental Army Medical Department, but because of constant quarrels with Congress over support for the medical department, he was ousted in early 1777. Amidst the organizational chaos, it is likely that nearly all dispatches from Washington to Morgan would have been ignored or misplaced. It is not surprising that no report of Alex Grant's groundbreaking work was

disseminated to the American Army Medical Department.

Chapter 20 - The Patrol
Thursday, February 20 to Friday, February 21, 1777
Northern New Jersey

Late on Thursday, February 20th, Lieutenant Colonel Caleb Gibbs and four other troopers ascended a hill north of the hamlet of Bound Brook. They had been riding from Morristown since dawn. Gibbs was tired and frustrated. He said to the junior officer riding beside him, "Last night, General Washington gave me intelligence that the wagons would be leaving Brunswick today, but we've had no luck finding them. I've sent out three patrols on other roads, but we've gotten no message from them either."

The junior officer added to Gibbs's worries by asking, "Sir, do you suppose the wagons could have slipped by us? Could our intelligence be dead wrong? Could the plotter's plan have been changed?"

"Yes, all of those are possible," grumped Caleb Gibbs uncharacteristically. "Look, rather than riding back to Morristown, we'll make camp around here and range closer to Brunswick tomorrow. Maybe that will allow us to find the wagon shipment."

Caleb's troop rode a few miles farther south and with dusk nearing made camp in a clearing, just above a brook. Caleb had an unusual relationship with his Life Guards. They all admired him and looked up to him both as their officer but also as an older brother. One of the troopers came up from the stream and shouted, "Look here, I've caught three catfish. I'll roast them over the fire." After they finished eating, Caleb advised, "Listen, lads, tomorrow will be a demanding day. You get to sleep. I'll take the first watch." Caleb walked carefully around the campsite. He looked skyward noting heavy, gray clouds moving in from the west. He double checked their horses to be sure they were secure.

The air felt heavy and damp. He sensed they would find their prey in the morning.

****

That same evening, a few miles away, the Williamsons repaired the wagon wheel. Charles unhitched their horses, and William took four blankets from a chest to prepare the bedrolls. Between the second and third blanket, he found a broken, small glass vial. "Charles," he called out, "What do ya' make of this?"

Charles looked at the shards. "Ah, those clumsy buggers at the storehouse! Just shake those pieces off. I'm gettin' very tired." William placed the bedrolls under a wagon because of threatening, dark clouds. Around their campfire, they hurriedly ate a meager supper of salt pork and cheese that they found in another chest. The brothers washed it down with whiskey from Charles's flask. Tarleton smelled the smoke of the Williamsons' fire and stealthily followed the road until he could hear their voices clearly.

William inquired, "Brother, should we take turns guarding the wagons? The supplies are of high value."

"I suppose. I have my old Brown Bess if we need it," Charles responded as he gazed into the campfire. "Look, here are the directions the quartermaster major gave me to the outpost. Neither of us has been in these parts, but the route seems straightforward enough. We'll get there easily tomorrow. I'll take first watch. Good night, Will."

From the exhaustion of the day and the whiskey, William was asleep in minutes. Charles's chin fell to his chest shortly, and he too drifted off to sleep a few minutes later. Once Tarleton saw them both asleep, he backtracked a short distance and laid his bedroll under a dry, rocky outcropping. He ate an even more scanty meal of pemmican and water. Cursing the Williamsons for making him spend the night so miserably and worrying about the delay, he could not sleep for more than a few minutes off and on. "Those stupid oafs, they better get the job done bright and early."

At dawn, on Friday, February 21st, Tarleton awoke in a dense fog. He could see only a few feet through the woods, but his ears perked up when he heard Charles Williamson's voice as he woke his brother and called to their horses. Charles bellowed, "Come on, Will, we must get out of this buggerin' damp. We've got to get to that outpost." Will quickly folded the blankets and stashed them back in their chests. Charles's wagon led the way along the fog-enshrouded road. He called back to Will, "At least the road's dry and wide, Will. I want to be in my own warm bed tonight."

With the woods silent in the fog, Tarleton intentionally trailed well behind the wagons. "I know exactly where those bumpkins are headed. I'll give them plenty of space this morning," he said to himself.

Before leaving the storehouse, Tarleton had given Charles Williamson written directions. For his plot to succeed, Tarleton needed an American patrol to intercept the Williamsons and bring the wagonloads of supplies and blankets into Morristown, unknowingly infesting the American camp. Tarleton had thought, "The Williamsons have never been to this part of Jersey. They won't know. I'll tell them that these are directions to the outpost, but they'll be headed right toward Morristown. The bloody fools will be caught for sure! My Trojan Horse cannot fail."

When he left Brunswick, Charles read Tarleton's directions twice and placed the written copy in his torn vest pocket. As his wagon now lumbered along the road, Charles reached into his pocket to double check the route. He felt once, then twice, but could not find the paper. He called to Will, "Last night, when I showed ya' the directions, did ya' return them to me?"

Will thought for a few seconds and recalled, "Right, I handed the paper back to ya' while ya' were having a whiskey 'round the fire." Charles stopped the wagon, climbed down, and searched every pocket. "For the love of Jesus, I cannot find the directions. Check your pockets." Will could not find it either. Charles muttered, "Bullocks! Here we are in country we don't know, in a hell of a fog, and without directions. This is a cursed trip if I ever saw one. What possessed me to deal with that blasted quartermaster son of a bitch?" To his brother, Charles said dejectedly, "Well, no choice now. My memory is we stay on the main road, and that we'll do—through this bloody fog!"

****

That Friday morning, Caleb's troop of Life Guards began to stir at dawn. A thin fog had settled over their campsite. To ward off the damp chill, they made tea over the campfire and ate a few stale biscuits. "Lads," said Caleb, "It's likely clear up on the ridge to the south—towards Brunswick. Let's get out of this fog. After all, I don't want you to be too homesick for misty New England!"

The road Caleb took climbed to a high ridge and into bright sunshine, but as he looked south, he muttered, "Bloody hell, as far as I can see, there's nothing but heavy fog covering the road below. It's still early though. We'll stay on the ridge and hope the fog clears a bit." While waiting, Caleb thought of the intelligence he had received just before leaving Morristown. It was from Lieutenant Martin Walker's letter, naming the Williamson brothers as the civilian teamsters hauling the blankets.

No more than thirty minutes later, through the quietness of the fog, Caleb heard the jangle of metal and the distant clomp of hoofbeats coming from the valley to the south. "Wait," he said softly to the four guards, "Look immediately to the west. There's a break in the fog. Hang on, my boys."

Caleb's patience was rewarded as the fog cleared momentarily over the road. Caleb peered through his telescope and whispered, "Two wagons headed up the valley. This is our day! After me!"

But just as Caleb had spotted the wagons, Charles Williamson squinted at the ridgeline. "Will, do ya' see mounted men up there? In these parts, they may be buggerin' rebel cav'. Look, the fog is still thick just behind us."

The Williamsons turned their wagons around. Charles snapped his whip at his team and raced back along the fog-covered road. In no more than two hundred yards, Charles spotted a narrow trail leading into dense woods to the left. The brothers drove their wagons in, and the thick foliage closed behind them. They climbed down from their wagons to quiet their horses.

Minutes later, they heard the troopers race by, headed further south down the road. Charles grinned widely. "Will, the troopers'll head back this way soon, but they'll be checkin' every side trail. This is our only chance. Move!"

They climbed back onto their wagons and drove them back down the trail. When Charles turned his team onto the road, his grin morphed into a look of horror. His lips drew apart, and he sucked air between his clenched, yellow teeth.

Chapter 21 -The Devil Himself
Friday, February 21, 1777
Northern New Jersey

To his dread, Charles Williamson stared through the lifting fog at three menacing horsemen astride the road. The middle rider's pistol was squarely aimed at Williamson's head. The two riders on either side pointed their carbines at his chest. The middle horseman commanded, "Charles Williamson, you and your brother will slowly bring your wagons to the clearing on the right. Then, unhitch your horses, and be quick about it, or we'll blow your brains out!"

Charles recovered enough to recognize the men as Washington's Life Guards. He stammered, "But...but, Sir, how do ya' know my name?"

Lieutenant Colonel Gibbs barked, "Never mind how I know your name. I know a great deal about you two. Now, get your wagons over to that clearing."

Just a few minutes earlier while still on the high ridge, Caleb called out, "Gentlemen, it's the Williamsons all right up ahead. Look, they can't outrun us. They'll likely duck into the first side path they spot, hoping we'll charge right by them. Lieutenants Yorke and White, you two, ride down there first. Yell at the top of your lungs! The three of us will stay behind you. When the Williamsons think we have all passed them, they'll return to the main road. We'll give them the surprise of their lives."

The Williamsons fell right into Caleb's trap. While the Williamsons drove their wagons to the clearing, Lieutenants Yorke and White returned to join the other Life Guards. Caleb greeted them. "Excellent job, my lads! You made it sound like an entire squadron was racing down the road. Our ruse worked perfectly! Now, let's carry out the rest of our mission."

Charles waddled toward Caleb, who remained mounted. Will Williamson followed anxiously. Caleb warned, "That'll be close enough, Mr. Williamson. Now, exactly where were you headed?"

"Why, Sir, we're headed to the new British outpost, on the road west. Aren't we on that road?" asked Charles innocently.

Caleb ignored Charles's question. "Now, Mr. Williamson, I know you're hauling blankets and great coats. What else is in those chests?"

Bewildered that an American trooper could know this, Charles simply replied, "That's the main cargo, but there's also some cartridges, salt pork, cheeses, and whiskey."

"And where did you spend last night?" inquired Caleb.

"Don't know exactly where it was, but we slept in the open near a stream."

Caleb continued, "Was it not cold last night? How did you two stay warm?"

Not comprehending Caleb's line of questioning, Charles replied openly, "Yeah, it was bloody cold alright. Just took some o' them blankets from the chests and made bedrolls."

"I see," replied a concerned Caleb. "And did you notice anything when you opened the blankets."

"No.... Not really," responded Charles, but then William whispered in Charles's ear. The older brother added, "Oh, yeah,

William found some bits of broken glass in the blankets. Why's that so important? I figured it was a clumsy bloke at the storehouse."

Caleb was now convinced that the Williamsons had received a heavy exposure to the smallpox debris, but he had more pertinent information to get. Caleb drew his mount three steps closer. His horse pawed the ground threateningly. He glared down and growled, "Tell me who paid you to make this shipment."

"I...I ...I don't know, Sir."

Caleb drew his saber from its scabbard and placed the tip right on Charles's rotund belly. "How in heaven's name can that be?"

"I...I...never got his name, Sir, but he's a quartermaster major, a little heavy 'round the middle and gettin' gray in his head. He gave me ten pounds in gold coin as a bonus. I couldn't read his signature on the requisition, but here it is," replied Charles reaching into pouch.

"Get your hand out of the case, Williamson. Toss your pouch to the Life Guard to your right. One more move like that, and it'll be your last!"

"Beggin' your pardon, Sir. I ..I ...I was just tryin' to be helpful," quivered Charles.

Life Guard Major Samuel Webb quickly read the requisition from Charles's pouch. "Colonel Gibbs, it's just as Williamson says. And one more thing, the signature....it's illegible, but it's got a left handed slant."

Caleb smiled at how the pieces were fitting together. "One

more question for you both," snapped Caleb to the scruffy brothers. "Have either of you had the natural smallpox or the inoculation?"

"Why would that matter?" asked a flummoxed Charles.

Caleb now replied sympathetically, "It matters nil to me, but it will to you and your brother. So, you had better tell me."

Thinking for a minute, Charles recalled, "I had the smallpox when I was a wee lad, but I don't think William had it.

"That's true, brother, not the pox, not the inoculation," recalled Will.

Behind the Williamsons, the two junior Life Guards, Lieutenants Peter Yorke and Benjamin White, opened the chests atop the wagons and liberally spread gunpowder onto them. At Charles's last answer, the guards fired their carbines at the powder-covered trunks.

Though unhitched from the wagons and tied up over fifty yards away, the teamsters' horses brayed and kicked their hind legs nervously. Charles Williamson jumped at the crack of the shots. His eyes widened as he saw their wagons burst into flame. "Bullocks," cried Charles, "why are ya' doin' that?"

Caleb dismounted. "Mr. Williamson, go over to the corner of the clearing. I'll be there momentarily." Caleb then told his troopers, "Keep William here and be sure the fire doesn't spread to the woods. The fog's beginning to lift. Good Lord, the fire's sending up a huge black plume of smoke. We'll want to get moving as soon as the chests and wagons are completely burned."

Caleb stayed several feet from Charles Williamson but spoke softly. "Mr. Williamson, I have grievous news for you."

Charles's eyes widened with fear. "What, are you going to shoot us?"

"No, we aren't going to harm you," replied Caleb empathically as he prepared to deliver devastating information. Before leaving Morristown, Caleb received specific instructions from General Washington about what to tell the Williamsons in the likely event of their capture. Caleb proceeded accordingly. "You see, you and your brother have been victimized by the man wearing the British Quartermaster officer's uniform. He instructed you to drive the supplies to a newly-established British outpost to the west, but there is no such garrison. He wanted you to head toward Morristown, knowing that you'd be intercepted by American troops."

Dumbfounded, Charles's jaw dropped. "Why in hell's name would a British officer have wanted all the blankets and goods to get captured by his enemy?"

"Indeed, that's the main question," acknowledged Caleb. "And you just confirmed our intelligence. Before you left Brunswick, the officer infested the shipment with smallpox. He must have left one of the vials in the blankets you used last night. He expected the blankets would be used immediately at Morristown leading to a huge outbreak in the American camp. The officer wanted his plot to cripple the American Army."

"That means my brother….is he gonna' get smallpox?"

"Mr. Williamson, I don't know about William, but I am going to give you a letter. You must take it directly to Dr. Walker, Director of the Main British General Hospital in New York. He'll give William the best care. You are in no danger because you had the pox."

"You mean, you're gonna' let us go?" asked Charles incredulously. Caleb replied sincerely, "Yes, you and your brother have been deceived by a pernicious rogue. You have told me all you know. You may ride your draft horses back to New York. Two of my troopers will escort you most of the way to the British lines."

Charles added, "Colonel, we're thankful for the letter and for our release. Ya' wouldn't know if we'll get our haulin' fee from the quartermaster, or who will pay us for our wagons, would ya'?"

Caleb chuckled, "I'm afraid the hauling fee is not in my power to say. As for your wagons, you should just be thankful you are not prisoners. Well, here's the letter for Dr. Walker. Please give him my personal regards."

By now, the flames had consumed the wagons, chests, and their contents. Only gray ash, a few smoldering timbers, and red-hot metal fittings remained. The heat of the fire decomposed the smallpox debris, rendering it harmless. With shovels rescued from one chest, the troopers piled dirt from the damp ground on the residue.

As the Williamsons and their escort rode east, Caleb called to his junior guards, "Lieutenants Yorke and White, Take them no further than Elizabethtown. From there, they'll know the way. I want to get the news back to General Washington as quickly as we can. His Excellency will be very relieved. We'll see you in camp before nightfall." Caleb and his two senior Life Guards, Majors Samuel Webb and William Grayson, rode toward Morristown. On route, Samuel Webb asked, "Sir, I was just wondering, why did you decide not to take the brothers as prisoners?"

"I did think about that, but I am confident they were just innocent dupes, completely tricked by that British rogue officer. I'm certain Charles Williamson gave me all the information he had. He was so scared he could not have been holding anything back. What's more, I also have the false requisition in the plotter's handwriting. Besides, young William is at dreadful risk of smallpox. The poor souls, they've had enough troubles."

The carbine shots and the smell of smoke attracted the attention of another rider. Because of the fog, Banastre Tarleton had lost track of the wagons but was now drawn toward the clearing. Unable to make his way through the dense woods, he rode cautiously along the road, stopping repeatedly to listen for approaching riders. He memorized the road's twists in case he needed a quick retreat. Tarleton checked that his pistol was loaded and thought, "Bloody hell, this is not what I expected! Shots, smoke—for the love of mercy, could the bumpkins be dead? Are the wagons burning? I must find out." Within a few minutes, Tarleton heard hoof beats moving slowly toward him. A trooper peered through the dense fog and yelled, "Halt, who goes there?" Lieutenants Yorke and White saw a flash of a green uniform. "It's the devil himself," cried Yorke. "After him!" yelled White leaving the bewildered Williamsons by themselves.

On his favorite horse, Tarleton raced headlong down the road. Ahead he saw a large, jagged rock overhanging his path. Tarleton quickly pulled off the road, concealed by the rock. "I'll show these rebels how the king's best fights!" The troopers rode past him but shortly walked their horses back to look for his trail. With both guards scouring the ground, Tarleton charged from behind the rock and fired his pistol from three feet away into Peter Yorke's chest. The shot rang through the quiet forest as the ball tore into the young trooper's lungs and heart. Yorke fell to the forest floor in a dead heap. Caught by surprise, Benjamin White reached for his saber with his right arm, but Tarleton was already upon him. With a mighty slash, Tarleton cut so deeply into White's arm that it hung limply. White screamed in anguish as in his last moment he saw the fiendish look on Tarleton's face. The dragoon's eyes were wild and his mouth agape when he thrust his saber almost up to the hilt into his Benjamin White's chest. The thin blade slid between the guard's ribs, punctured his lung and lacerated his aorta. Blood instantly poured into his chest. Tarleton laughed insanely as he withdrew his saber, drenched in blood. The trooper's head lolled, as bright red froth billowed out of his mouth, and he tumbled to the ground. But White's left foot was caught in the stirrup. His startled horse bolted up the road, dragging the young trooper's body and grotesquely smashing it against rock and tree.

Lieutenant Yorke's horse charged back up the road. Tarleton looked down from his mount and thrust his saber into the Yorke's motionless body—just to be sure. He dismounted and sat the corpse upright against a tree at the roadside. He did not want the other Life Guards to miss his skillful work. Tarleton then continued carefully up the road. Shortly, he found Lieutenant White's hideously battered body. His foot had slipped from his boot, and he mercifully came to rest on the roadside. White's face and head were smashed beyond recognition, and his right arm ended in a bleeding stump. Tarleton ghoulishly sat the lieutenant's corpse against a tree and continued to ride through the fog.

Caleb and his two senior guards had not ridden very far toward Morristown when they heard a faint crack. Caleb said, "Major Webb, I swear that sounded like a pistol shot. Our two lads are back there. We'd better check." The three galloped back to the smoldering clearing but saw no one there. Another quarter mile down the road, they heard hoofbeats of several horses approaching. They drew their sabers and trotted ahead. Caleb was momentarily confused when he saw the Williamsons riding toward him on their draft horses and in their hands the reins of two other horses. "In God's name, what happened?" he shouted to the teamsters.

Charles looked fearful and cried out, "We made out at least

one horseman, wearin' a green uniform ahead of us. The two lieutenants gave chase. A little while later, I heard a single shot. Then, their horses raced back to us, but we haven't seen the guards. I loaded my old musket, and not knowin' how many of them there were, we headed back hopin' to find you. Am I ever glad we did! But better have a look for yourself, Colonel. Both saddles... they're covered in blood."

Caleb added, "Williamson, have you seen any other British soldiers?"

"None at all, Sir."

Caleb thought, "This cannot end well."

Major William Grayson, riding ahead of the others, peered through the lifting mist and saw a Life Guard sitting upright against a tree. Grayson yelled back to the others, "Here's one of the lads!" But as Grayson came closer, he cringed at the hideous wounds. The Life Guard's skull was battered. His legs were broken at grotesque angles, and his bare left foot was bloodied. His uniform was shredded and covered with mud. Caleb dismounted and sighed, "What could have happened to you, my boy? I vow to find the culprits and avenge your death!

Caleb knelt next to the fallen guard and wiped the blood and dirt from his head. "The young guard deserves a decent burial. William Williamson, would you stay here with him? We'll get him back to Morristown, but for now I'm going ahead with the others to find Lieutenant Yorke."

As they cautiously proceeded down the road, they began to put the events together. They found the trooper's left boot, small shreds of his uniform, and blood splattered on jagged, gray rocks. When they came to a sharp turn in the road, Caleb's heart sank as he found the remains of Peter Yorke, also placed in an eerie sitting position. He had a blackened powder burn and a bullet crater over his heart. "My God, my God," cried Caleb. "Not you too."

Now the fog had lifted, and one hundred yards away, but hidden by the dense woods, Banastre Tarleton watched every move. He had wisely positioned himself on the far side of a stream. He thought to himself, "So that's it. A troop of Washington's own Life Guards must have intercepted the buggering Williamsons, and the smoke—they must have burned the blankets. Mother of Christ, how could the guards have found out? Bastards, I cannot afford to have Charles Williamson tell the rebels anything more." As Tarleton aimed his carbine at Charles's chest, a flash of bright sunlight reflected off its muzzle. Just before Tarleton squeezed the trigger, Caleb shouted, "Down!" A puff of white smoke gave away Tarleton's position an instant before Caleb heard the shot. Tarleton saw Charles slide from the draft horse as his ball found its mark.

Tarleton's mount dashed through the woods to the road. Caleb spotted the green tunic of a lone dragoon and shouted, "Grayson, come with me. Webb, look after Williamson."

Caleb charged to the stream bank and eased his mount into the fast-flowing waters. William Grayson followed right behind. At mid-stream, the water was over three feet deep, and slippery, moss-covered rocks lined the stream bed. Caleb fumed as the guards' pace slowed as the horses had to pick their way carefully across the stream. By the time they had crossed, they saw the dragoon had already ridden out of the woods and was racing across a broad meadow. "Blast!" yelled Caleb. "We'll never catch that devil now."

Forced to give up their pursuit, Caleb and William Grayson returned to find Samuel Webb had tended to Charles Williamson's wound. "Luckily," Webb rejoiced, "Charles

Williamson was already sliding off his horse. The ball was no doubt aimed at his chest, but it hit his right shoulder—only a deep flesh wound, at that. It'll need our surgeon's care as soon as possible. I've also cleaned up poor Lieutenant Yorke with some stream water. He was such a good young officer."

Caleb lost his characteristic optimism for a moment as he said, "This has been a bloody awful day, hasn't it? We break the plot to infest Morristown with smallpox, but I lose two of my finest young guards—and to a scoundrel who manages to escape from my clutch! At least Charles Williamson will come through.

Major Webb added, "Colonel, it's a sad day, but sooner or later we'll get that rogue, I'd bet. Should we head back to camp, Sir?"

"Right, Major Webb, indeed. And now there's no way the Williamsons can get to Brunswick or New York. So, Mr. Williamson, let's collect your brother, and you're both coming with us. Drs. Grant and Hobbs will get you all fixed up, and then we'll see what to do."

Tarleton laughed aloud when he saw that the Life Guards had to give up their pursuit. But then as he rode toward the military ferry, he took stock. "Christ, my weeks of work all wasted! Well, I did have the utter thrill of dispatching those two lieutenants from Washington's Guard. The Americans will remember that."

Yet, Tarleton was not aware of the trail he had been leaving nor of Lee's betraying him to General Howe. He rode toward Paulus Hook thinking, "I would like to know how those rebels found out about the shipment of blankets coming in those clumsy brothers' wagons. Well, with General Lee as my only confidant, no one will ever be able to identify me as the mastermind." As he boarded the last ferry of the evening to Manhattan, Tarleton's knotted mind churned. "I'll gain the recognition I'm due."

Chapter 22 - Repercussions
Friday, February 21 to Monday, February 24, 1777
Morristown and Brunswick

As Banastre Tarleton crossed eastward over the Hudson, Caleb Gibbs's troop ascended the plain into Morristown. The sentry welcomed him. "Sir," he said snapping a smart salute, "Good to see you back." Solemnly, Caleb returned the salute and looked straight ahead. Only then did the sentry glance down the line, past the wounded Charles Williamson, past the shabby William Williamson, and to Majors Webb and Grayson, who each led a mount carrying the body of a lieutenant in its saddle. The sentry muttered, "Oh, no, not both." Caleb led the procession to headquarters where he spoke softly to the Life Guards on duty, "Two of our colleagues were killed in action today. Would one of you get blankets so that we may cover them respectfully? I have urgent news for His Excellency. Please announce my return."

Within minutes, General Washington appeared at the door, exchanged salutes with Caleb's troop, and walked to the bodies of Lieutenants Yorke and White. He removed his tricorn, and his head hung down as his hand gently touched the young guards' heads. "They were fine young officers. Please, Colonel Gibbs, come in and speak with me. Major Webb, would you kindly take our fallen comrades to the hospital where they may be properly received? I believe Drs. Grant and Hobbs are there this evening." Then, looking at Charles Williamson, Washington said graciously, "I see we have a guest who also needs care in the hospital. Please escort him and our other guest there as well."

Washington's office was dimly lit by banks of candles and the glow from the fireplace. The general signaled Caleb to one of the chairs in front of his desk. "Now, Colonel Gibbs, please fill me in with complete detail."

As Caleb reported on how his troop had hunted down the Williamsons' wagons and then burned the infested cargo, Washington nodded admiringly, interjecting "Well done, well done" three or four times.

When Caleb paused, Washington concluded, "Colonel, you foiled a heinous attempt to disable our army. I shudder to think what would have happened if the plot had not been uncovered in time and if the shipment had not been destroyed. Now, please tell me what happened to our brave lieutenants and what you know of the perpetrator."

As Caleb finished his account, Washington rose from his chair. "What a cruel mind the plotter has! Mocking the young dead, indeed. I vow to catch the cunning demon if it's the last thing I do."

Regaining his composure, Washington put his arm on Caleb's shoulder and said, "I want to see the lieutenants. Would you kindly accompany me to the hospital?"

Earlier at the hospital, Alex and Hobbs examined Charles Williamson's gunshot wound. "You're a lucky man, Williamson," noted Hobbs. "The ball's gone clean through and didn't even hit the muscle. We will get it fixed up in no time." Alex added, "Dr. Hobbs will take care of you. I'm going to oversee the preparation of our poor murdered lads. When Dr. Hobbs is finished, he'll find a place for you two to stay for now." Alex whispered to Hobbs aside, "Keep the Williamsons to themselves, knowing of their likely smallpox exposure."

Caleb and the commander in chief entered the hospital operating theatre quietly. With his back to the door, Alex was at one table mending Lieutenant White's broken and battered body. Tench and Samuel Webb stood at the table's head gently stroking their colleague's arms. At the adjacent table, Jesse and a surgeon's mate washed Lieutenant Yorke's remains. Major Grayson choked back tears. Washington cleared his throat and said, "May I pay my respects to our young heroes?"

Alex recognized the voice immediately but was still surprised to see the commander in the hospital. "Good evening, Your Excellency, this would be a very good time. We have nearly completed preparing our courageous young officers for burial rites."

Washington continued, "Colonel Gibbs has given me an account of today's actions. I trust that Major Webb and Major Grayson have provided you all with the details as well. Please accept my humblest gratitude in halting this diabolical plot. Colonel Tilghman, would you please provide for a fitting burial for Lieutenants Yorke and White and prepare letters to their next of kin? Gentlemen, I am most grateful for your brave and bold efforts today and grieve for our lost young Life Guards. You are family to me."

While Caleb escorted General Washington back to headquarters, Tench efficiently began his preparations. "The burial will be at one o'clock tomorrow afternoon. There's only one fitting place, and that's the churchyard. Major Webb, it's getting late, but please see the vicar this evening to locate the exact burial sites. Ask the vicar if he might choose the appropriate Bible reading. And, oh, yes, ask him where to get two caskets. If he has none, go over to the engineers and have them construct them. Then, arrange a detail to dig the graves. Have them start at eight o'clock in the morning. Major Grayson, please find a suitable carriage and team of horses to carry the caskets to the churchyard. Dr. Grant, it looks like the bodies are nearly prepared, but what can you do for poor Lieutenant White's distorted head?"

"Don't worry. My mate will have them dressed in fresh

uniforms, and I'll restore his face as well as I can."

Tench concluded, "Very good, everyone. Thank you. General Washington will be there, punctually, you may be sure."

At one o'clock the next afternoon, the clouds broke over Morristown as bright sunlight warmed the living souls gathered in the churchyard. The pallbearers placed the oak caskets on straps over the two adjacent gravesites. The vicar was tall, distinguished, and graying. In a resonant voice, heavy with an Irish lilt, he intoned, "Ladies and Gentlemen, I read from the One Hundred Twenty First Psalm:

> I will lift up mine eyes unto the mountains:
> From whence shall my help come?
> My help cometh from the Lord,
> Who made heaven and earth.
>
> The Lord is thy keeper;
> The Lord is thy shade upon thy right hand.
> The sun shall not smite thee by day,
> Nor the moon by night.
> The Lord shall keep thee from all evil;
> He shall keep thy soul,
> The Lord shall guard thy going out and thy coming in,
> From this time forth and forever.
> Amen."

The pallbearers lowered the caskets, one at a time, into the graves. General Washington unfolded a note from his pocket and recited words adapted from an ancient prayer:

> "Tender memories fill our thoughts as we stand here by the grave of our young brothers-in-arms. Precious was the blessing that God gave us in their brief lives. Brothers indeed were they at all times, kind and considerate in

their words, brave and honorable in their deeds."

Each of the Life Guards, in turn, took a shovelful of earth and dropped it onto the coffins. The dull thud of the damp earth upon the caskets mimicked drumbeats and the haunting finality of death. General Washington expressed his gratitude to the vicar and led the cortege from the churchyard.

****

Early the next week, Lieutenant Martin Walker arrived at the Brunswick military storehouse at nine o'clock but found the door still locked. "Strange," he thought, "my clerk is always here by eight to prepare for the day." Martin opened the lock with his own key but still saw no sign of his clerk. A few minutes later, a disheveled, red-headed woman ran into the storehouse. She blurted, "I mus' see Lieutenan' Walker. M' 'usband...'e is not well this mornin' ...up all nigh' w' chills, pains in 'is 'ead and throwin' up."

Martin Walker replied inquisitively, "It's all right, madam. Was he having a few with his chums last night?"

"Not at'all, Sir!" she fired back indignantly.

"Well, tell him to rest and go to hospital if he's not feeling better. Tell him not to worry about the storehouse."

Although Lieutenant Walker was aware of a brewing plot, his clerk's symptoms were not yet indicative, to a layman, of smallpox. Martin Walker had no idea of what was to befall his storehouse unit. Walker called his assistant clerk to handle the front counter because he had other matters needing his attention that morning. He had not seen the civilian teamsters return and, with his suspicions aroused, decided to pay them a visit. He had no trouble finding their house and office on the road to the east of town. The fence sign read "Williamson Bros, Teamsters" in crude painted black letters. Walker knocked on the front door, but when there was no answer, he went to the rear entry which was unlocked. Upon entering, he called out. No one answered. He found the rear windows partially opened and the floor still wet from the previous night's rain. "Good grief, it looks like no one's been here in days. I wonder where they are. What could have happened to them?"

It was late afternoon when he returned to the Brunswick storehouse and felt an abrupt, shaking chill. A half hour later, Martin had another chill, this one causing him to shiver violently. He called to his junior clerk, "I'm not feeling so well myself. I'm going to my quarters. Would you mind checking on our senior clerk after you're finished for the day? You could leave early if you need to."

Martin shivered as he walked two blocks to his barracks, took off his uniform, and got directly into bed. His forehead began to throb intensely, and he retched twice. Martin fell asleep but awoke with severe pains in his back and legs. He felt restless and hot. Through the night, he had more chills and occasional drenching sweats. Just before nine o'clock, Martin awakened to knocking on his door. "Come in," he said weakly.

His junior clerk's mouth dropped as he took in the lieutenant's distressed condition. "Sir, last night, I went to the senior clerk's billet, but his wife said he was asleep. She wouldn't let me in. This morning, I went back, and I saw him. My Lord, he could not even recognize me. He even thought he was back in England! Sir, if you don't mind my mentioning it...you don't look very good yourself. Shouldn't we get you to hospital?" As the assistant clerk helped dress the lieutenant, he said, "Sir, please wait here. I'll run to the storehouse and get a wagon to take you." As the young clerk climbed aboard the wagon, he thought to himself, "With all the misery surrounding us, I'm glad I had the inoculation before leaving England!"

Shortly, the assistant clerk returned and held Martin upright as he walked unsteadily to the awaiting wagon. Martin covered himself with three blankets for the short ride. At the Brunswick General Hospital, Surgeon's Mate Blackfield examined Walker carefully. "Sir, I can tell from feeling your forehead that you have fever and seeing your other symptoms, we must take precautions for smallpox. It's too soon in the course for a rash, but Sir, have you had the inoculation or the natural disease?"

"No, I've had neither, I'm afraid not. We lived in a village where the pox rarely occurred, and my regiment somehow missed the inoculation before we sailed for America. And where's the surgeon?"

"Sir, our surgeon sailed for home weeks ago. You see, he got a letter that his wife was deathly ill. They have five small children. It's just the three surgeon's mates, but we expect one of the surgeons from the Main General Hospital in New York tomorrow or the next day."

Martin perked up at this news. "Would you happen to know the name of the surgeon who's coming from New York?

"Afraid not, Sir. But they're all good up there. For now, you'll be in the isolation ward. Don't worry, we have plenty of laudanum to control your pain, and we'll keep you on a light diet: broths, teas, and barley-water. And when your fever gets high, we'll use cool sponging. For now, let's get you a fresh set of bedclothing."

Martin felt reassured by Mate Blackfield's confident manner as they walked to the isolation ward. He said to the mate, "My assistant clerk from the storehouse is still waiting outside. Would you please ask him to inform the quartermaster general of my condition? And, what's more, I can't recall whether he's had the inoculation. Would you please ask him about that or the natural infection back home in England?"

When Martin looked around the smallpox ward, he was at first comforted. There were only two other soldiers there, each at a corner of the large room and lying on a clean straw pallet. All the unnecessary furniture and the curtains had been removed. A fire blazed to keep the invalids warm. After Martin changed into the linen bedclothes, he heard the soldier in the far corner cry out repeatedly. Martin could not see him but heard the lad moan, "Mother, please take me home. Mother, I don' wanna' die." The mate rushed to the invalid's pallet and gave him medication. In a few minutes, the lad was quiet.

Martin's alarm worsened that afternoon when the surgeon's mate brought another soldier into the isolation ward. Blackfield placed him at the remaining corner and set up a screen around the pallet. Even the veteran mate was aghast at the grotesque appearance of the man's face. His eyelids were markedly swollen with thick, yellow pus exuding between them, and his face, mouth and throat were covered by sores. The patient's breathing sounds were harsh and labored, and he coughed in long, painful spasms. When Blackfield saw the papules and pustules over his whole body, he thought to himself, "Of all the luck, this soldier's in for it. It looks like confluent smallpox with, I'd guess, pneumonia."

Martin looked toward the door as a frightened, red-headed woman burst into the isolation ward. She screamed, "Where's m' darlin'? Where is 'e?" Mate Blackfield rushed out from behind the screen and reprimanded her. "Madam, you are not permitted in the isolation ward. I insist you leave immediately!"

"I've 'ad th' 'noculation, back in London. 'ere's m' scar. That mus' be m' 'usband you've put in th' corner. I mus' spend 'is last 'ours with 'im!"

Through his own febrile confusion, Martin vaguely recalled her appearance. He racked his brain and then his eyes widened. "My Lord," he thought. "She's my clerk's wife. She came into the storehouse just the other day, and now she says my good clerk is at death's door! Such a tragedy. And it's horrific to think the same lies ahead for me." Martin tried to steer his thoughts in other directions, without success.

****

At the same time in Morristown, Hobbs was concerned about the Williamson brothers' exposure to the smallpox debris, and at his direction, the brothers did not attend the funeral. That afternoon, William began to feel vaguely ill. Later, he felt a wave of nausea and vomited. William looked up, his face now greenish, and replied, "Charles, my head throbs, my back hurts, and I just had a chill. I want to go to the hospital. I cannot bear these pains any longer."

When Jesse received them at the Continental Army General Hospital, she noted William's symptoms and obtained the brothers' medical histories. After she learned of their sleeping among infested blankets and William's susceptibility, she put the picture together. "Please wait right here. I'll be back with our doctors."

As Alex examined William Williamson, he confirmed Jesse's suspicions. "Mr. Williamson, your findings strongly suggest early smallpox. Even though you don't have a rash yet, I'm going to place you in the isolation ward. I'll keep you warm and comfortable and watch your course carefully. After all, you've probably had quite an exposure sleeping in those blankets the other night. Do you have any questions?"

Through one more teeth-chattering chill, William asked, "Sir, what about m' brother? ...Will he have to be placed in isolation too? And ...can I get the inoculation now?"

"Your brother Charles has had the natural pox a long time ago; he'll be fine. As for the inoculation for you, I'm afraid it's too late for it to do any good. You should get as much rest as you can. You'll be here several days."

Alex left the isolation ward thinking, "Good Heavens, if William slept in those infested blankets, then he's in for a bad time of it. Poor lad, doubly victimized by that devious rogue... tricked out of their fees and exposed to the pox!"

Chapter 23 - Vengeance
Friday, February 21 to Saturday, February 22, 1777
New York City and Northern Jersey

Tarleton disembarked from the military ferry at Murray's Wharf in lower Manhattan. Exhausted from the long day of riding and the close in-fighting, he rode slowly through the darkening town to his billet, drank a few ounces of brandy, and fell asleep still in his clothes. He hadn't even noticed the large, dried blood patch on his right sleeve and the spatter of red on his green tunic. Towards dawn, he awakened with a scream, rapid breathing, and sweat soaking his garments. He sat up in bed and thought, "What a nightmare! Bloody hell, as I was dispatching one of those lieutenants, the other ran me through with his saber. My mouth filled with red blood just before he blew away my face with his pistol shot." Tarleton often had violent dreams after battles, but never had he been the victim. He was distraught, not so much from his killings but by the thwarting of his plot. He sneered as he noticed the American's blood on his green jacket. He threw the stained uniform on the floor, washed the old blood from his hands and nails, and put on a fresh tunic. With the sun now rising, Tarleton went to the officers' mess for breakfast and then rode to see his lone confidant.

Charles Lee was at his desk when Tarleton knocked at the general's quarters. Lee's one guard peered through the window, opened the door, and saluted the senior officer.

"I have official business with General Lee," barked Tarleton. The sentry let him in and then returned to his post inside the door. Tarleton spotted specks of egg and breadcrumbs on Lee's dressing gown. *Spado* sat at his feet, licking yolk and ham morsels from the plate Lee had placed on the floor. When Tarleton approached, *Spado* growled threateningly. Sensing Tarleton's discomfort, Lee asked encouragingly, "Well, Colonel, what do you have to report about your...adventure?"

Tarleton began with uncharacteristic reticence, "Sir, I did get all the pieces in place, but I'm afraid the plan did not succeed. You see, the wagonloads of infested blankets were intercepted by Washington's Guards just before the shipment reached the American encampment."

Lee reacted with genuine surprise. "What? You mean that the Americans somehow uncovered the plan—in the buggering nick of time. I never thought that Washington's bumbling intelligence oafs could have figured it out. Give me the full story, Tarleton, and we'll see what in bloody hell happened." Lee kept to himself his own betrayal of Tarleton's trust when he had disclosed the brewing plot, in part, to General Howe. Tarleton completed his detailed account: disguising himself, collecting the smallpox debris, duping the Williamsons, infesting the blankets, learning of the capture and burning of the wagons, killing the two Life Guard lieutenants, shooting Charles Williamson, and escaping the senior Life Guards. But he intentionally left out one detail, too small in his mind to mention: the breaking of the vials.

"Alright then," Lee consoled, "I'd say the plan was victimized by the fortunes of war. You tried your best. If you couldn't do it, no one could have." Then, putting an arm on Tarleton's shoulder, Lee concluded deceitfully, "Rest assured. I will reveal your role to no one. Now, get yourself a good day's rest. *Adieu*, Tarleton."

Lee changed into his uniform and called in his sentry. "Go take a piss break, private. In a few minutes, you are going to escort me to headquarters."

****

At two hospitals less than a day's ride apart, the

unanticipated consequences of Tarleton's plot were about to crash upon three unintended victims on Saturday morning, February 22nd. At the British General Hospital in Brunswick, Mate Samuel Blackfield still awaited the arrival of the senior doctor from New York. The mate, though experienced from many years of service, looked in horror at the senior storehouse clerk lying motionless on the pallet. Exhausted from the ordeal, the clerk's wife was propped in the corner, sleeping deeply. "For the love of Pete," Blackfield muttered while examining the ill-fated clerk. He thought to himself, "His neck glands are greatly swollen, and his pulse is rapid and feeble. There's no more I can do. I'll awaken his wife to tell her after I complete my rounds."

On the road from the Perth Amboy ferry dock, a senior surgeon cantered the last miles to Brunswick. Familiar with the town from previous inspections, he rode directly to the Brunswick General Hospital, dismounted, and entered the foyer. Surprised to find no one there, he called out, "Hellooo. Hellooo. Anyone here?"

Mate Blackfield rushed from the isolation ward to greet the surgeon. "Sir, it's so good to see you again. I've been almost beside myself."

"No doubt, you have. Take me to your sickest patients," requested the surgeon.

Blackfield led him to the senior clerk's pallet where the surgeon quickly assessed the patient's moribund condition and softly gave the mate instructions for comforting care. "I'm afraid he's got a fatal case," concluded the surgeon. The clerk's wife awoke, dis-oriented and startled to see the tall, graying doctor. Mate Blackfield introduced him, saying. "Madam, this is the very best doctor in the entire British Army. May I present Dr. Walker?"

From the opposite corner, Lieutenant Martin Walker

listened incredulously. "Uncle Tim, can it really be you?"

Dr. Walker barely recognized his nephew's voice, strained as it was from dehydration and fever. Always courteous, especially to those of lower class, Dr. Walker said, "Madam, please excuse me. I'll return in a moment." He exclaimed, "Good Heavens," as he bolted to Martin's side.

Dr. Walker knelt by his nephew, immediately taking in his feverish brow and multitude of red spots. Grasping his uncle's arm, Martin cried out, "Thank you, Lord, for sending my uncle to save me!"

Even though Dr. Walker knew Martin was headed for a stormy course, the doctor offered encouragement. "Martin, my boy, you're a healthy young man. You'll come through just fine. But tell me, do you know how you got exposed to the pox?"

"Uncle, the man behind the screen—he's my senior clerk from the storehouse. I reckon we got the pox from the same source. Several days ago, he cut himself while emptying a refuse barrel. My clerk even sucked the blood from his cut finger. It had to be the morning the Williamsons' wagons left to deliver the blankets to the outpost. I inspected the trash and found that it was not thorns, but glass shards wrapped in a handkerchief. Who could have thrown that in the barrel? It could have been the Williamsons, or the only other person around was the quartermaster major...the officer who ordered the blankets."

"Martin, can you recall anything about the major?"

Martin closed his eyes tightly in thought. "As I wrote in my letter to you, his requisition was written with a left-handed slant. And, oh, yes, he was on the heavy side and getting gray hair. Does that help?"

"Yes, Martin, it helps a great deal. I'll have our mate give you a sponge bath to cool your fever and laudanum for your severe pains. I'll be nearby if you need anything else. Get rest, my boy."

From behind the screen, the clerk's wife screamed, "Doctor, doctor!"

Dr. Walker and Mate Blackfield arrived to see the clerk having jerking motions of his head, limbs, and trunk. The woman looked on in absolute horror, her hands alongside her face, her mouth agape. To Dr. Walker's touch, the clerk's head was burning hot; his breathing was shallow and rapid. Dr. Walker reached for the sponge to cool his patient, but two more seizures followed in quick succession. The clerk's racked body stopped breathing. Dr. Walker felt no pulse and pulled the sheet over the body. He looked at the clerk's wife and offered, "Madam, the soul of your good and honest husband is now with the Lord."

She dropped to the floor, pulled back the sheet, and hugged her departed husband. "Lerd," she wailed, "Why was 'e taken from us? 'e was a good man. Oh, why, Lerd, why?"

Martin Walker heard the cry of his clerk's wife and shuddered. When Dr. Walker returned to Martin's side, he tried to comfort his nephew. "Martin, your exposure was much less than your clerk's. Remember he cut himself with the glass—it was certainly contaminated with smallpox debris—and then he put his bleeding finger into his mouth. He inoculated himself heavily. Trust me, lad. You're going to pull through."

Dr. Walker knew he was painting perhaps too rosy a picture, and over the next few days, even the senior doctor began to have doubts. Martin continued to have hectic fevers and the red spots progressed. There were dozens of them on his face and extremities, and they became fluid-filled, circular and umbilicated. Then, they changed to painful, grayish-yellow pustules. Martin looked exhausted and took only a small amount of broth. Dr. Walker was by his side regularly to encourage him. "Martin, you must take more broth." "Martin, these pustules are to be expected." "Martin, I will keep you comfortable with laudanum."

And then in two more days, at last, Dr. Walker beamed as his awakened his nephew. "Martin," he said, "Your fever has disappeared, and the pustules on your face are beginning to dry. You are recovering!"

Martin clutched his uncle and wept openly. "Thank you, Uncle Timothy. Thank you, Lord. I was sure I was going to die."

Dr. Walker called in Mate Blackfield to show Martin to him. "Feast your eyes on Lieutenant Walker, who is now making his recovery. We'll have to keep him in the isolation ward until all the pustules dry and healed, but he's certainly out of danger."

Martin smiled for the first time in nearly two weeks. He said, "Is the cook here? I'm so hungry."

"Certainly," replied Blackfield. "The cook will prepare eggs, ham, coffee and biscuits. How does that sound?"

Martin had only to smile once again. He devoured the wholesome breakfast, wiped his mouth, and then called for his uncle to return. "Now that I'm on the mend I have one other matter. How do we find the blasted quartermaster major or whoever he really is? There must be justice."

****

Also on Saturday morning, February 22nd, at the American General Hospital in Morristown, Alex and Hobbs reviewed William

Williamson's course from the past night. The surgeon's mate's note read,

8:00 pm - Brow and body hot to touch. Sponge bath given.

Midnight - Cool brow. Sleeping. No complaints.

4:00 am - Brow feels very hot again. Gave sponge bath. Chills repeatedly. Complaining of severe backache. Dose of laudanum administered. Fell asleep afterwards.

6:00 am - Delirium noted. Thought he was in his mother's house. Vomited. Twitching of arms and legs noted for first time. Pulse 130-140, feeble.

8:00 am - Diffuse red spots have appeared. Bleeding from nose and rectum. Doctors called.

Softly, Alex concluded to Hobbs and the mate, "Mr. Williamson's course is extraordinarily severe. The worst sign is his bleeding. He's likely developing hemorrhagic smallpox." To his surgeon's mate, he added, "Please get Charles Williamson. I must apprise him of these dire complications. He's not susceptible to smallpox."

When Charles arrived, he immediately called, "William!" but his younger brother stared vacantly, not responding. Distraught, Charles asked, "Dr. Grant, will he make it?"

Alex took the older Williamson aside and replied, "Mr. Williamson, when these findings appear so early, they do not bode well. You might want to spend the next hours with William."

"For God's sake, you mean I am fully protected by the inoculation, but because William did not get it, is he goin' to die?"

Alex placed a hand on Charles's shoulder. "He has a very grave course, but there is always room for prayer and hope."

"I'm not very good at prayer. Would someone please call the vicar?"

Hobbs was at William's side when the young teamster's body jerked violently. Hobbs called, "Dr. Grant, he's having a seizure. I'm trying to restrain him." Within the minute, the seizure stopped, but bright red blood flowed from his mouth. Hobbs said to Alex, "I gather he's bitten his tongue."

"I hope that's all," replied Alex, "but with earlier bleeding from his nose and rectum, this might be generalized hemorrhage, now including his lungs."

Twenty minutes later, fulfilling Alex's prophesy, William vomited copious dark material, looking like coffee grounds, and passed tarry stools from his rectum. Hobbs felt for his pulse but said, "It is so rapid and weak I cannot count it. He's no doubt bleeding internally." (1)

William's skin promptly turned white. His eyes rolled back, and he took one last gasp. Hobbs said, "I no longer feel his pulse."

The vicar walked into the hospital to find Charles in disbelief. "Dr. Grant, Dr. Hobbs, has my brother really passed? He was perfectly healthy just...yesterday."

The vicar tried to comfort Charles, saying, "We cannot always understand the Lord when He takes a loved one. Come, Charles, we will pray."

Although Charles had asked for the vicar a few minutes before, now he wanted neither comforting words nor understanding. Charles shook his head and hissed, "I will have my revenge!"

---

(1) Fatal cases of smallpox took several forms including hemorrhagic disease which William demonstrated. In these cases, bleeding occurred into the gastrointestinal tract, lung and brain, causing vomiting of the "coffee ground" like material; black, tarry stools, coughing up bright red blood, and seizures.

Chapter 24 - Fear of a Dire Situation
Saturday, February 22 to Friday, February 28, 1777
New York and Brunswick

Charles Lee walked quickly to General Howe's Headquarters, his British guard barely able to keep up. From Lee's previous visits, the captain of the headquarters guard recognized the American officer. "General Lee, what business do you have here this Saturday afternoon?"

"Just let General Howe know that I have urgent intelligence to report," snarled Lee.

The guard captain felt Lee's condescending manner but made no issue of it this time. The captain disappeared into the mansion and reported to the British Commander in Chief. "Oh, for Pete's sake," muttered Howe, "I'm getting quite annoyed by Lee barging in here whenever he thinks he wants to tell me something...real or imagined. It will do him good to wait a bit. Put him in the foyer until I'm good and ready."

Lee took a seat in a straight-backed chair but in a few minutes began to pace around the entrance hall. His hands clasped behind him, he looked out the window for a while and returned to the chair. After an hour, Lee grew more anxious and asked the guard at Howe's door, "Did General Howe say when I would be able to see him?"

"Just as soon as he could. That's what General Howe told me," The guard replied indifferently.

Inside his office, the British commander leisurely wrote three long, personal letters to England: one to his wife Frances, one to his sister Caroline, and one to his aging mother Charlotte. After two hours, he told the guard to bring Lee in.

Still recalling the verbal wounds from his last visit, Lee approached Howe obsequiously and waited for Howe to begin the discussion. Not bothering to rise from behind his massive desk, Howe looked Lee up and down. Lee saluted, but the British commander did not bother to acknowledge it. He simply motioned Lee to a wooden chair before the desk. "General Lee, I am quite busy this afternoon. I understand you may have new intelligence to report. Be quick about it."

"Your Excellency, when I last reported, I told you of a plot by Lieutenant Colonel Tarleton's against the American Army."

"Yes, yes, of course, I recall that," responded Howe impatiently. "Go on."

"Well, Sir, Tarleton returned last night and told me just a few hours ago that his plan was...uhm, went a bit awry. It was unsuccessful."

Howe rose from his desk and walked behind Lee's chair. Lee continued to look straight ahead, sweat forming at his neck and armpits. "Well now that the matter is over," Howe demanded, "I am authorizing you tell me what you know of his scheme."

Lee began, "Sir, Tarleton developed a detailed plan to spread smallpox into Morristown."

"What?" exclaimed Howe, "Spreading the dread disease among Englishman? As an officer and a gentleman, I would never condone so despicable a plot! Why did you not tell me? I would have cut it in the bud."

Dumbfounded by Howe's disavowal, Lee stumbled, "But, Sir, I tried to inform you..."

The British commander cut him off. "I have no recollection of your telling me anything whatsoever about a smallpox plot. Good Heavens, that's unthinkable!"

Lee was now in the exact position he feared: Howe's complete denial of knowledge of the plot but Howe knowing Lee knew about it all along.

"This is outrageous but for the record, I must hear from you all you know, down to the last detail."

When Lee finished, Howe commented, "You don't find Tarleton's failure surprising, do you, General Lee? It was hare-brained to begin with. But tell me this: has Tarleton returned safely? And, have there been cases of the pox in our ranks? With Tarleton carrying the smallpox debris from New York to the Brunswick storehouse and spreading it into the blankets, I am concerned about our men having been exposed."

Lee hadn't given the latter point a thought but replied assuredly, "Sir, Tarleton is in perfect health, even after dispatching those two Washington's guards. As for smallpox among our men, well, Tarleton did not tell me of any."

Howe blustered, "Well, of course, he wouldn't even if there were hundreds of cases. Tarleton's too crafty. He wouldn't have confided this to you. General Lee, you may return to your quarters. I'll consider what my response will be to the foiled plot, but I needn't remind you—for your own good--say not a word of this to anyone. Clear?"

As Howe watched Lee walk towards his quarters, the commander in chief knew that he, himself, could not be incriminated in the plot or for failing to stop the plot. He thought, "If Lee tries to implicate me, it will my word versus his, and who would believe that conniving traitor?"

****

Later that afternoon, General Howe's coach, escorted by a guard of 17th Dragoons, rolled north from British Headquarters along the Boston Post Road. The general tapped the roof of the cabin to signal the coachman to stop at Horn's Hook. William Howe and Elizabeth Loring alighted to take in the confluence of the Harlem River running south and meeting the East River flowing in from Long Island Sound. The water coursed rapidly between two large jagged rocky points, called Buchanan and Barren Islands, in mid-channel. Closer to Horn's Hook, Hancock's Rock jutted majestically from the East River. The current swirled wildly around these natural obstacles, making for treacherous navigation and giving the confluence its name, "Hell's Gate." When they were alone, General Howe whispered, "How I have missed these outings while you have been recovering. I am excited to be here with you at last at one of my favorite sites in North America."

Elizabeth placed her head on his shoulder and purred, "Indeed, I am so glad to be feeling completely well and alone with you." But even in this idyllic setting, Elizabeth sensed Howe's discomfort. "Darling, when we've come here before, you always have enjoyed it immensely. It's a place where you could relax. What's troubling you this evening?"

Howe looked over his shoulder to be sure the guards were beyond hearing. "Elizabeth, I received disturbing news today about one of my officers, but I am not at liberty to share this even with you."

Elizabeth suggested, "Come, let's take a stroll along the path. It's still very mild for this time of year. Bring a blanket. We'll get a better view of the cataracts." When they were concealed from the dragoons, Elizabeth leaned against a tree, unlaced her bodice, and pulled William against her body. She kept her abdomen covered to conceal her freshly healed scar which she thought was disfiguring. William, aroused quickly He unfolded the blanket on the grass, covered themselves with another, and completed their lovemaking hurriedly. Elizabeth was relieved that she had no pain. "Mmm, did that make you feel better, darling?" she whispered to William.

He flashed a boyish smile and nodded slowly. As they walked hand in hand along the path, Elizabeth asked innocently, "Would you feel even better if you said what's disturbing you?"

After their lovemaking, the commander in chief often liked to regale Elizabeth with stories reflecting his power and position. Elizabeth encouraged his tales by seeming full of admiration while taking keen mental notes. Aware of his own potential culpability, Howe acknowledged only part of the story, "Well, now...I suppose I can confide in you, but you cannot mention a word to anyone."

Elizabeth nodded in agreement, her heart racing as she was about to get new pieces of critical intelligence. He did not want his lover to think he had any role—either active or passive—in the plot and conveniently modified the account. "You see, just this morning, I found out about a rogue plot by a British officer to spread smallpox into the American camp at Morristown. Mind you, in the previous war, the army used smallpox against enemy native tribes, but never as a weapon against English colonists or European soldiers."

Elizabeth pried for more details, innocently asking, "What British officer could ever have stooped to such villainy? You pride yourself on the code of honor among your officers."

Wanting to avoid his missed chance to nip the plot in the bud, Howe implicated his expedient target. "Elizabeth, I suspect that the American prisoner of war, General Charles Lee, has stirred the pot here. He's been a scoundrel his entire career: previously a British officer, now forsaking his mother country and selling his services as a rebel general, and always crude, foul, and self-centered."

Elizabeth dared to probe a bit further, "But darling, didn't you say the plot was by a British officer?"

William Howe was now deep into his own account of the plot. "Well, yes, but I believe that Charles Lee put the British rogue up to it. Lee found a cunning and ambitious officer who had something to prove. And Lee himself had details of the rebel army officers and organization. I wouldn't put it past him. He could even have been plotting to assume the American command if Washington faltered again on the battlefield or ran into a crisis from smallpox incapacitating his army."

Elizabeth was astonished to be getting this intelligence from Howe. She did not want to appear overeager and said, "My love, it's getting chilly. May we walk back to the coach and have a quiet evening together?"

It was dark by the time they reached Howe's headquarters. General Howe stepped from the coach and held Elizabeth's hand as she followed. Quickly, they dashed inside the mansion. Howe returned the salutes of the sentries and the captain of the guard. Disapproving of the commander in chief's blatant affair with an officer's wife, the captain stifled his smirk until the couple were past him.

William poured brandy for Elizabeth and himself as they sat by the fire. "This should take the chill away, my love," he promised. But she had one more piece of intelligence to gather before the night was done. While William was so amorous, she led him to his bed. "It was so rushed this afternoon. Now, could I have my pleasuring more...deliberately?"

William was eager to comply. Afterwards, she murmured, "It's getting very late. I must get home." She kissed William passionately and dressed for the coach ride. "It was a splendid day together. I'm so glad you found relief from your disturbing news."

As he embraced her once more, Elizabeth asked seemingly offhandedly, "Darling, I've been thinking. Does anyone know who that British rogue officer is?"

Caught off guard, Howe blurted, "It is surely that sly fox Tarleton of the 16th Dragoons, but he doesn't know that I'm suspicious nor what I have in store for him."

The commander in chief's carriage took Elizabeth down Manhattan to her house. She entered quietly, peeked into her husband Joshua's separate bedroom, and found him soundly asleep. Earlier that day, Joshua had told her he was having dinner with the Senior Commissioner of Prisoners. Elizabeth knew that meant Joshua and his immediate superior would be drinking heavily and returning home soused.

Behind the locked door of her own bedroom, she removed a tattered codebook from the recesses of her desk. On a tiny paper, she wrote an encoded message intentionally making it short so that, if intercepted, it would be more difficult to decode. It read:

velcivqphleaqqp.unemmrqzmpvqnqllcuvqyp

She crept to the ground floor and awakened her trusted manservant. "James, my note is so small you can hide it in your sock. It's almost midnight. Take this immediately to Agent 111 at his usual contact immediately. He'll be there until one o'clock. Tell him it's for 711."

From her bedroom window, she saw James leave through the side door, cross Broad Street, and walk north toward his clandestine rendezvous. As Elizabeth was about to close the curtain, she glimpsed a tall figure appear from a dark archway across the street. James did not see him, but the man watched James carefully and then cautiously followed him. Elizabeth was alarmed that she had no way to warn James.

****

In the days after the storehouse clerk's death from smallpox, Dr. Walker worried about the growing number of cases at Brunswick General Hospital. The first deaths were the clerk's neighbors, all family members of British military personnel. Then, he began to care for a few cases among camp followers and civilian workers. Within days, the cases burgeoned as smallpox spread to uninoculated soldiers, mainly Loyalists from rural colonial areas, Hessians from farms and remote villages in Germany, and then occasional uninoculated British troops. Dr. Walker and his mate set up a smallpox ward to isolate the cases, but he knew this would be inadequate. Because the Brunswick General Hospital was far too understaffed for him to see General Howe in New York, Dr. Walker settled for an urgent dispatch to the commander in chief, dated Friday, February 28th.

After describing the sentinel smallpox cases arising in the Brunswick storehouse, Dr. Walker detailed how the pox was rapidly spreading to both civilians and soldiers. His letter concluded,

Sir, with the greatest admiration for your strategic and tactical skills and for your concern for the army's health, I fear a dire situation in New Jersey with widespread disease among colonists, few of whom have been inoculated, and then spreading throughout large portions of His Majesty's Forces here. Notably, the Loyalist militia and Hessians are susceptible as well as selected British troops. I humbly request that you consider an order to inoculate all vulnerable soldiers, camp followers, and civilian contractors. Sir, as you know, even when most of the troops are already inoculated, an outbreak can still jeopardize an army's fighting strength. I shall leave final decisions to Your Excellency, but pray you consider the adverse impact of mass troop movements in New Jersey upon the health and fighting ability of His Majesty's Forces.

Signed,
T. Walker, Surgeon.
Director, British General Hospital, New York
Acting Director, British General Hospital, Brunswick

Dr. Walker took the dispatch himself to the military post office, just one block away. To the postal clerk, he said, "Private, please get your commanding officer right away. I am Doctor Walker."

Shortly, a lieutenant came out to greet him. "Good morning, doctor. How may I help?"

Walker replied urgently, "Lieutenant, my dispatch is for Commander in Chief General Howe. It is a matter of high importance. I would take it myself, but we are nearly overwhelmed with sick and dying at the hospital."

The lieutenant responded, "Well, your timing could not be better. I have two other top-priority dispatches for headquarters, and I'm riding there myself today. I'll be certain General Howe sees this as soon as possible."

Hours later when the lieutenant arrived at British

Headquarters, he handed the dispatches to the captain of the guard who replied, "Lieutenant, very good timing. General Howe is beginning an evening council of war meeting in thirty minutes. I'll get these to him right away."

The captain rapped on Sir William's door, handed him the dispatches, and returned to his post. General Howe read the top dispatch carefully. It was Walker's. Howe's face turned crimson as he read it. When he finished, he muttered under his breath, "Tarleton, you dog. You'll regret ever conspiring with Lee on this loathsome plot when I'm done with you."

Chapter 25 - The Noose Tightens
Saturday, February 22 to Monday, February 24, 1777
New York and Morristown

In the quiet of the night, Elizabeth's manservant James was convinced he heard footsteps some distance behind him. Knowing the city well, he quickly turned right for two short blocks and crossed William Street. After one more block, James turned north onto Gold Street, ducked into an alcove, and stooped behind a low brick wall. Within a few seconds, he heard the footsteps go past the alcove. Then as if his pursuer were searching for him, James heard the steps circling up and down Gold Street and finally trail off into the distance. James thought to himself, "It must be getting close to one o'clock when my contact will leave the rendezvous point. I haven't heard anything in perhaps ten minutes. Has he given up, or is he just nearby, waiting for me to emerge? I must take a chance." James peeked over the wall and stepped onto Gold Street. He took a deep breath when he saw the street was empty. He continued a short distance up Gold Street until it became Princess Street and opened the unlocked door at the two-story house at number 242. From inside a darkened room, the deep voice of Agent 111 inquired, "James, have you been followed?"

"Why do you ask?" James quivered.

"Through my curtains, I saw a tall man, dressed in black, pacing up and down the street. He must have been looking for someone."

From his right boot leg, James took a crumpled paper and handed it to Agent 111. "Sir, I was followed up Broad and onto Gold Street, but the tall man lost track of me when I hid in a dark alcove. I'm certain no one saw me enter here."

"I hope you're correct," replied the agent, "for your safety—and for mine. To be sure, leave by the rear door. Follow the narrow lane to Queen Street and turn south. When you're a few blocks away, take any of the cross streets back. And for God's sake, James, be careful. Are you armed?"

"No, Sir, I don't have any weapons."

"Well, then, take this pistol. At least it will provide you with some protection. I'll be leaving in a few minutes. I have your paper and other dispatches for the general. A skiff will ferry me to Paulus Hook. I'll get to Morristown by late afternoon. Fortunately, it's a moonless night, and these lazy redcoats rarely patrol the Hudson during the wee hours."

Agent 111 bolted the rear door behind James and unfolded the encoded note. From inside his Bible, he took a copy of the code. Down the righthand column were the coded letters, and opposite them were the letters of the English alphabet in order. Below each of the thirty-seven letters in the message, the agent wrote the decoded letter. When he was finished, he said aloud, "That degenerate Tarleton! General Washington must see this as soon as possible." He saddled his horse and rode toward the Hudson River.

In the meantime, James walked briskly down Queen Street. Even though he saw no one at this early hour, he carried the pistol in his right hand. James crossed over to Broad Street and continued south. He was relieved when he saw the candlelight still burning in the Loring's parlor. Suddenly, James lurched in horror as the tall dark man appeared instantly in front of him, warning, "That will be as far as you go!"

James started to raise the pistol at the tall man, but from behind him a brute grabbed James's arm and drove his left knee into James's back. As James fell to the ground, the second assailant smashed the butt of the pistol into James's skull. Within seconds, a carriage sped around the corner. The two assailants dumped James's limp body in the back, and they jumped aboard as the carriage raced north. Twenty minutes later, the carriage turned quietly into the rear entrance of British headquarters. Waiting at the door even though it was approaching two o'clock in the morning was Howe's spymaster, Major Stephen Kemble. To the driver, Kemble hurriedly asked, "Do you have him?"

The driver nodded slightly as his two partners carried James from the rear of the carriage. They had looks of fear. Kemble knew instantly what this meant. On James's head, he saw the sickening gash and crater left by the pistol butt. James 's body was gray, still and already cold.

Usually mild-mannered, Kemble now roared, "You blundering fools! I needed him alive. He was our key to finding out where our leaks have come from...and, for Pete's sake, to convince Howe of *her infidelity*. Now you've killed him! Get your bloody asses out of my sight, and make sure no one will ever find his body. And Lord help you if you don't get that right!"

****

Agent 111 crossed the Hudson on a barge run by another agent in Washington's extensive network. They knew that in this part of the river the Royal Navy did not patrol after midnight. Disembarking on the Jersey shoreline, Agent 111 used back roads to avoid any British patrols. He arrived untouched at Morristown in the afternoon and was admitted to Washington's headquarters in Freeman's Tavern. The Life Guard immediately showed him into the general's office. Washington looked tired and greeted him abruptly. "What news do you bring from New York?"

A veteran of many trips to see Washington, the agent took no offense. "Sir, I bring a coded message delivered to me at one o'clock the morning by Mrs. L's manservant James. I decoded it immediately and perceived it was urgent. Your Excellency, I got here as fast as I could."

Showing his usual calm exterior, Washington replied, "Very good work, and please pardon my inhospitable reception a moment ago. Well, let's see the message."

Washington recognized Elizabeth Loring's cursive on the coded line:

velcivqphleaqqp.unemmrqzmpvqnqllcuvqyp

Below in the agent's heavy block letters, the message read:

TARLETONDRAGOON.SMALLPOXINMORRISTOWN

The general's face showed no hint of the anger he felt. Looking kindly upon the agent, the general explained, "Thank you for getting this valuable intelligence to me. It puts all the pieces together about a heinous plot. We now have confirmation of the culprit and his intensions. My aide will arrange for you to get feed and rested. He will also see to your well-deserved reward. I humbly express my sincerest gratitude. I ask that you stay to attend a small meeting I will host this evening."

Washington scratched a few words on a slip of paper and handed it to his valet. "Billy Lee, please take this list of seven names to Lieutenant Colonel Gibbs and ask him to assure that these men will meet here at six o'clock. And please arrange a light supper for all. Thank you."

Solemnly, Washington began the meeting looking deeply into the souls of the seven men—Life Guards Gibbs, Tilghman, Grayson and Webb, Drs. Grant and Hobbs, and Charles Williamson—and what he was about to ask of each one. They had already finished their simple supper of cold ham and potatoes. "Gentlemen, tonight I will describe a decisive mission to you. It will be fraught with danger, but each of you brings your unique skills—and extraordinary motivation. Billy Lee, please bring me the New York City map. Gentlemen, come around this side of the table."

The commander in chief unrolled the exquisitely detailed map drawn two years previously by the senior British engineer and printed in London in 1776. Washington continued, "The twin objectives are to rescue Elizabeth Loring for, I fear, British intelligence has uncovered her as my prized agent and to capture Tarleton. Our own intelligence service has provided detailed information. Mrs. Loring lives here in a white house to the right of the Protestant Church on French Church Street."

Washington saw that all eyes were following carefully and continued, "Tarleton's lodged on the second floor of Number 2 Beaver Street, here at the intersection with Broad Street. As you see, they live about three short blocks apart. If you each agree to volunteer for this assignment, you will acquire disguises as British officers and carry out the rescue and capture, respectively. I need not remind you that if caught, you will be treated as a spies and face certain hanging. May I please have your responses: Yea or Nay?"

The general nodded appreciatively as the seven men responded in unison with a thunderous shout, "Yea!"

Billy Lee distributed seven copies of the orders which he had transcribed from General Washington's dictation just prior to the meeting. The commander in chief opened his copy and explained, "You will work as two parties. Lieutenant Colonel Tilghman, you will lead Major Grayson and Dr. Grant to rescue Mrs. Loring. Dr. Grant is essential as she knows and trusts him. Lieutenant Colonel Gibbs, you will lead Major Webb and Dr.

Hobbs to capture Tarleton. I have attached Dr. Hobbs on case you need to sedate Tarleton with laudanum for the crossing by ferry. I want him alive. Dr. Hobbs also knows his way around the city from having been stationed there last year. And I have attached Mr. Charles Williamson. He asked that he join you since he has a score to settle with Tarleton. Mr. Williamson will be valuable since he knows the city thoroughly from his years of hauling there. Mr. Williamson, I emphasize that we will take our revenge on Tarleton after his capture. We have provided captured British uniforms for you on the rack in the rear. Gentleman, I leave the details of your assignments to Colonels Gibbs and Tilghman to be arranged prior to the operation. I have chosen you for your loyalty and bravery as well as your ability to think on the run.   My trusted Agent 111 will lead you safely back to the city. I had hoped to get you there tomorrow night, but as you can see, ominous snow clouds have built up all around. We'll have to await clear passage. When ready, Agent 111 will take you to his home until you are set to carry out your assignments between midnight and three o'clock. He informs me that the last ferry to New York City leaves Paulus Hook at ten o'clock in the evening. The first ferry from New York back to Paulus Hook is at five o'clock in the morning. You'll plan your mission accordingly. Gentlemen, your country is most grateful that you have taken on this mission. I ask that Providence look over your mission and your safe return."

Chapter 26 - The Mission
Saturday, March 1 to Sunday, March 2, 1777
New York City

Because of the late February storm that engulfed Morristown, the mission had to be postponed. Three days later, Washington brought the men together. "I know that the delay has been hard to bear, but the roads through the passes to New York will be clear tomorrow, Saturday. Tonight, you will all stay in a private home across the square. Get a good night's rest for you will be facing a cold journey to New York. You will need all your physical and mental strengths during the mission. Are there any last-minute questions?"

Caleb asked, "Sir, has there any word from our agents in New York?"

The general shook his head. "Because of Mother Nature's behavior, we have had no contact from New York. I can only presume that our intelligence has not gone stale. Our plan remains unchanged. If there were any development, I'm certain our senior agent in the city would get word to Agent 111's home upon your arrival." Washington said warmly. "Gentlemen, look out for each other. I will see you all upon your safe return...with the two prizes in hand. Good night."

Tench fell asleep quickly but awakened in the dark. He heard the grandfather clock in the living room faintly chime three o'clock. He tried going back to sleep but could not stop his mind from racing. "What if we get intercepted by a redcoat patrol?' he thought. "What if our identity is uncovered? What if the road is not clear and we miss the last ferry? Can I really trust Williamson? What British troops will we encounter in the city?" He looked to the bed across the room and saw Caleb sleeping soundly. "You lucky bloke. I wish I had your composure."

Despite Tench's worries, the journey from Morristown into New York went uneventfully. Shortly after 11 o'clock that Saturday evening, Agent 111 led the seven men, all in captured British uniforms, to the back entrance of his house on Princess Street. They hitched their horses in the stable but did not unsaddle them as they planned to begin the mission shortly after midnight. The agent lit a lantern and opened the rear door leading to a small kitchen and parlor. He looked under the door for any information from the senior American spy. He found none and concluded that there was no change in the intelligence gathering.

"Gentlemen, please rest here while I prepare coffee and brandy."

Caleb Gibbs, the ranking officer, sensed everyone's worry. Concealing his own anxiety, he began positively, "Thank you. The coffee and brandy will be perfect! Lads, so far, our mission has gone without a snag. We made it to the last Paulus Hook Ferry to New York in plenty of time and were not even challenged by the guard on the Jersey side. With the streets empty, no one even saw us come in here. This bodes very well. We'll move out at thirty minutes past midnight, allowing time for late British patrols to complete their rounds. That's an hour from now. Maybe the snowstorm did us a favor, after all, by delaying the mission until Sunday. Maybe the redcoats will be enjoying the Lord's Day. Let's go over the operation one more time."

Caleb Gibbs and Tench Tilghman reviewed every detail they had worked out—the streets each party would take, the role each man would have, what they would say to Elizabeth and to Tarleton, contingencies for the unexpected, the rallying point back at 242 Princess Street while awaiting the five o'clock in the morning ferry, and how to drug Tarleton.

Tench concluded, "In operations like these, unplanned

events are bound to happen. Keep calm; keep your wits about you. Be confident. You've all been in tight fixes before. General Washington has total faith in each of you. We will have complete surprise. Remember: we're going to save a damsel in distress, so to speak. And we're about to get even with a roguish knave. We are the gallant knights of yesteryear!"

Tench's analogy brought a sorely needed chuckle from Alex, Hobbs and the Life Guards, but Alex saw that Charles Williamson sat silently, sweat forming on his brow. "Mr. Williamson," asked Alex empathically, "how are you feeling?"

"Truth be told, Dr. Grant," Charles responded, "You men are the officers. I've not been in fixes anythin' like this a'tall. I'm just a hauler, but I'll tell you one thing: I can't wait to settle my score, and I can't wait see the look on Tarleton's face when he sees us! Thank you, I'll be fine just as soon as we get goin'."

Caleb reminded Williamson, "Our objective is to take Tarleton alive. This is only the first step in settling the score with him."

Alex added, "Dr. Hobbs and I had the opportunity to rescue Elizabeth Loring's life twice before, once from her tumor and then from her wound infection. She is the bravest of the brave and has put her own life on the line for our new country in ways none of us can even imagine. Now, she is in great danger. It is an honor to be with our party. With the Lord's help, we will be successful and will all come back with her."

Caleb Gibbs's scarlet-coated party mounted their horses and left the stable at precisely half past midnight. Fifteen minutes later, Tench Tilghman's similarly disguised party took its planned route the short distance to French Church Street, one intersection east of Elizabeth's house. The streets were silent. Through his telescope, Tench saw one British private guarding the entrance.

"Blast," he whispered, "I wasn't expecting that General Howe would have set up a guard already. I don't see any other guards. Let's see how well our forged orders work."

The sleepy private was surprised as the party approached but snapped to attention. Using his best upper crust London accent, Tench commanded, "Private, I have orders to take Mrs. Loring into my custody and conduct her to a safer location. You are relieved and may return to your billet."

The private, a country lad, gave no thought to these orders other than to beat a hasty retreat to his bed. "Yes, Sir," he said thankfully. While Tench and Grayson waited outside, Alex ran to Elizabeth's bedroom. Elizabeth was already astir and peaked out the window. She greeted Alex at her door and grasped his arm. She whispered, "Oh, Dr. Grant, I've been at my wit's end. James disappeared after I sent him with a message to General Washington two nights ago. I was certain I was going to be arrested as a spy. Are you here to rescue me?"

"Indeed, we are. We brought a British officer's uniform for your disguise. Put it on quickly. I'll prepare your horse. And where is your husband?"

"No need to worry about Joshua. He was carousing this evening. He'll be stuporous until mid-morning."

Within minutes, the rescue party was on route back to the rendezvous on Princess Street, Elizabeth safely in hand.

Three blocks away, Caleb's party dismounted in front of Number 2 Beaver Street. Leaving Webb with the horses, Caleb, Hobbs, and Charles Williamson dashed through the unlocked entrance and tried the door to Tarleton's second floor apartment. Finding it locked, Caleb put his shoulder to the door and crashed in expecting to capture his prized quarry fast asleep. In the dim light, Caleb could see the bed, but it was neatly made. Hobbs lit a lamp and gasped. "Well, for the love of Pete, someone's beaten us here!"

The three searched the apartment but found no trace of its occupant. The closet and chest were empty, and the small writing desk contained neatly stacked blank paper with a quill pen and ink bottle. "Son of a bitch," muttered Williamson. "He's been tipped off."

The crashing noise awakened Tarleton's second floor neighbor, a British infantry lieutenant who, half dressed, opened his door. Surprised to see superior British officers inspecting Tarleton's apartment, the lieutenant volunteered, "Sirs, if it's Colonel Tarleton you're looking for, you're a bit late. You see, he left yesterday—under guard."

"Lieutenant, my orders are to take Colonel Tarleton into my custody. Did you hear where he was being taken?"

"I'm afraid not, Sir. I peeked through my door. All I can tell you is that he was taken from his apartment by six officers, a lieutenant colonel commanding. When the colonel spied me, he said, "Close your door, son, this is none of your affair." I did see Tarleton. His hands were tied behind him. How strange, I thought. I've been billeted here three months but never had a more than a few words with Colonel Tarleton. He often came in soused and frequently had lady visitors, usually late at night. I could hear their...their celebrating."

Boiling inside, Caleb calmy replied, "Thank you, lieutenant. Sorry to have disrupted your sleep. Gentlemen, let's return to our barracks. I'll obtain a full explanation shortly."

On route to their rendezvous point, Charles Williamson asked Caleb, "What is the meanin' of Tarleton's arrest by his own army?"

Caleb replied, "He's gotten himself in deep trouble from both sides. I'll wager the redcoats are furious about his dishonorable conduct and now endangering their own troops. He'll have a court martial undoubtedly."

When Caleb's party entered the rendezvous on Princess Street, they were greeted robustly by Tench's party. Hobbs's eyes lit up when he saw Elizabeth, especially in the scarlet uniform. She smiled affectionately and bowed in mock formality. "And here is my other favorite doctor! Dr Hobbs, I am glad to see you so well."

Not seeing Tarleton, Alex asked hopefully, "Is your captive outside?"

Caleb sighed and explained sadly what they had found at Tarleton's apartment. He concluded, "There's no more to be done here. We'll stay here until half past four and then leave in two parties for the five o'clock ferry. I'm proud that we've rescued Mrs. Loring. With luck, she will not be missed until we are safely in New Jersey. As to the mystery surrounding that degenerate Tarleton's disappearance, well, we'll have to see what General Washington's other agents can find out."

Neither Caleb nor Tench's parties raised suspicion from the sleepy guards at the ferry. Still in their captured British uniforms, the party disembarked at the Paulus Hook terminus at first light and rode quickly to Elizabethtown. Good fortune looked over them as there were no British patrols along the road. Caleb observed to Tench, "Those lazy redcoats must be sleeping in this early Sabbath morning." At Elizabethtown they changed into their Continental uniforms and by mid-afternoon were back at Morristown. The American sentry recognized Colonels Gibbs and Tilghman and waved the party through. At Washington's Headquarters, Caleb entered first and debriefed the commander in chief. When the rest of the party entered headquarters, Elizabeth Loring was the first to be greeted by the general. In an extraordinary display of public emotion, Washington took her hand and whispered, "Thank the Lord Almighty for your deliverance!" Alex was astonished to see tears glistening in Washington's eyes. Then turning to the others, Washington said, "Mrs. Loring has been my most valuable agent, at great risk to herself. I express my heartfelt gratitude to all of you for your bravery and skill in her rescue. And as for the whereabouts of that scoundrel Tarleton, I already have a good idea."

Chapter 27- Flight
One Day Earlier
New York and Brunswick

On Saturday morning, March 1, General William Howe urgently met with Stephen Kemble, his Chief of Intelligence. "Major, I have just received a dispatch, written yesterday, from Dr. Timothy Walker, Director of the General Hospital. You have met him and know he is a fine and honorable man. Dr. Walker is presently in Brunswick, inundated by sick and dying soldiers and their family members—all with smallpox. I have no doubt these are consequences of Tarleton's plot gone awry. I want you to go to Brunswick immediately and find out what Dr. Walker knows and what is happening there. I swear on my valiant brother's memory, I'll have Tarleton's fool head on a platter."

Arriving in Brunswick by afternoon, the intelligence chief took detailed notes as Dr. Walker revealed his precise knowledge of how Tarleton implemented the plot—how he had secretively gathered the smallpox debris, how he had cunningly arranged to spread it into the American camp, and how the smallpox accidentally took hold in British-held Brunswick. Walker told Kemble of his care of Tarleton's unintentional victims including the fatal case of the senior storehouse clerk and the near-fatal case of his own nephew Martin. In the ensuing days, dozens of other smallpox cases had developed. Dr. Walker concluded, "When Lieutenant Walker recovered, we vowed to see Tarleton brought to justice. I want to see him court martialed and then dangled from a noose! Is there anything else I can tell you?"

"Good Lord," Kemble cried out. "I never would have imagined a British officer so dishonorable. And moreover, endangering to our own army. The information you have provided confirms our suspicions. Now, tell me, what are you doing to protect our lads?"

"Major Kemble, even before I could get an order from General Howe, I have had my surgeon's mates search out all the troops in Brunswick and their family members who are susceptible to smallpox. We have been inoculating every last one of them, and I have instituted strict quarantining and isolation of those with smallpox. Fortunately, because the army is still in winter encampment, there has been no perceptible spread to other parts of the Jerseys. Yet, the troops are quartered tightly together, many packed in houses in Brunswick. The returns from regimental surgeons are still showing increasing numbers of cases, mainly among rank and file, their wives and children. I pray Tarleton's epidemic will start winding down soon."

"I pray for that as well. And thank you for your excellent initiative in trying to contain the outbreak, Dr. Walker, truly excellent! I'll report to the commander in chief straight away. Goodbye and good luck."

That evening when Kemble returned to British Headquarters in New York, he saw light coming from under Howe's door and heard the crackle of the logs in the fireplace. He rapped on the door and entered upon Howe's command.

"Ah, Major Kemble, come warm yourself by the fire and pour yourself a brandy from the bar. You have had a long day. Tell me, what did you learn from Dr. Walker?" The commander in chief was eager to find out not only whether smallpox was spreading among his troops in Brunswick, but also whether Walker had any inkling of Howe's own unspoken knowledge of the plot. As Kemble debriefed his chief, Howe's facial expressions were hidden in the dimly lit office by a large snifter of brandy. When Kemble was finished, Howe rose from behind his desk and placed his arm on Kemble's shoulder. "I am concerned about the growing numbers of smallpox cases. I am going to have Tarleton arrested immediately. I will draft the warrant. In the meantime, please go to the commandant of my guards and select five officers. Tell him I want a lieutenant colonel as the official head, but Kemble, I want you to lead the arrest and put that conniving scoundrel in prison. Go now, I don't care what time it is. Report to me first thing in the morning."

Nearing midnight, Kemble and five officers we stationed outside Tarleton's house on Beaver Street. They saw no light in the window. "Very good," Kemble surmised, "Tarleton must be asleep. Follow me."

The party rushed up to Tarleton's second story apartment door, and in a falsetto, Kemble chirped, "Ban, it's Kate. Pardon th' 'our, but I mus' 'ave left m' purse 'ere. Open up, please."

Still groggy from the night's drinking, Tarleton staggered from bed. Rubbing both eyes with his palms, he unlatched the door. The lieutenant colonel of the guard startled the dragoon and thundered, "Banastre Tarleton, in the name of the King, I have orders to place you under arrest!"

Tarleton's jaw dropped, but he rapidly regained his wits about him. "What in the hell is wrong with you? This is preposterous! I demand to know what baseless charge you have."

"Banastre Tarleton, you are charged with dereliction of duty, endangering the lives of His Majesty's troops, and conduct unbecoming an officer." Not knowing that Charles Lee had informed Howe of his role in the plot, Tarleton was caught completely by surprise. He fumed as two guards held him at bayonet point and oversaw him as he dressed in his uniform. They then bound his hands behind him. The two other guards threw Tarleton's clothes in his haversack, made his bed, and straightened the desk. They wanted no trace of Tarleton being there. One guard searched the desk and in the back of the bottom drawer found a leather shoulder case. Inside was a tightly fitting wooden block with six one inch in diameter holes. Protruding from one hole was a stoppered glass tube containing crusted brown debris. Knowing precisely what the case contained, Kemble thought to himself, "Ah, just the evidence I was hoping to find." He leaped in front of Tarleton and demanded, "What is the meaning of this?"

Tarleton pretended to inspect the device. He lied, "I did not use the desk and never saw that case before. It must have been left by the previous occupant. I haven't the slightest idea what it is."

Kemble shook his head in disbelief. To the commandant of the guard, he advised, "Be very careful with that case. Wrap it in these towels and bring it with us to headquarters. It's good that all your men were selected for having received the inoculation before leaving England."

Kemble's guards locked Tarleton in a tiny and dank military holding cell near headquarters, pending transfer to one of the prison ships anchored in Wallabout Bay. At eight o'clock that morning, the intelligence chief was on route to General Howe to report his mission's success. When Kemble entered the commander in chief's office, he saw General Charles Lee sitting by the fireplace, at the side of General Howe.

"Oh, Major Kemble, please join us for tea. I invited General Lee to discuss likely American strength in the spring campaign. But tell us, how did your... *exercise*... go early this morning?"

"Perfectly, Sir, perfectly. Our prisoner is already secured in a cell, ready to be tried. We recovered incriminating evidence in his possession: a case containing tubes of smallpox debris."

"Thank you, Kemble. Outstanding operation. You may return to your other duties." Having dealt for the present with

Tarleton, General Howe worked his deception on his American prisoner of war. Howe reasoned that it would be better to keep Lee close and appear to let him back in his good graces. After all, Lee still had high-level information about the American Army. Lee also had revealed part of the plot to Howe. Yet, if it ever came down to Howe's word versus Lee's, the general would easily win. Taken in by Howe's chicanery, Lee leaned back in his overstuffed chair, a self-satisfied look on his face. Lee thought to himself, "Tarleton, you fiend, you will owe me!"

****

Two mornings later, Tarleton awoke, racked in pain. He tasted blood coming from his nose, and with his left hand he felt swelling and tenderness around both eyes. Both arms were bruised. When he inhaled, his chest felt on fire. Through his foggy brain, Tarleton remembered being kicked and punched mercilessly. He had tried to protect himself by curling into a ball, but the beatings seemed endless. He could not tell where he was now but recalled being escorted from the military holding cell during the nighttime. When his senses began to return, he heard the chiming of bells and felt the room rolling. He could make out dim light entering his musty quarters. Outside, he heard gulls squawking. As daylight brightened his surroundings, a gruff voice bellowed, "'ere's yer breakfas'. Take it 'r not. Makes no diff'rence t' me." A small bowl cold gruel slid under the heavy wooden door. Only then did Tarleton see that iron bars ran vertically through the opening in the door.

He forced down three mouthfuls of rotting gruel but then gagged when he saw maggots crawling in the bowl. He kicked the bowl across the room, and for the first time since childhood he sobbed. Minutes later, he heard the jangling of keys and the squeaking as the door opened. Two men faced him from the doorway, back light making it impossible for him to see their faces.

"Banastre Tarleton, I am Major Richard Leffingwell, senior aide de camp to General Howe, and with me is the ship's surgeon. He's here to help mend you."

"Where in hell am I, and what has happened to me?"

Leffingwell admonished in an even voice, "I'll decide what information you will receive and when. Right now, the surgeon is going to tend to your injuries. I'll return when he's finished."

The ship's surgeon gently cleaned the blood from Tarleton's face and limbs. "All in all, you're a lucky lad. Your nose is not broken, and neither are your arms or legs. You have bruises around your eyes. They'll be swollen and discolored for a few days, but nothing worse than that. You no doubt have a cracked rib or two; they'll heal in time too. You have a few lacerations which I'll cover with fresh dressings. I'll see if I can get you better rations. Good day."

When Leffingwell returned, he began, "You are in a cell aboard the ship of the line, *HMS Asia* sailing from New York harbor to Jamaica Island in the Caribbean."

"What is the meaning of this abduction?" Tarleton demanded.

The senior aide continued calmly, "I remind you that you are prisoner of the Royal Army under most serious charges. You were placed in the military prison prior to a court martial and no doubt would have been convicted. I need not tell you of the ultimate sentence you would have received, correct?"

Wearily, Tarleton nodded in understanding, adding, "How did I get here?"

"A benefactor of yours interceded in your case with General Howe. He pleaded that, despite your charges, you were still a bold and resourceful officer, if presently somewhat...*misdirected*. He argued that, after a period of rest, you would be more valuable to the general alive than dead. He begged the commander in chief not only to spare you from a court martial and certain hanging, but also to spirit you from New York. You see, others have a score to settle with you. Those you harmed and friends of those who died of smallpox are determined to avenge their loved ones. The general's intelligence service also found out that just after your arrest, a band of rebels disguised as British officers came to capture you at your billet."

Tarleton's head hung down as his narrow escape sunk in. "Well," he asked, "why did I get beaten?"

"That happened the second night you were in the military holding cell in the city. Word travels fast in army circles. I presume that someone wanted to get even with you for the death of a friend or family member. They must have had connections with the prison guards and paid them handsomely. We got you out just in time. *HMS Asia* is now approaching Sandy Hook on the Jersey coast. I'll be transferring to a cutter and returning to New York City. My assignment was to make certain you were secure. Once *Asia* gets into the Atlantic, General Howe has granted that you may resume your rank of lieutenant colonel with all the attendant rights and privileges. Here is a letter which you will give to the major general in command in Jamaica. He is an old friend of Sir William's, and he'll see to it that you will be looked after for a few months. Stand clear of any...and I emphasize, *any* trouble. General Howe will send for you when he's ready. Tarleton, you are indeed a fortunate soul."

With new-found insight, Tarleton replied humbly, "I am most appreciative of this second chance. I am thankful for your kindness and of General Howe's faith in my future as an officer.

But who was that *benefactor*? Was it my father or one of his trading assistants here in New York?"

"Your father may be very influential in London, but he could not possibly have known yet of your troubles. It had to be someone in New York, and your father's helpers here would not have had sufficient connections or resources. No, it had to be someone much closer to Howe. Think about it. *Au revoir*, Tarleton."

Leffingwell walked down the gangway to the cutter and signaled the naval lieutenant to head for the East River. Only then, from inside the cell, came the faint call, "Was it Lee?"

Chapter 28 - The Rogue's Epidemic
Thursday, March 20, 1777
American Headquarters and British Headquarters

In the village of Morristown, the deciduous trees were still barren, and brown leaves carpeted the forest floor. At higher elevations, deep snow packed mountain crevices, and large, white patches remained in the shade of rocks. Yet, this Thursday afternoon was pleasant, with the first shoots of new growth breaking through winter's ground cover. Alex and Hobbs walked along a trail leading north from a small lake while Elizabeth and Jesse sat nearby on a log, viewing a beaver family at work.

"Good heavens," Alex sighed with relief. "Today is the last day of winter. Can you believe all that has happened since Christmas?"

Hobbs replied, "Indeed, and the arrival of spring means that the military campaign will be getting underway shortly. We'll need to be getting the hospital ready for the field. Who knows exactly what old Howe has in mind?"

"Well, Dr. Hobbs, I'm glad to hear of your planning. I had some fears that you would have had enough campaigning and would return to life in Albany." Teasingly, Alex continued, "After all, a man of your age has to slow down a bit."

"But even at half speed, I'll still run rings around much younger surgeons. Dr. Grant, I'm in to see this war to its just end."

At the lake, Elizabeth was eager to know more about Hobbs and Alex. "Jesse," she inquired, "where did Drs. Hobbs and Grant meet?"

"Dr. Hobbs was a regimental surgeon from upstate New

York, one of the few with excellent experience and good judgement. Last September, he was appointed Assistant Director of the General Hospital when Dr Grant was made Director. The two of them make an incomparable team."

"And where did Dr. Grant learn his skills?"

"Mrs. Loring," she replied formally, "He's from a family of physicians, going back to their time in Ireland. He's from Maryland but attended medical school in Philadelphia. Before the war started, he wrote the first American book on treatment of injuries and wounds. Dr. Hobbs says that he has innovated surgical practice in North America. He's a Professor of Surgery at the Medical College of Philadelphia. As you have seen, despite all his achievements, he is a humble and compassionate doctor."

Elizabeth surmised, "Jesse, you admire him a great deal, don't you?"

For a moment, Jesse thought she might have revealed far too much of her personal feelings. She added in a matter-of-fact tone, "Oh yes, he's a fine physician and splendid to work with."

Elizabeth then added innocently, "I've not heard him mention a family."

"That's a sad tale, Mrs. Loring. Before the war, Dr. Grant's wife delivered a stillborn baby, and there was a double tragedy when a few days afterward she died of fever and bleeding. He rarely speaks about her death."

"How sad, indeed. He would certainly make the perfect husband," she said out loud, even surprising herself. Elizabeth turned her head so that Jesse would not see her blush.

When the men returned to the lake, Elizabeth said, "The

sun will be setting soon. I 'd like to be getting back."

"So would I," added Hobbs, but Alex replied, "I like the light at this time of day. I think I'll stay a bit longer."

"Then that will make two of us. Would that be all right with you, Dr. Grant?" asked Jesse. Elizabeth smiled politely, wondering if she had been outmaneuvered by this skilled nurse.

After Hobbs and Elizabeth left, Alex broached a subject he had been thinking about for weeks. "Jesse, I would hope you will remain with Dr. Hobbs and me for the coming campaign. I suspect this will be the decisive year of the war. Ours is noble work." Alex could not reveal that he hated the thought of her leaving. His admiration for her grew daily, but when he began to dream, his mind had to shut it down.

"Dr. Grant, may I please give this a bit more thought? I am most grateful for what you have done for me and what I've learned, but as a free Black woman, I must think about my future."

Jesse and Alex walked along the lake for a while in silence, neither exactly certain of what to say and both anxious about their growing feelings. The sun was setting when they turned back toward Morristown. On the uneven forest trail, Alex reached for Jesse's right arm to steady her. She clutched his arm not letting go until they arrived at the encampment.

As they walked past Washington's headquarters, Alex broke the silence. "Look at all the lamps burning. Do you see General Greene through the window? I also see a young man wearing a heavy, dark brown coat. I don't recognize him from here. There must be three or four senior officers there as well. The commander in chief must be having a council of war."

A few moments later, after Alex escorted Jesse to her quarters and returned to his quarters at the General Hospital, a junior Life Guard was awaiting him. "Dr. Grant, His Excellency wishes your immediate presence at headquarters for a council meeting."

****

The previous week, the Brothers Howe retired to Sir William's office for brandy after dining together. Lord Richard began affectionately, "Savage, it's been a hard winter, but thank the Lord, Tarleton is taken care of, for now." The older brother dealt delicately with the escape of Elizabeth Loring by saying, "And with the... erm...*security matter...inactivated*, we can at last concentrate on the spring campaign." Lord Richard hobbled to the bar to refresh his brandy and to spare William the embarrassment of having to look directly at him. The admiral thought to himself, "No one would have the nerve to rebuke William about his affair." Then, aloud, he changed the subject, "Ah, my gout's doing better lately, but the pain sometimes still makes my toe feel like a beast has been gnawing on it."

Sir William had been flogging himself since his intelligence chief uncovered Elizabeth Loring's long-standing spying. Since his affair with her was so widely known, Howe felt humiliated. He confessed to his older brother, "What a juvenile I was. What a fool!"

"Look, Savage, other than Kemble, very few on our side even know what she was up to l

Lord Richard paused for a moment and once more redirected the conversation, asking, "By the way, I see a packet ship arrived from London today. Anything from Lord Germain?"

"Indeed, there is," replied William at last breaking his funk.

"I did not expect Secretary Germain's reply this quickly. The ships must have had favorable winds for their winter crossings, and Germain clearly treated my request immediately. Germain acknowledged my rationale for reinforcements. Although not sending the full fifteen thousand I requested, he promised to send an additional eight thousand officers and men, some from Ireland and some from the home island. Germain expects them to set sail in early April."

"By Jove," jumped in the admiral. "With those reinforcements, you'll have half the King's men under your command for the campaign."

"That's exactly my calculation as well. We'll have a total strength of thirty thousand here in North America, leaving a slightly larger number divided among Ireland, Britain, the West Indies and India. Germain also gave General Burgoyne approval for his expedition from Canada but gives me discretion in coordinating that campaign and mine." Rubbing his hands together, William went on, "That's perfect. As commander in chief, I am now clear to capture the rebel capital and defeat the main rebel army. That over-inflated Burgoyne can fend for himself, and if he winds up getting into trouble, I'll be done in Philadelphia in time to turn north and rescue him.

"Very well, then," Lord Richard recalled, "when we last discussed the route of approach, you favored transporting the army to the Amboys in my naval vessels and then a quick march across New Jersey to Philadelphia. Still feeling the same?"

"Dick, the situation is different now. My Director of the General Hospital, Dr. Timothy Walker, is gravely concerned about large numbers of smallpox cases among the troops in Brunswick and vicinity—an unexpected complication, shall we say, of Tarleton's blasted, cock-eyed scheme. Dr. Walker intimates that I should not be moving our troops through there. Thus, I want to revise the plan and keep my troops well north of Brunswick. If the Royal Navy will kindly transport my men across the Hudson to Paulus Hook, I am certain that we can draw the rebels from their stronghold in Morristown onto the plains below. They are likely to think we are still on route to their capital. Then, I will meet them and crush them!"

"Savage, it will be the Royal Navy's pleasure to oblige your transportation needs. We have large numbers of bateaux to get all your men, horses, wagons and artillery wherever you want them. It will not take me long to prepare."

Beginning in the next few days, His Majesty's Forces in New York began to stir from wintertime inactivity. Seamen removed dozens of red-painted bateaux from their boathouses, washed off winter's grime, and rowed the craft to staging positions at the Manhattan ferry dock, across from Paulus Hook. Infantry regiments turned out to polish their accoutrements and clean their muskets, before beginning their afternoon drills in public squares. Artillery units tended to their trusty field cannon, removing dirt and spider webs, and then burnishing the brass pieces. The gunners replaced worn and cracked parts of their gun carriages and added a fresh coat of paint. In the fields north of the city, cavalrymen began to put their heavy steeds through their paces. All this activity suggested a single interpretation: As spring was officially arriving, General Sir William Howe's Army was preparing to take the field.

George Washington's two remaining senior spies in the city carefully noted all these endeavors. When they had a solid picture, the spies arranged to meet secretly with their contact. Early one morning, while the street was still quiet, they entered the rear door of Queen's Head Tavern. They knocked seven times, then six more times on the door of the side office. A voice responded softly, "*Entrez.*"

Samuel Fraunces, Sr. listened intently to the agents and then probed their observations to be certain that he had as accurate a report as possible. When satisfied, Fraunces replied, "*Très bien, très bien!* I will get your intelligence to General Washington by this evening. Please wait at the bar while I prepare your rewards."

The senior Fraunces unlocked his strongbox and removed two silk bags, each containing identical gold coins, equivalent to a working man's annual salary. On the side of the room, a young man drew back the curtain. "Father," said Samuel Fraunces, Jr., "Those agents provided critical intelligence. I remember every detail. We must get it to General Washington in Morristown."

"The British have relaxed their guard now, and the *Asia* has sailed back down to the lower bay. If I use my back road route, I'm certain I'll have no difficulty in getting to Morristown this time."

"God speed, Samuel, and return safely as soon as you can."

****

By the time Alex arrived in Washington's council room, the senior officers were already seated. Graciously, Washington said, "Dr. Grant, so good you have joined us. You already know everyone here except perhaps for my special guest who has just ridden from New York." Reaching out his arm to the young man in the heavy brown coat, the commander in chief made the introduction. Please have a seat next to Monsieur Samuel Fraunces. He brings fresh intelligence, gathered by my top agents in the city. We are meeting to analyze our responses. I have called you here because of preparations you'll need to make for the General Hospital."

Samuel Fraunces nodded to Alex, who leaned to Fraunces's

ear and said quietly, "Very good to meet you. I have heard of your invaluable service."

After Washington briefed the council, Fraunces provided his detailed report. Immediately, General Greene opened the analysis. "First, we need to determine what General Howe's intent is. Will he move directly to capture Philadelphia and our Congress? Will he attack our fortified encampment here? Will he parade his forces south of Morristown, hoping to draw us from our stronghold? Yet, Howe's a sly old warrior. Is he gathering the bateaux as a mere ruse to conceal his real intent: to sail up the Hudson in Royal Navy warships to rendezvous with the force from Canada? If I were Howe, that's exactly what I'd do. It would split off New England from the rest of the country and give him an overwhelming force. Or does the British commander in chief have yet another objective in mind: perhaps rallying the Loyalists in the South with a powerful expedition to Charleston or Savannah?"

Washington nodded, "Indeed, these are all possible, as General Greene so clearly states. On this last day of winter, we do not know, but it will eventually become clear. My senior officers, this campaign will likely determine the outcome of the entire war and the future of our young country."

He looked around the room. It was perfectly silent as Washington continued, "Once again we face great odds as this campaign is about to unfold. Once again, the enemy has a larger, better equipped force. With control of the seas and waterways, they once again have greater mobility, and they once again have the initiative. Our best preparation is to begin mobilizing and be ready to respond to General Howe's opening moves. Mind you, we are not without our advantages. Our army and officers are more experienced than we were a year ago. We expect new recruits shortly, and we have acquired adequate materiel for the beginning of the campaign. Our intelligence is excellent, and we have one other advantage."

His face looking deathly serious, he quipped, "My brother officers, we are fighting...General Howe!" The council roared.

Later, back at his quarters in the General Hospital, Alex raised a glass of brandy with Hobbs and Jesse. "Tonight, we heard the possible moves the enemy may take to open this spring campaign. General Washington does not know yet which option Howe will follow. Howe has always been slow to follow up, and we can expect opportunities on the battlefield. But we should expect heavy casualties, and our hospital must be ready."

Cheerfully, Hobbs replied, "Never mind, Dr. Grant, we'll be ready all right, but for this evening, let's celebrate a bit. I raise my glass first to your saving Mrs. Loring's life and for her bold rescue."

Hobbs and Jesse downed the brandy and cheered, "Huzzah! Huzzah! Huzzah!" Alex smiled humbly.

Hobbs continued, "I'm far from finished with my toasts. I raise my second glass to your success with the novel Calcutta inoculation. You've saved many a lad's life! And third, you were essential to disrupting the plot of that scheming Tarleton!"

With Hobbs's glowing toast complete, the three rose, steadied each other arm in arm, and each drank a few more ounces of brandy. Alex returned the compliments. "My dearest colleagues, I would not be here without you. Jesse, when I was at death's door, you gave me hope and nursed me back to health. I am eternally grateful. You both were essential to Mrs. Loring's surviving from her tumor and wound suppuration. It was together that we perfected and carried out the Calcutta method. And many of us helped to uncover and thwart Tarleton's plot. I just wish we had captured that... that...bloody scoundrel. As for now, I think we must have a song to conclude our celebration. Jesse, do you have a favorite?"

"Dear doctors, there's probably only one song we can all recall at this moment. On the count of three, let's begin. Follow my lead."

Outside, two off-duty sentries who were passing Alex's window of Alex's laughed heartily when they heard the inebriated threesome singing aloud. The sentries ran into the hospital and added their voices to the slightly slurred words:

" Yankey doodle keep it up.
Yankey doodle dandy
Mind the music and the step
And with the girls be handy."

When Alex awoke the next morning, he rejoiced at his great fortune since Christmas. Throughout the American camp, he sensed that everyone was eager for the pivotal, upcoming campaign. Indeed, from its opening days until well into the fall, the American armies fought the British-Hessian enemy on fields from far northern New York State to Chesapeake Bay. The campaign turned out to be decisive in unimagined ways, and even when the last arms were laid down at the campaign's end in autumn 1777, its full impact was still not known.

THE END

Postscript

The Rogue's Plot is written as a stand-alone, historical novel but is a sequel to *The Long Shot* (2020). *The Rogue's Plot* begins just as *The Long Shot* ends, even with a little overlap. For old and new readers, I wish to state a few central points to both novels. First, my intension is to weave real history, gathered from a lifetime of reading and travel, with plausible events and characters from my imagination. Indeed, I was delighted when many readers of *The Long Shot* said they regularly went to Wikipedia or other sources to find out what the actual history was. *The Rogue's Plot* asks: *what if* a ruthless British officer schemed to incapacitate General Washington's Army through Eighteenth Century germ warfare? *What if* the rogue officer spread smallpox into the American winter encampment prior to the critical 1777 fighting season? It is a point of true history that European armies used smallpox against indigenous peoples of North America, but use of smallpox back then against people of European stock was a far different matter. Only cold-blooded characters would have conceived of such a diabolical plot. Yet, history provided me with not one, but two, such scoundrels: British Lieutenant Colonel Banastre Tarleton and the British prisoner of war, American General Charles Lee. Tarleton did come from a wealthy merchant family involved in the slave trade, and he was arrogant and ruthless. Charles Lee was at times foul, bullying, and scheming, but at other times charming, scholarly, and worldly. It is the product of my imagination that they conspire in the heinous plot. I have described the historic events and characters to the best of my ability to set the backdrop for the germ warfare plan. Thus, the opening actions at Trenton and Princeton are real. The King's senior officers including Commander in Chief Sir William Howe, his brother and naval commander Lord Richard Howe, General Charles Cornwallis, Hessian General Baron Wilhelm von Knyphausen, and the spymaster Major Stephen Kemble are all real and are depicted based on historical descriptions although I have taken some liberties in the interest of plot development. General Howe did indeed have an open affair with Elizabeth Loring, the American wife of his officer, Joshua Loring. However, I imagined that Elizabeth was a top-secret agent for General Washington. On the American side, the senior officers are also real and are described faithfully. These include Generals George Washington, Nathaneal Greene, Henry Knox, Israel Putnam, John Sullivan, and Hugh Mercer and Lieutenant Colonels Tench Tilghman and Caleb Gibbs. It is pure coincidence that the latter lieutenant colonel and I share a surname. We are not related. Tench Tilghman served as Washington's military secretary beginning in summer 1776, but I portray him as a Life Guard for flow of the story. Washington's Life Guards Samuel Webb and William Grayson were real officers. To tell the story, I created the central characters: American surgeons Dr. Alexander Grant and his side kick Dr. John Hobbs, their stalwart nurse Jesse Jones, and master British senior physician Dr. Timothy Walker. Other Americans playing smaller roles including Kate, the brothel owner; Surgeon's mate Willem Vander Voort; Elizabeth Loring's manservant James; the teamsters Charles and William Williamson ; and the two unfortunate Life Guards, Peter Yorke and Benjamin White are fictional as are English characters with smaller parts including surgeon's mates Samuel Blackfield and Tom Smart; engineer Major "Red Jack" Redmond; Surgeon Timothy Walker's nephew, Lieutenant Martin Walker; and aide-de-camp Major Richard Leffingwell. I give cameo roles to two historical figures. As portrayed, Alexander Hamilton was truly a captain of New York Artillery at The Battle of Princeton. Shortly afterwards, on March 1, 1777, he became Washington's military secretary and aide-de-camp, a position Hamilton held for over four years. With his new position, Hamilton rose to Lieutenant Colonel and became a valued advisor to the commander in chief. New York tavern owner Samuel Fraunces was also real and probably was an agent for Washington, but I imagined his son, Samuel Fraunces, Jr, as an American spy.

Second, the practice of medicine in the late Eighteenth Century predated the modern era by roughly one hundred years, but it is plausible that innovative physicians like Timothy Walker and Alexander Grant could have employed techniques well ahead of their time. Accordingly, I depict: Timothy Walker incising Alexander Grant's tonsillar abscess to save our hero's life; Walker diagnosing Elizabeth Loring's acute abdominal pain and Alex operating on her emergently; Alex treating "Red Jack" Redmond's arm wound conservatively and thus avoiding amputation; Alex and Walker doubting the effectiveness of bleeding as a therapy; and Alex brilliantly instituting the "Calcutta method" of smallpox inoculation. Medical history of the late 18th and early 19th Centuries includes frequent citations of physicians making treatments that were seventy-five to one hundred years ahead of their time only to have these innovations forgotten until re-instituted by others much later. I made up the term "Calcutta Method," but nasal inoculation had been used in Asia for centuries. It was a distinct possibility that an open-minded physician-scholar like Grant could have heard about the Asian practice and adapted it. However, to fit the plot, I shortened the true timelines for actual smallpox infection and inoculation effectiveness.

Third, in *The Rogue's Plot,* there is a great deal of dialogue including frequent expletives. I have tried my best to be true to dialects of the time. For the most part, I use these dialects for persons of the social underclasses of the Eighteenth Century and use modern English for the officers and educated. For ease of reading, characters whose first language was German (General von Knyphausen) and French (Samuel Fraunces) speak in modern English peppered with an occasional expression in their native language.

Fourth, as a life-long cartophile, I used period maps, mainly from my family's collection, for my descriptions of waterways and terrain as well as for place names of some towns and New York City streets. Some current day names are different from the 18th Century location. For example, today's New Brunswick, New Jersey was more often simply called Brunswick in the late 1700s. In the front of the book, I have also included period maps so that the reader may better envision America of nearly 250 years ago.

Fifth, I have made some additional adaptations and have taken some liberties. In *The Long Shot,* I used the term "African" to describe Jesse, to be consistent with Eighteenth Century language. In this novel, I describe her as "Black" to reflect current usage. Banastre Tarleton is looked down upon by fellow British officers because of his family's taint with the slave trade, but the year 1777 was too early for such social concern among British aristocracy. Yet, I allow this slippage to develop Tarleton's character.

Sixth, because the Eighteenth Century was a formal time socially, in the novel even good friends speak to each other using their titles, rather than more familiar first names or nicknames. I have made an exception for how the Howe brothers address each other, as one would expect of siblings even then.

To conclude this Postscript, I return to the beginning. In the *Preface,* I stated that the British commander in chief made a bewildering strategic decision that fatally determined the outcome of the war and the future of the United States. I promised that *The Rogue's Plot* would provide a new explanation for what led to that strategy. In fact, we did not get to learn of Commander in Chief General Sir William Howe's bewildering decision—at least not yet—but we do learn what influenced the general's thinking. As described, the smallpox epidemic that British rogue Lieutenant Colonel Tarleton intended to have decimate General Washington's Army boomeranged and begins to spread widely among the British camp and throughout the civilian population of Central Jersey. *The Rogue's Plot* ends on

March 20, 1777. In the immediate weeks afterwards, General Howe will have to deal with these developments as he plans his campaign for the 1777 fighting season. The straightforward strategy will no longer be the best option.

Acknowledgements

In the thousand days since I started writing *The Rogue's Plot,* I've spent about a third of them, at least in part, immersing myself in the Eighteenth Century. Every day, whether researching, writing, or editing, has brought me great joy (as well as panic every once in a while) in creating my second novel. Along the way, I got great help from many. As with *The Long Shot*, I express my heartfelt admiration and gratitude to Amy Benedicty for her friendship and editing the manuscript. She provided encouragement and raised innumerable comments and questions that were essential to a detailed, plausible and consistent story. Nothing escaped her attention. My good friends Judith and Jerry Klein and Barbara and Howard Bomze once again provided talents in design for the book and in preparing the final version for publication. For the new headshots and the map images, I thank my creative friends and photographers, Michael Chanover and Tom Paper, respectively. To Jacquie Laskey, I extend my great thanks for her immeasurable assistance in preparing the final manuscript. I thank Myles Margolin for his life-long friendship and encouragement in my writing. I also wish to thank Richard Melnicoff for hours spent advising and working on promotional strategies. I relied on Stuart Gibbs for many ideas during the book's development, and I asked good friends and family for a critical reading when the story was almost done. To Suzanne and Darragh Howard and Albert Sukoff, I express my gratitude for their commentary and excellent suggestions. To develop the fictitious medical characters, I have, once again, drawn heavily upon colleagues going back as far as fifty-five years. I want to note my three great physician role models: Richard Schwarz, Joseph Seitchik and E. Stewart Taylor, and my close physician friends: Alan Decherney, Mike Mennuti, Richard Sweet, Marvin Amstey, John Hobbins, and Ches Thompson. Finally, for all my hours spent writing, I thank Jane for her unending love and understanding. This past year marked the 60th anniversary of our first date, and we are coming up on our 58th wedding anniversary. Jane has been a passionate partner in all my life's endeavors, and she has been an unmatched role model as a mother, grandmother, and advocate. We recall our loved ones who are no longer in our midst: our parents, my brother, our nephews, dear friends, and our daughter-in-law. We cherish their memories as blessings. We are thankful for our many friends and our incomparable family, Stuart, Suz, Darragh, Ciara, Dashiell, and Violet, who bring us a world of love and happiness.